CLARA THORN

THE WITCH THAT FOUGHT

DON JONES

PRAISE FOR CLARA THORN, THE WITCH THAT WAS FOUND

"Clara shines as a spunky protagonist who is grown-up enough to accept her destiny.... Jones links math and magic in a way that makes math seem cool.... Fresh ideas, some welcome diversity, and memorable character work enliven the material."

— BOOKLIFE

"Jones' series opener brims with wonderful characters. ... While a school for magical youngsters has become a popular subgenre all its own, this novel unfolds as an engrossing mystery. ... Clara's...synesthesialike power showcases the author's radiant prose."—Kirkus Reviews

— KIRKUS REVIEWS

"This is the kind of book that, when you send your child to bed, you know they're making a tent out of blankets and reading by flashlight so they can continue to read."

— RAY HAYES (BETA READER)

"...an incredibly well written Young Adult Fantasy—using magical realism to bring the enchanting world of Underhill to life. The lore of the world...is easy to understand, as [Jones] reveals it in dribs and drabs, allowing the reader to learn about this new realm at the same speed as Clara.... He has hit on all of the typical tropes including found family and magic schools, while managing to create something completely and utterly unique."

— REEDSY.COM DISCOVERY

For the family I found:
Christopher, Donavan, and Corentin

"My own heroes are the dreamers, those men and women who tried to make the world a better place than when they found it, whether in small ways or great ones. Some succeeded, some failed, most had mixed results... but it is the effort that's heroic, as I see it. Win or lose, I admire those who fight the good fight."

— GEORGE R. R. MARTIN

ALSO BY DON JONES

CONTENTS

CHAPTER 1

A PALADIN PROBLEM

"How did they find us so fast?" Ed panted as he and Clara dashed down the sidewalk, dodging a homeless man who'd stretched out in front of a bus stop.

Clara didn't reply, saving her breath for running, but she wondered the same thing. *Maybe they can see the Border with those goggles. Perhaps they just got lucky.*

She and Ed had emerged from the new Las Vegas Border—located in an archway that framed a rather embarrassing statue at the D casino—and had barely stepped onto the sidewalk before a Paladin had spotted them. The witch hunter had shouted at them to stop as he ran bolted toward them from across Carson Avenue. Clara and Ed had immediately taken off running in the other direction, heading North toward the busy Fremont Street Experience. *We should have gone into the casino,* Clara thought ruefully, but perhaps the presence of all the tourists on Fremont would deter the Paladin.

"They probably recognized our faces," Clara said, slowing to a trot as they rounded the corner and turned right onto Fremont, heading toward Clara's home. They scurried along the casino's long

1

outdoor bar, weaving their way through the people waiting in line for drinks. Clara's eyes darted back and forth, looking for someplace they could hide. "Duck in here," she said as they passed a small souvenir shop. They were both short enough to hide behind the racks of t-shirts, peering through to watch the Paladin clatter to a halt a moment later, his head swiveling back and forth as he looked for them. His face was half-covered by heavy, steampunk-looking goggles that they knew let him see magical auras.

Auras like Ed's.

"I can do an illusion," Ed offered. "Make us look like someone else. I got really good at it."

"No!" Clara hissed. "Sorry," she added as Ed tensed next to her. "No, it'll make it worse. We'll both be lit up like flares that way. Mom —bio-Mom—said the goggles fluoresce, so maybe he won't be able to—"

The Paladin cursed loudly, drawing curious looks from a few tourists, and pulled the goggles down, letting them dangle around his neck.

"What happened?" Ed whispered.

"I don't—no, wait," Clara mused. "It's so bright out there with all the signs and the overhead video. . ."

"Maybe the goggles are useless here?" Ed ventured.

"Possibly," Clara said hesitantly.

"He's leaving," Ed whispered. The Paladin was stalking slowly to the east, his head still swiveling slowly back and forth as he moved through the crowd.

"He's trying to spot us," Clara said distractedly. She unfocused her eyes, looking at the trail of magic that had been leaking out of Ed, drawn to the iron plates in the Paladin's trenchcoat. As the Paladin moved away, less and less of Ed's energy was being drawn toward him, and after a few more seconds the drain tapered off completely. Clara sighed, her shoulders relaxing a fraction, as she refocused on the real world. "I think we're safe now. At least in here."

"You think he's gone?"

Clara shook her head firmly. "He knows we ducked into a shop or a casino. All he has to do is stand out there and wait for us to come out. He obviously knows what we look like." Outside, the shops and pavement were bathed in flickering lights from the blocks-long arched video screen overhead.

"I don't think he had the goggles on when he spotted us coming out of the Border," Ed said.

"He didn't," Clara agreed, thinking hard.

"I don't suppose anyplace down here is haunted?" Ed asked hopefully.

Clara snorted. She'd gone to visit Ed and his mother in New Orleans over a school break, and they'd run into a team of Paladins there as well[1]. They'd run into a bar to find help—and found more than they'd expected, in the form of the spirit of Jean Lafitte. The Paladins had seen the ghost too, and had backed out quickly. Ed's mother had pulled up a few minutes later and driven them home. "They say the Apache Hotel is, but it's at the other end of the Experience. We'd never make it if he spots us." The Vivavision overhead screen outside changed again, soaking the streetscape in bright yellows and oranges. *Hmm.* "I wonder. . ." VELLUM CHECK FOOTNOTE

"What?"

"Illusions. Could you do something to make it even brighter? The big overhead screen, I mean?"

Ed frowned as he thought. "This counts as self-defense, right?" Their school had a strict policy about students using magic on their own.

"I should certainly think so."

"So, there's a spell called *Ilumina, realza, brilla.* It's Spanish, they'd use it for spelunking. Exploring caves."

"I know what spelunking is. What's the spell do?"

"Brightens all available light. I don't know if it'll cover the whole thing, though," he added, doubt creeping into his voice. The Fremont Street Experience covered four city blocks.

Clara looked around. "Just do as much as you can then. We just need him to keep the goggles off so he can't see your aura." As a mathemagician, Clara didn't have an aura, because she didn't gather magic into herself like other witches.

"He'll still recognize us," Ed protested.

"I have another idea. And my debit card."

Ten minutes later, the two walked out separately, each clad in tacky new "What Happens in Vegas Stays on Facebook" shirts, cheap shorts, hats, and sunglasses. Their gray and burgundy school uniforms were bundled into a new drawstring sack that Clara slung across her back.

They both headed east on Fremont, and spotted the Paladin halfway down the block, his head still slowly turning as he scanned the crowd. He stood out like a sore thumb with battered black engineer's boots and dusty black trenchcoat, in a sea of people wearing shorts and tees. The tourists strolling along parted around him, coming back together when they'd passed him.

Clara's heart began pounding as she ducked behind a large group of people who'd stopped to watch one of the performing street crews, forcing herself not to look toward Ed. He'd moved to the other side of the street, walking behind the performers as they balanced on their heads and leapt about in time to loud, thumping music. Clara walked close to an older couple, keeping them between her and the witch hunter, hoping he'd just take her as their kid. She risked a quick glance and saw that Ed was hugging the building opposite, darting from one group of people to the next.

The Paladin didn't notice the two teens. In fact, as Clara stole a backward glance, she saw he'd started to move west on Fremont, toward the Four Queens casino.

Luck was on their side: the light to cross Fourth Street turned white just as they approached, and they hurried across, joining up on the far side. Clara directed Ed through the Neonopolis building, speed-walking past a hot dog shop and into the confines of the outdoor mall's courtyard. A few minutes later, they popped out of the building's opposite side and ran across Las Vegas Boulevard, dodging cars rather than waiting for the light at the crosswalk. Glancing over her shoulder and seeing no sign of Paladins, Clara ran up to the high-rise her parents had recently moved into, thumbed the combination code into the back gate, and ushered Ed into the building's loading dock.

"I wish we could have cell phones," Ed muttered as the heavy gate clanged shut behind them.

"You know they fritz out almost right away," Clara sighed. While she didn't store magic like other witches, most technology still wouldn't work around her for long. "C'mon, we'll use the freight elevator."

"Clara, that's terrifying," Mom gasped. Clara had waited until she, Mom, Ed, and Dad were seated on the new sofa and chairs before telling them what had happened. "Whyever did you put that portal all the way over there?"

"Border, Mom," Clara corrected. "And I didn't. This is the one that originally went out into the desert near the dam, the one Oberherr fell into last year. But it wasn't stable. It's like. . . it didn't want to be there. So I had to re-anchor it, and that's just where it wanted to go."

"Next to that silly statue," Mom said, pursing her lips in disapproval. Clara shrugged.

"I think next time we'll need to arrange to meet you there," Dad said calmly. "And we'll certainly be escorting you back."

"Thank you, Mr. Thorn," Ed said gratefully. He'd collapsed into his chair and accepted a glass of water from Clara's mother. A bit of color was already returning to his face, Clara saw, relaxing a bit.

"This place is looking really nice, Mom," Clara said, trying to change the subject. "I thought you guys wanted something out in Henderson, though?"

"That's where the office is," Dad said with a nod. "But. . . we really like it down here. And your Mom's new job is actually close enough to bike to, and this condo came on the market at a really good price, so. . . we did it."

"It's really great," Ed offered, sipping his water.

"Once we get all these boxes unpacked, it'll be great," Clara's Mom chuckled.

"Where'd you get the furniture?" Clara asked. They'd been sitting on the floor just three days ago when Clara had completed her eighth-grade final exams in the Ordinary school just a couple of blocks away.

"While you were off making new port—sorry, Borders," Mom said with a grin, "we discovered Ikea. And they were having a sale. We've got a new bed frame coming tomorrow."

"Wow, really settling in!" Clara said approvingly. She looked around. The two-bedroom condo had a decent-sized kitchen-dining-living area, fronted by floor-to-ceiling windows that faced south toward the Las Vegas Strip. A spacious main bedroom suite occupied almost half of the remaining footprint, also featuring full-height, south-facing windows. Behind the kitchen was a smaller bedroom. As they'd walked past it from the entry door, Clara had noted it contained a work desk and bookshelves. "So you're using the other room as an office?"

Dad laughed. "See, Arlene, I told you she'd notice."

"Notice what?" Clara asked.

"As if we'd kick you out at your age," Mom chided. "That desk folds up against the cabinet, and then the whole thing drops down to the floor. It's a Murphy bed. So when you're here, that's your room. All yours, and it's got a good-sized closet to boot. And when you're off at your magic school, Dad can use it as an office and work from home some days."

"I promise to keep it clean," Dad added with a smile.

"You had all that installed in the past three days?" Clara asked.

Mom nodded. "It took them like four hours, actually. Really efficient."

"You know, Clara," Ed pointed out, "you could stay at Linginbaum's all year if you wanted to. I'm thinking about it for next term. Just commute to Ordinary school."

"Well," Mom said before Clara could reply, "I suppose we could think about it." She didn't sound certain. "If that's what you want."

"Only with an escort," Dad reminded her.

"I'll think about it," Clara mused. "It might be easier, at least until the rest of the Borders are restored. So I don't have to keep running back every other weekend."

"They're working you too hard," Mom protested.

"I don't mind, Mom," Clara said. "Actually, I really like it. It's neat to get to see so much of Underhill."

"Well, you've got months to decide," Dad said, shooting his wife a glance. "When's the term start?"

"A week from today," Ed said. "Tenth-years have to be back a few days before start of term to help the professors set up."

"I still can't wrap my head around ninth grade being tenth year," Dad chuckled.

"They don't have kindergarten like we do," Ed reminded him. "So everyone does the same thirteen years, they just count it differently, is all."

"Sure, sure. Just can't keep it in my head," Dad said. "My little girl, already starting high school!"

"Will you stay here until the term starts?" Mom asked.

Clara nodded. "No more Borders for a month at least, they said. They've got crews prospecting for the right spots Underhill, and then I go in and figure out where that spot wants to connect to in the Ordinary. Here, I mean. Headmaster Dimmick said they're getting down to the last handful, and it's harder to pinpoint the proper spots."

"Is your Mom helping with that?" Dad asked.

"Theo," Mom warned.

Clara sighed. "It's fine. I don't know, Dad. I haven't seen Mom much. Maybe four or five times. She's. . . I guess off trying to find Dad. My other Dad, I mean. Sorry."

"Don't be sorry, Clara Beara," Dad said gently. "You have two sets of parents who love you deeply."

"Even if one of them can't seem to find time to—" Mom began with some heat.

"Arlene," Dad said.

"Sorry."

"It's fine," Clara said again. "She's nice and all. Just very. . . intense."

"Has she talked about. . . before?" Mom asked softly.

Clara shook her head. "Not much. She and Dad were captured. Oberherr did it, handed them over to the Paladins. They escaped, but Dad got hurt and didn't get away." Clara had shared all of that with her adoptive parents shortly after her bio-Mom, Jessamine Holdaway, had told her the story. "She's been trying to find him again ever since." Clara suddenly felt tired. The encounter with the Paladin, the weight of her missing bio-Dad, all the work she'd been doing to raise new Borders. . . "Hey, would you guys show me how to open the bed? I could use a nap." Then she looked around the room. "Is that a sofa bed?" Her parents had invited Ed to stay with them for the remainder of the school break, but—

"Well," Mom said, a mischievous expression stealing across her face. "No, but that's because we kind of had a little surprise for you both."

"I can't believe you're living in a *resort,*" Johanna gushed, wiggling slightly in her lounge chair.

"It's just for a couple more days," Clara said. "But it's *awesome.*"

"I can't believe it's *free*," Harriett said.

"The room is," Clara corrected her, "and this cabana. Mom still has to cover anything we eat or drink. But it was pretty cool of the hotel to give it to her. And they're discounting the food, even."

"Cool is her letting you invite us over for the day," Idalia added. "Thank you again, by the way."

"You should *see* the room," Ed said. Unlike the girls, who'd taken the four lounge chairs in front of the cabana—all in full sun—Ed and his ultra-pale skin were tucked back in the shade of the cabana itself. "It's huge! Two full bedrooms, each with their own bathroom. A dining area, a living room, it's got everything! It's like a condo!"

"Vegas, baby," Clara said with a laugh. "This is their slow time of year, so when I asked if Ed could stay with us, Mom asked her boss and they said it was no problem. I figured we'd just sleep on the floor of the condo or something!"

"So it's just the two of you?" Idalia asked.

"No, Mom and Dad are in the one bedroom. It's got the bigger bed. Ed and I are sharing the other one since it's got two beds."

"Which are still huge," Ed added.

"Isn't it a little weird, sharing a room?" Johanna asked.

Clara gave a little shrug and sipped her iced tea. "Not really. Not for me, at least. The last city we were in, we were in a studio apartment. Everything was in one big room, the kitchen, everything but the toilet. Mom just hung some curtains everywhere to make rooms, but it's not the same as walls."

"I've always shared with cousins when they visit," Ed said. "Which in our family is like six times a year. No biggie. Until I started at Linginbaum's I didn't even know having your own room was a thing that happened. How did your family manage? There's like twenty of you."

Harriett snorted. "There's ten, and I guess we've always shared. But it was always just the three of us. That's not. . . it doesn't feel like sharing, I guess."

Clara sat up, swinging her legs to one side of the lounger so she could see the triplets. They'd followed their usual dress code, all wearing the exact same one-piece swimsuit in slightly different shades of blue. "You guys aren't using sunblock?" She knew their pale, freckled skin wouldn't stand a chance in the Vegas sun.

"There's a spell for that," Idalia said slyly. "Mom taught us. *Red mijn huid tegen de zon,* it's called." She struggled a bit over the difficult Dutch words. "We've been taking turns casting it on each other all morning."

"Want us to teach you?" Johanna asked.

"You know it won't work. But wait a sec." Clara stared at the three girls, letting her eyes slip just out of focus. The magic eddying around them was bright and clear even in the intense sunlight, and Clara quickly spotted the blue-yellow equations of the spell. "Oh, it's not that hard," she murmured. She looked down at herself and began twisting some of the ambient magic into the same forms and colors. "Oooh, it actually takes the heat down a notch, too. Nice." She tugged the equations into the same lazy loops she saw around the girls.

"It took us literally half the night to get that right," Idalia sighed. "I'm more than a little jealous of you right now."

"That's how it was all last school year," Johanna said. "Everyone else bangs their head against it until they get it, and then Clara just watches and copies it." She sighed. "I've accepted it as our lot in life. At least we don't have to bounce all over Underhill setting up Borders."

"I kind of enjoy seeing everywhere," Clara said defensively.

"Yeah, but with Dimmick's Border crew? Ugh, no. Too many old people."

"I wouldn't mind going with you next time," Ed offered.

"They said no," Clara sighed. "I asked. And to be fair, it's been a lot easier with grownups. They're better at holding their magic in a pure form and feeding it to me. Once we're prepped, I can usually get the Border up in a few minutes, now."

"Does your Mom ever go?" Johanna asked.

"Rude," Idalia snapped.

"No, it's okay," Clara said with another sigh. "No, she hasn't. She's been off looking for Dad." Clara pivoted back into her chair, stretching her legs out and hoping that would end the conversation.

Then her eyes grew wide behind her sunglasses.

"Girls," she said in a low, hard voice, "drop your spell." She snapped at the magic surrounding her, feeling her skin warm a bit as the protective spell faded.

"I'm not out here to fry to a—" Harriett began.

"Now," Clara hissed.

"It's a Paladin," Ed said, walking up behind Clara's chair.

There, across the pool, was a tall man wearing one of the Paladins' signature black trenchcoats. His goggles were pushed up onto his clean-shaven head, but he was slowly scanning the people in and around the pool.

All five of them quickly scrambled into the cabana. Clara checked to make sure the triplets' spell had dissipated, and quickly scanned everyone's magic. "He's not close enough to pull your magic, yet."

"And he's not wearing the goggles," Ed noted. He slowly drew one of the cabana's front curtains closed, and they all huddled behind it.

"What's he doing—" Idalia began to ask.

"Why are you all hiding in here?" Clara's Mom, dressed in a crisp gray business suit, ducked into the cabana. She frowned as she saw Clara's expression. "What's wrong."

"A Paladin, Mom," Clara said.

Arlene turned and quickly spotted the man in the black trench-coat. Clara peeked around the curtain and saw that the Paladin was still moving slowly and deliberately through the pool area, carefully looking at each guest and staff member he passed.

"I think not," Mom said firmly. She withdrew a small handheld radio from the pocket of her blazer. "Security, Operations. This is Arlene Thorn. There's a man in a black trenchcoat stalking around the lower pool, across from the cabanas. He's acting suspicious—I think he might be casing guests for theft."

"Copy," the radio replied at once.

"That will keep him busy. As soon as Security rounds him up, I'm taking you back to the room. Girls, you're coming with us."

"Okay," Idalia said.

"He wasn't wearing those goggles," Mom noted quietly.

Clara peeked around the curtain again and saw four uniformed guards surrounding the Paladin. "They have to have our photos or something."

"Let's go."

Mom led everyone around the back of the cabana and into a service corridor. "I'll take you up in one of the housekeeping elevators."

"You won't get in trouble?" Ed asked.

"It's fine. We do this with VIPs."

A brisk ten-minute walk and a quick elevator ride later and they were all relaxing in the enormous suite. "You all stay here," Mom instructed. "I'll have some lunch sent up. Girls, you're welcome to stay as long as you like, but if you leave, have your parents or someone come up and get you. The valet can hold your car up front, just give them my name."

"What exactly *is* your job here, Mom?" Clara asked. "You sound important." A year ago, Mom had been taking the bus to clean other people's homes, and now you could just give her name to the hotel valet?

"Senior Director of Hotel Operations, baby," Mom said with a smile. "Medium-big shot. You knew I had a degree," she added as Clara's eyebrows rose.

"I guess," Clara said softly. Even Ed looked impressed.

"Dad will be back around three, and you text me if you need

anything, but do not leave this room. I'm going to go see what Security found out."

"You three staying?" Ed asked as Clara's mother left and the heavy door *clacked* shut.

"Are you kidding?" Harriett asked, grabbing the television remote and plopping into the plush leather sofa. "She said 'room service.' I don't care if a Paladin brings it, I'm in."

CHAPTER 2

BACK TO SCHOOL

"Wow, they really tore everything down," Clara observed as she and Ed emerged into Underhill. "It looks good, though."

Her parents had escorted them both from the condo to the Border, and Mom had even floated the idea of having one of the resort's security people accompany them. Dad had nixed that idea. "How in the world would we explain that, Arlene?" he'd chuckled. But he'd insisted they go directly down Fremont Street and through the D hotel, ensuring they'd be on camera and around a crowd for the whole walk. Fortunately, they hadn't spotted a single trenchcoated Paladin.

"They'd said they would tear it all down during the break," Ed replied, stopping and looking around.

They'd emerged into Underhill from the first Border Clara had erected almost exactly a year ago. It was an enormous stone monolith, rising a dozen feet directly from the center of what had once been the school's playing field for Wizard's Rules Football. Now that it was in place, it couldn't easily be moved, so the school had been forced to relocate the field—and its attendant locker room facility and spectator stands. That work had apparently been completed while the students were finishing their term of Ordinary school through the winter and spring because the Border was now surrounded by nothing but fresh green grass.

"It's all so flat now," Clara said as she and Ed began walking again. The stone pathway from the field to the school was still in place, snaking through small flower gardens. "Although I guess I never really got used to this area." For the entirety of Clara's last term, the school had used a temporary field.

"They probably finished rebuilding everything around the new one," Ed said. "The teams were getting pretty tired of those temporary shacks they put up."

"I was getting tired of those wood grandstands," Clara said. "They hurt my butt."

Ed laughed as they wound through the last of the flower beds and approached the school's main entrance.

Linginbaum's School for Magic Users occupied a tall, imposing, fairytale castle that was modeled after the Ordinary-world Neuschwanstein castle in Bavaria. The school's upper structures, with its light-pink towers and stone crenelations, also looked like a giant version of Disneyland's Sleeping Beauty castle, a fact that made Clara giggle a little every time she saw it.

The heavy wooden entry doors had been thrown wide open as students trickled in. Ed and Clara stepped into the imposing main hall, blinking as their eyes adjusted to the dim lightning.

Clara couldn't see anything different since the last term. The main hall's ceiling soared several stories overhead, and long galleries stretched off along either side of the hall. Almost every part of the school could be accessed from those galleries: classrooms, the dining hall and kitchens, and even the main library were on the ground floor, magically occupying far more space than the castle's physical structure contained. The second level led to more classrooms, staff offices, and the student dorms. At the end of the main hall rose the imposing spiral Stairs, a semi-intelligent magical construct that—if it was in the mood—would take you to the faculty offices and other restricted places.

Bolted to the walls was a twisting spaghetti of bronze and copper piping, conduits for the various mundane magics that kept the castle operational. The Bavarian architects had, at some point in the school's history, become enamored of a Jules Verne-like steampunk aesthetic, relying on magically enhanced steam and other mediums to run the school's equipment, lights, kitchens, and more. The contrast between the metal pipes and the ancient-looking stone walls had seemed very strange to Clara during her first term here last year, but now it all seemed completely normal. She'd even—

"Hello, children."

Ed and Clara jumped at the steely tone of voice. They turned to see a tall, sharp-featured woman whose white hair was gathered into an impossibly tight bun at the back of her head. She wore a trim burgundy suit, long pants extending nearly to the floor, providing just a peek at a pair of chunky-heeled black shoes. Her gray eyes caught the light from the chandeliers overhead, glinting with shrewd intelligence.

"Oh, hello," Clara stammered, caught off-guard by the woman's severe demeanor.

"I am Professor Herrera," the woman said smoothly. "Your new Headmaster. Your reputation, of course, precedes you, Miss Thorn. I presume this is Mr. Langsdale?" Ed nodded mutely. "Very good. I look forward to working with you this term."

Clara's mind was doing flip-flops. Where was Headmaster Dimmick? *I saw him less than two weeks ago! He never mentioned he was leaving!* "But—" she managed aloud. Herrera merely cocked an eyebrow. "Where's Headmaster Dimmick?"

"Professor Dimmick has taken up a special project on behalf of the government here in Underhill," Herrera replied, the eyebrow rising slightly higher at Clara's sharp tone. "I am, of course, honored to follow in his footsteps. I will also be taking over as liaison for your Border-raising activities, which I understand should be nearing completion."

"Oh," Clara said, not sure what else to say. She'd been comfortable with Headmaster Dimmick, and this new, sharp-edged woman. . . she couldn't imagine getting along quite as well. Dimmick had been. . . warm. Stern, when he felt the need, but he'd been something of an uncle-like figure to Clara through the past year. "What about Mr. Mayer, Mr. Thomas, Miss Cook, and Mrs. Harrington?" The foursome of witches had been instrumental in helping Clara locate just the right spot for the new Borders, and feeding her the purified magic she used to raise them.

"My understanding is that they've joined in the special project."

Clara's heart fell. She'd be starting all over.

"I'll call you to my office tomorrow, perhaps," Herrera continued, "and we can review your Border work so far and plan out what comes next. We'll have a new team of witches leading the effort to locate appropriate positions for the next Borders. They're very much looking forward to meeting you."

"Ok," Clara said even more softly. She'd gotten used to working with the last set of four, and they'd grown very efficient and friendly. *Why is everything changing all of a sudden?* she moaned in her head.

"Excellent to meet you both," Herrera said. "Is it safe to assume you had no problems with the Border?" Her tone remained even, but her gaze bored into them—this wasn't idle curiosity. Clara's breath caught in her throat.

"Not coming back, no," Ed said, finally speaking up. "Clara's parents escorted us."

"Not... coming back? But at another time?" Herrera took a step closer to them, and Clara repressed an urge to step backward as the woman loomed over them.

"There was a Paladin when we got to Las Vegas," Ed said. "And we saw another one. . . later."

The Headmaster nodded, her lips compressing into a grim line.

"We've received numerous reports of increased activity. Just one, each time? Not a group?" The teens nodded. "That fits the reports as well. We believe they've spread themselves thin in an effort to find more witches. You are, of course, to remain Underhill unless accompanied by an adult."

"Of course," Ed mumbled.

"And when you say your parents, Clara," Herrera asked, her voice exhibiting slight concern, "you mean your *adoptive* parents?" Clara nodded. "Hmm. I might advise. . . caution, next time. It would be better if a witch accompanied you to and from the Ordinary, if possible. Your hum—that is, your adoptive parents would be essentially defenseless against a Paladin. We're not sure they'd be above taking human hostages, if they felt it would advantage them."

Clara's heart grew tight. She'd never thought of Mom and Dad being in danger. "Oh."

"Just be careful. I'm sure we can find an appropriate escort at need." Herrera gave them a quick, decisive nod before continuing. "You'll be heading to your dorms, then?" Clara and Ed nodded. "Off you go. Best wishes for the new term."

The two teens scurried away, angling toward the mundane staircase that could be relied upon to lead to the upper floors without having to be cajoled.

"That was sudden," Ed said as they walked.

"Someone could have said something," Clara muttered as they headed up the stairs. "I saw everyone like two weeks ago."

"I wonder if something happened."

"Obviously *something* happened."

"Could you get a message to Dimmick? Ask him?"

"Maybe." Clara fell silent, her stomach roiling with concern. "I mean, fine if he took another job, I guess," she added, although her tone suggested it definitely wasn't fine. "But the entire team? All of them? All at once?"

"Possibly something to do with the Paladins? Apparently, we weren't the only ones who saw one."

"Maybe," Clara repeated, chewing her bottom lip.

They stepped through the archway that led to the dorms. This long hallway led to entrances for each dorm's common room. Every class of students stayed in the same dorm through their entire time at Linginbaum's, but the dorms themselves rotated physically. That meant first- and ninth-years were at the start of the hallway, on the right and left sides, respectively. The annual rotation had already happened, and so they walked past the first doors to the tenth-years'. They pushed through the brass-bound door into their common room.

Clara inhaled deeply, reveling in the smell of the leather-bound books that lined almost every wall, the slightly musty smell of the old furniture, and the indescribable brassy scent of magic that pervaded the room.

"Clara! Ed!" The triplets were already there, and Idalia bounced up from the battered old sofa that occupied the middle of the room. "You're here!" She dashed over to meet them, followed closely by her sisters.

"I thought you guys weren't coming in until tomorrow," Ed said, giving Idalia a quick hug.

"Mom and Dad wanted to bring us personally, and yesterday was the only day they could both get free," Johanna explained, giving Clara a squeeze.

"Who else is here?" Ed asked.

"Finlay. He's in his room already. And you won't believe it, but—
"

"Hello."

Clara's eyes widened as the owner of that soft, sure voice stood and gave a small wave from one of the threadbare armchairs. "Brinley?"

"Brinley's staying in the dorm this term," Johanna whispered loudly.

"But I thought—" Clara started. Brinley Marsh was—well, had been—one of the "in" crowd, a follower of the rich, spoiled, holierthan-thou Phoebe Witcher. The Witcher family maintained a private residence on the school grounds, open to all of Phoebe's coterie. Brinley had always seemed like an odd fit for that clique, with her gentler demeanor and strong, subtle grasp of magic. She was certainly pretty enough to blend in, but—"I mean, last year you—"

"It's a long story," Brinley said quickly. "I just. . . I hope we can be friends now."

Clara's eyebrows climbed into her hairline. "Of course," she said softly. Brinley had never been overtly mean. She'd simply been *with* the kids who were.

"Elsie's here too," Johanna said. "She's—"

"Unpacked," Elsie Green announced as she strode through the door on the opposite side of the common room. She'd doubled down on her Goth look, with what looked like freshly dyed black hair and even more severe eyeliner than Clara remembered. "Didn't bring much. Hi, Clara. Hi, Ed."

"Hey," Ed replied with a wave. "How was Ordinary school?"

"Moms pulled me after a week," Elsie said with a shrug. "All the Paladin stuff freaked them out. So I homeschooled until it was time to come back here."

"I'm jealous," Harriett sighed. "Our parents still have this nostalgia for Ordinary school, I think."

"Don't be," Elsie said firmly. "Moms' ideas of education involve a lot of pagan stuff. Dancing naked under the new moon kind of thing. If I never burn a sage branch again, I'll be very happy."

"Did you guys know Dimmick is gone?" Clara asked.

Everyone nodded. "We met the new one on the way in," Harriett said with a grimace. "Bit of a statue, isn't she?"

"She did seem very. . . firm," Ed agreed. "Do you know what happened to Dimmick?"

"He's on a special project," Brinley said. Everyone turned to look at her. "My father's working with him. Well, under him. It was all just settled this past week."

"That's pretty fast," Clara said.

Brinley nodded. "It was. But Dad was. . . you know he worked for the Witchers?"

Clara blinked. "I did not. Is that why you're. . ."

"It's related," Brinley said with a sigh. "I'm just glad he has a good job again. Apparently, Dimmick's been snatching up people left and right to work on the new effort."

"What is it?" Idalia asked.

Brinley shrugged. "No idea. Dad won't talk about it. Not even a clue." She paused. "But I think it's about Paladins. He was. . . really cagey when I asked him point-blank." She paused again, as if weighing her next words. "Clara, do you know if your Mom. . ."

Clara's shoulders tensed. "I haven't heard from her," she said, struggling to keep her tone even. "But if it's an anti-Paladin thing, she's probably in on it. It's all she thinks about. That and. . . Dad."

An awkward silence stole over the room as everyone exchanged uncomfortable glances.

They were saved by Finlay entering through the door Elsie had just used. "Hey, guys," he said in his soft Irish lilt.

Now Clara's heart quickened and butterflies filled her stomach. "Hey, Finlay," she said warmly. She walked over to him and gave a tight hug.

"Oh, hey," he said, stiffening. Clara let go at once and took a step back. "How's, um. . . stuff?" he asked, taking a step away from her.

"Good?" Clara asked, frowning slightly. She'd been excited to see Finlay since the end of last term. The two of them had been. . . close, she'd thought. *Did I do something wrong?*

"Are you still putting up Borders?" Elsie asked.

Clara turned back to the room as Finley edged past her and sank into a worn armchair. "Yeah. Last week. They think I have about a dozen to go. But Dimmick was in charge. And now even the witches who were helping me are changing, Herrera said."

"So that means. . ." Harriett asked with a frown.

Clara sighed with frustration. "I don't know. But it's like starting over. The old team had gotten perfect, we were standing up Borders really fast, once they found a spot." Clara's unique skills as a mathemagician let her wind together magic from other witches, and use it to dig deep into Underhill's roots to create a permanent connection between the Fae world and the Ordinary. "Herrera said she'd talk to me tomorrow about it."

"Idalia, you guys didn't have any more Paladin problems, did you?" Ed asked.

All three triplets shook their heads. "Haven't seen any since the one at the resort. But Clara's Mom called our parents, and they wouldn't let us out of their sight unless we were in the house."

"You saw Paladins?" Brinley asked, her voice suddenly tense.

Clara nodded. "One chased Ed and me when we got to Vegas. My Mom put us up at the resort she works at, and we saw another one at the pool there. He didn't see us, and Mom had hotel security walk him out or something."

"Moms said there was one wandering around our village," Elise said.

"Dad pulled me out of Ordinary school two weeks early," Brinley said. "He said there'd been sightings everywhere."

"Ma did the same," Finlay said. "She and Da wouldn't let me leave the house until I came here, and they insisted on coming with me."

"Which Border did you use?" Clara asked.

"The one in Dublin."

"That comes out. . . near the Underhill capital, doesn't it?" Clara said, trying to remember. She'd set up more than two dozen so far, and had started to lose track pretty early on.

"Aye. But they've got Anchors everywhere now. None here on the castle mesa yet, but there's one straight to Linginham, and Da was able to use travel magic from there."

"Funny, translocation Anchors and travel magic working Underhill," Ed mused. "Long distances used to be risky."

Clara had never heard the term *Anchor* before. She filed it away for later investigation.

Brinley nodded. "Underhill is more. . . stable, somehow. Geographically."

"Interesting," Ed said. "I wonder if—"

"Classes don't start for five days," Elsie groaned. "Let it go, Ed."

"Hello, Clara!"

They all whirled to see Phoebe Witcher strolling into the common room, her long, perfectly straight black hair gently framing her perfect, heart-shaped face. The rest of her clique streamed in behind her: Phoebe's minion, Lucy Strout; the unremarkable Augustus Webb; and Phoebe's perfectly vapid boyfriend, Sinclair Hunt.

"My goodness, it's crowded in here," Phoebe continued in an artificially bright, saccharine-sweet voice. "Clara, however do you cope?"

"Hi, Phoebe," Clara sighed, edging next to Finlay's chair. "What're you doing here?"

"Well, it seems we have an empty bedroom in the residence," Phoebe chirped, sending a hard look at Brinley, "and Father suggested you might want to get out of this. . . *common* room and have some space to yourself!"

Clara was losing the battle to not roll her eyes. "No thanks, Phoebe. I actually have my own room here, and this is where my friends are. We have a ton of fun here, right, Brinley?"

"Uh, right," Brinley said quickly.

"Well," Phoebe huffed, her face locked into a fake-cheerful smile, "I'm sure it's just like a big sleepover every night. But you know, we *do* have a private chef and—"

"I'm good, Phoebe," Clara said firmly. "But it's almost lunchtime. Would you like to head down to the dining hall with us?"

Clara watched Phoebe's jaw muscles clench as she fought to maintain her smile. "That's ever so nice of you, of course," she got out, her teeth barely parting. "We'll have to pass. If you change your mind, you know where to find us! Come on, all." She whirled and pushed through her posse, who quickly fell in behind her.

"What," Ed asked as the door *clanked* shut behind them, "was that?"

Clara let out an exasperated sigh. "She started doing that toward the end of last term. Her father's making her do it. He keeps trying to have input into where the new Borders come out in the Ordinary."

"Why?" Harriett asked.

"One of the Border team witches said he's trying to set up isolated resorts on islands and stuff. Obviously gives him more control if there's a Border that goes directly there."

"It's worse than that," Brinley said quietly.

All eyes turned to her. "How so?" Clara asked.

"Aaron Witcher still believes in the Oberherr Doctrine." The common room seemed to grow a bit colder at that. Minister Oberherr, in an unlikely alliance with the Paladins, had managed to destroy nearly all the old Borders between Underhill and the Ordinary. His plan had been to implement tight control over the remaining ones, setting up checkpoints and controlling the movement of witches between the worlds. His ultimate goal was to have all witches living Underhill, under his "benevolent" control.

"So he wants to control who uses them," Harriett said in a flat voice.

"And he still thinks we should all live Underhill, yes. The resorts would be for the wealthy, a place they could go for a change of scenery." Brinley's face looked troubled. "It's why Dad quit working for him."

"So he was pressuring you, Clara?" Ed asked.

"Yeah. Oh, he was super nice about it. I didn't know. . . well, it doesn't matter."

"So you told him no?" Idalia asked.

Clara shrugged. "I told him it's really not my decision. On the Underhill side, the Borders need to go where there's a strong flow of magic. That usually corresponds with someplace in the Ordinary, but the Border basically finds its own way there. If I try to have it come out anyplace else, it doesn't hold long." She thought about it for a moment. "And you know, I don't think they like being in isolated places. They seem to like… being around people." She had a theory or two about *why,* given what had happened to Underhill's magic when the old Borders started coming down. It was at least obvious to her that magic *originated* in the Ordinary and flowed into Underhill through the Borders.

"So they're all in big cities?" Elsie asked.

Clara nodded. "Mostly. If not, then someplace pretty bustling, at least." She was convinced it had something to do with people. Humans, specifically. The more there were in a given area, the more strongly the new Borders were drawn to that area.

"Huh," Ed said, his brow wrinkling. "That makes me wonder if—
"

"Not class time, Ed," Elsie interjected. "And Clara's right, it's almost lunch—"

"Halloo, Tenth!"

The common room door burst open, and a loose knot of energy rushed through, in the form of the Tenth-Year football team: Darrell, Tark, Bernice, Selma, Roman, and Darcie.

Out of the corner of her eye, Clara saw Finlay slump further into his chair.

"Darrell!" Idalia cried, scurrying over to give the Center a hug. "It's so good to see you!"

"You're going to be seeing a lot more of me—of all of us—this term," Darrell chuckled.

"Why?" Harriett asked.

"They tore down the team houses to make room for grandstands and the new locker rooms," Tark sighed. "They're promising to rebuild new houses next term, but meanwhile it's back to the dorms for all of us."

"Oh, great," Harriett sighed. "Just be quiet in the mornings?" The main reason for the football teams having their own houses was their pre-dawn, three-times-a-week practices.

"I commit to nothing," Darrell said with a grin.

The conversation continued as the students broke off into small groups and discussed what they'd done during breaks, how Ordinary school had gone, and more. Clara took the opportunity to crouch next to Finlay's chair. "Hey, is everything okay?"

"I'm fine," he said dully, refusing to meet her eyes.

"Finlay, I—"

"I'm fine," he repeated. Again, without even looking at her, he lurched out of the chair, moved swiftly toward the dorm's exit, and pushed out into the hallway.

Clara rose to find Idalia standing beside her. She'd always been the kinder of the triplets, Clara thought, and the expression on her face now was one of confusion and sorrow. "What's going on?" she asked quietly.

Clara shook her head sadly. "I don't know."

They stood for a moment before Idalia continued. "Are you worried about the new Headmaster?"

Clara sighed. "I don't know. She's so. . . sharp." Something occurred to her. "You know who she reminds me of?"

"Who?"

"Mycroft." Professor Mycroft had been similarly stern, her accent and fairytale witch attire disguising a seething loathing of all things human and Ordinary. She'd helped destroy the old Borders before Clara's first term started, and she'd been firmly aligned with Oberherr's plan to keep all witches trapped in Underhill.

Idalia tensed. "There are still a lot of people who think Oberherr was right," she admitted. "Do you think. . ."

"I don't know," Clara said softly. *Things had been going so well.* She'd looked forward to coming back to Linginbaum's, to learning more magic, to raising more Borders. . . to getting to know Finlay better. "I don't know."

Idalia laid a gentle hand on Clara's shoulder as Darrell loudly proclaimed his readiness for lunch.

"And the *küchenelfen* wait for no student," Elsie agreed, striding toward the door. "Let's eat."

Clara and Idalia followed the group out of the dorm, trails of chilled and dark emotions creeping around them as they went.

CHAPTER 3
SCHOOL DAYS

"Acceptable, Miss Green. But keep working on it." Professor Fitzgerald wandered amongst the students' workbenches, peering closely at the constructs they were building. Today's assignment was to create an amulet capable of holding a sustained illusion for at least a day, and nearly everyone in the class was struggling. Sparks and flashes of light danced everywhere as they tried to imbue their spells into the metal discs they'd been given.

Clara had stayed unfocused since everyone began, watching the ebbs and flows of glowing magical equations as everyone worked. She turned to Elsie now, seated on the bench next to her, intent on seeing what "acceptable" looked like. "It's wavering a lot," Clara cautioned. In Clara's vision, Elsie's magic was a tightly knotted stream of strange-shaped numbers and mathematical symbols pulsing uncomfortably between mauve-crimson and teal-emerald. Most of the symbols were firmly anchored to the amulet, but thin tendrils kept stabbing outward, as if trying to escape. Briefly refocusing on the real world, Clara saw an illusory bonsai tree sitting on the table where the medallion was lying.

"Can you help?" Elsie whispered. Clara's ability to see magic as mathematical equations often let her see where someone was feeding it too much power, or where they weren't visualizing the output correctly. In her mind's eye, Clara saw those errors as imbalances in the equations, and with concentration she could correct them.

"I'm not sure," Clara replied with a frown, switching her focus back to the magic. Most of the wavering colors seemed to be concentrated in two small areas, but the equations were spinning so quickly she couldn't make them out. That was compounded by a delicate fog of deep sapphire symbols that seemed to be emanating from the construct. "There are a couple of imbalances, but I can't tell which one is the illusion itself. It's bleeding energy everywhere, but that's the point, right?"

"Clara?" Professor Fitzgerald asked. "Are you getting it?" All of the professors had gotten used to Clara's unorthodox way of using magic—and her equally unusual way of learning it. Where other students learned gestures and words to help them focus their magic into the proper shape, Clara had to *see* someone perform a spell correctly before she could duplicate the effect herself.

"I think maybe?" Clara replied, more peering closely at the amulet. She was vaguely aware of Elsie's fingers twitching in the prescribed pattern, and the Welsh phrases the other girl was murmuring. *Excellent language for semi-permanent constructs,* the Professor had said at the outset of the lesson, *but more consonants than anyone really needs.* "It's supposed to be leaking energy as light, right?"

"Mmm, I wouldn't say 'leaking,'" Fitzgerald said. "It's meant to be a controlled release. Remember, we're investing energy in the metal itself, which is why we use brass or copper. They take very well to magic. Here, Miss Green, do you mind?"

"Go for it," Elsie sighed, taking a step back. "I haven't made it burst into flames yet, but if I keep pushing, I'm pretty sure that's what will happen." Elsie's magical quirk—something nearly every young witch learned to deal with—was summoning flame, whether that was her intention or not. She'd largely mastered it last term, mainly by being more patient and not pushing her magic as hard.

The professor's fingers started twitching as she said, *"Hud a fuddsoddwyd, egni integredig, delwedd wedi'i goleuo.* You really have to hit that *th* sound pretty hard."

In Clara's eyes the rainbow-hued symbols writing around the amulet suddenly got firmer, their colors stabilizing into blues and greens, and their swirls slowing to a more deliberate pace. Several of them shifted form, numbers distending in odd directions and letters ballooning into caricatures of themselves as the equations balanced. "Oh, I see," she said softly, mesmerized by the glowing spectacle. "It *is* more controlled. Elsie, you were coming in too sharp, I think. The professor's was more. . . rounded, if that makes sense. Softer."

"Interesting," the professor murmured. Then, more loudly, "Now that I've stopped the actual investment, do you see any difference?"

Clara looked more closely. "Yeah. It's eddying more slowly. And. . . hmm."

"What is it, dear?"

"I can definitely see the illusion part, for one." Indeed, the fog of dark blue symbols had thinned to a haze, magic bleeding out at a much more regular and sedate pace. "But. . . hmm." She leaned in more closely, trying to track the core equations as they spun lazily around the surface of the amulet.

"What else?" the professor prompted.

"It's like. . . some of the equations are simplifying."

"Simplifying?" The professor sounded intrigued.

"You know how you solve a complex algebra equation, right? You start by eliminating equivalent bits on both sides. Like, if both sides have a times-two, you just drop those since they cancel each other out. It's kind of like that. These ones are getting. . . simpler."

Fitzgerald chuckled. "I'm going to have to take your word for it, dear. Algebra was never my strong suit, even at your age."

"Well, that's what the magic is doing. It's like the spell is actually simpler, once you get it in place."

Professor Fitzgerald said nothing more, but her lips pursed. *Oops.* Clara had had a few months to forget how much adult witches disliked Clara telling them about magic.

"Can I try again?" Elsie asked impatiently.

"Of course. Just let me. . . actually, Clara, do you think you could dispel the investment? Now that you're seeing it?"

Clara nodded slowly, still staring intently at the amulet. "I think so." She prodded the formulae with her mind, but felt them resist. She hummed softly as she worked her way through the problem. There wasn't a weak spot, exactly, but the bit of the math that put out actual visible light might be. . . vulnerable. Clara tugged at it, and watched as the supporting equations flexed in an attempt to keep up. "I think I can overload it, actually." She pulled again, harder this time.

"Do be care—" Fitzgerald started.

"Oh!" Elsie exclaimed, just as Clara jerked back. The amulet's entire energy store—sufficient to cast a visible illusion for as long as a day—expended itself at once, resulting in a blinding flash of cerulean light.

"Well, that's one way to do it," the professor chuckled, rubbing her eyes. "Normally, you'd draw the energy back into yourself."

"I can't do that," Clara said apologetically. "Magic doesn't. . . I can't store it like you all can. I just manipulate what I see. Maybe I could ground it?"

"Perhaps," Fitzgerald said dubiously. "I suppose with a larger working that's what you'd do." She sounded uncertain. "Still, you've seen it now. Do you think you could do your own?" Fitzgerald asked.

Clara nodded. "I think so. I'd like to try."

"I'll get you a fresh amulet, then. Miss Green, you should be all set to try again with yours."

"Professor?" Phoebe Witcher's false-sweet voice cut across the room.

"Yes, Miss Witcher?"

"Could I ask you and Clara to check my work, please?"

Clara rolled her eyes as Fitzgerald agreed and led her to Phoebe's workbench. "The illusion seems strong," the professor said. Phoebe had chosen a small terrier. They hadn't worked up to *moving* illusions, and Clara thought the static three-dimensional image looked unrealistic. "Clara, tell me what you think." The professor chuckled. "You know, I've never been able to directly judge whether any of these would last the day or not. You can though, can't you?"

"Maybe," Clara said noncommittally. She unfocused her eyes and let the iridescent math appear. "It's good," she admitted reluctantly. And it was: Phoebe's equations were tighter even than the professor's had been, shining an even apricot-umber. She'd either cast the spell more directly or the equations had already simplified themselves, because Clara couldn't see any redundancy. The diffuse haze of magic that created the actual illusion looked incredibly stable. "I don't know if it'll last all day," Clara temporized, loathe to pay Phoebe any compliments, "but it looks as stable as yours did."

"A day or more then," Fitzgerald proclaimed. "Excellent work, Miss Witcher. Now—no, no, Mr. Webb, you're doing it all wrong I can tell from over here," Fitzgerald snapped as she hurried away.

"Thank you, Clara," Phoebe simpered.

"Don't mention it," Clara grumbled, turning to go.

"Clara," Phoebe said softly, the pretense vanishing from her voice. Clara stopped and looked at the other girl. "I really wish you'd consider Father's offer. He'd take care of you, you know. Your parents, too. The human ones."

"Mom and Dad are fine," Clara gritted out between clenched teeth.

"He gets what he wants in the end," Phoebe said. Was Clara imagining it, or was there a note of... *urgency* in her voice?

"I don't control where the Borders come out, Phoebe," Clara insisted. "They... *look* for places in the Ordinary to connect to. They like being around people. I just hold their shape and feed them power while they do it."

"You made that first one come out in the Nevada desert," Phoebe reminded her.

"I forced it. And it didn't stay, remember? People were popping out all over the place. I had to re-anchor it, let it find its own way. Your dad keeps asking me to put one on those islands he owns, but there's nobody there. I can't even get a Border within miles of them."

Phoebe frowned. "Really?"

"Really."

She shook her head. "He's not going to believe you."

"I don't care, Phoebe. *I don't care.* I don't want your father's money, or his approval, or any of it. Why can't people just use whatever Border they want and then translocate to your family's islands or whatever? It's what everyone else does."

A shadow passed across Phoebe's face, and Clara saw the other girl's shoulders tense beneath her gray school blazer. "You'll see."

FRIDAY AFTER CLASSES - SOCCER PRACTICE

"Please tell me you and Phoebe Witcher aren't becoming pals," Elsie muttered. She, Clara, Ed, and the triplets were trudging out to the new football field. The Tenth-year team was scheduled to have a practice match against the two Eleventh-year teams, and they'd decided to go cheer on Darrell and team.

"Don't even suggest that," Clara grimaced. "No, she's still trying to convince me to be her dad's pawn."

"The Borders?"

Clara nodded. "It's those islands of his. I keep explaining that I can't get a Border to anchor there, but nobody believes me."

"Can't they just translocate like everyone else does?" Harriett asked.

Clara threw up her hands in frustration. "That's what I keep saying! But then Phoebe goes all dramatic and says, 'you'll see.' What's that even supposed to mean?"

Johanna frowned. "The Witchers are used to getting what they want."

"Mom and Dad said to steer clear of them," Idalia added.

"Well, I keep trying to," Clara grumbled. Then her tone lightened. "Oh. Oh, wow. I had no idea."

They'd stepped out of the copse of trees that separated the castle from the new football field. Previously, this area had contained a half-dozen residences, used by each upper year's football team. The teams started their day early, before the sun even rose, with work-outs that ended with a run to the field, on the opposite side of the castle.

Those residences had been removed, and in their place was an incredible new football facility. The standard triangular field had been set in the dead center of the available space, with the three goals erected in each point. Along the sides, sturdy single-story buildings of stone had been erected. As they drew closer, Clara saw that each of them offered concessions along the field-facing side, and her nose twitched as she caught the distinctive scent of hot Bavarian pretzels. The back side of each building contained showers, lockers, and storage for whatever teams were playing at the moment.

Atop those buildings rose the new grandstands, likewise constructed from stone. Each was four stories high, and in each game every level would be reserved for a specific year of students. As one of the teams actually playing, the Tenth-years were given one of the third levels—high enough to see the entire game, and more protected from the elements than the open-aired topmost level.

The three teams were already warming up on the field as Clara and her friends collected pretzels, cheese dipping sauce, and mugs of chilled water, and began trudging up the stairs to their designated level.

Each viewing level was actually well over a story high, Clara real-ized as they stepped off the staircase, allowing the six rows of padded benches to be tiered and giving everyone a good view of the field. The Tenth-year class, for some reason one of the smallest in the school, fit handily on the first row with room to spare.

"Think we'll ever be able to field two teams?" Ed asked as they sat. Every year ahead of them and the one behind had enough players for two teams.

"Not unless we get a lot of transfers from other schools," Idalia sighed. "Pity, too. If we had a second team maybe Finlay'd finally get on it."

"That boy is mad for football," Johanna sighed. "It's killing him that he's not on a team."

"You know he practiced with this brother during break?" Elsie said. "He was *sure* he'd make the team this time."

"They're starting," Clara said. She unfocused her eyes and swept her gaze across the field.

"What did they pick?" Ed asked.

Prior to the game, each team got to choose a number of traps to embed in the field. The locations were randomized, meaning a team had as good a chance of setting off their own traps as the others, and it made for exciting games. Last term, they'd discovered that Clara could see the traps, and she'd now seen enough of the different types to tell them apart.

"Two tanglers, one of the ones with the little sprites in it, oh, a concussion wave over by the Blue goal. Um. One I don't know. A waterspout, that'll be fun if they trip it. And I think that one's a time-sludge, but I always get that mixed up with the gravity one."

"Where's the Ender?" Harriett asked, scanning the field as if she'd be able to spot it first.

The Ender was a special ball, buried beneath the field. If it was set off, it would start zooming around on its own, targeting players at random and attempting to bash into them. The players, in turn, would try to deflect it into a goal, ending the game.

"Way off on the Blue-Red line," Clara said. "It'll take a miracle to set it off."

"Too bad you can't tell them," Elsie sighed. "It made everything go so much faster." When their last term had started, Clara had been able to communicate the Ender and trap locations to their team's coach, who could in turn direct the team's Center accordingly. Midway through the term, that trick had been banned—not only at Linginbaum's, but across all magic schools and even in the professional leagues. Elsie, never a big fan of the sport, had enjoyed how much more quickly the game progressed once one team knew where everything was.

"There's the kickoff," Idalia said eagerly, leaning over the railing next to her sisters.

"Oh, nice drive," Ed said approvingly. The Tenth-year team was playing as the Blue team, with the Eleventh-years taking the Red and Green goals. The three-way kickoff was always a precarious moment as three Centers lunged for the ball, but the Blue's Center had cast his Dash spell at exactly the right time. He'd shot forward at double speed, slamming the ball toward the Red goal where the two Blue Wings were waiting.

The Wings passed the ball between themselves a couple of times, moving it carefully toward the Red goal and avoiding players from the other teams. A flash of light accompanied one of the Wings' Kick spell, which drove the ball at triple speed toward the Red goal.

The Red goalie had anticipated that maneuver, using her Pop spell to translocate directly in front of the incoming ball. She barely had time to brace herself before the ball arrived, but she managed to keep it out of her goal. The ball careened off down the Red-Green line, and several players fell behind it in hot pursuit.

"Early on to be using that," Ed observed. "Now she'll have to wait five minutes to use it again."

"Tangler!" Johanna cried, clapping with glee.

A Green player had passed over the trap, triggering an eruption of writhing green vines. These lashed out in every direction, entangling players from all three teams and batting the ball out of bounds. A referee blew their whistle, stopping the game clock. The two Red

Guards caught in the vegetal mass lashed out with Flame spells, quickly burning the vines to ash. The remaining players shook their heads and brushed ash from their uniforms as they regained their feet.

The ball was handed to the Red Center, who threw it back into play. A brief squealing noise cut across the field, making everyone cringe for a moment as the field's loudspeakers came alive.

"And they're off again!" an announcer's voice echoed. "Blue takes possession, moving the ball smoothly between their players. Red and Green are quick to apply pressure. And look at that! Blue's Wing is cutting directly through the center of the field, heading toward the Red goal."

"He's going to hit the waterspout," Clara said excitedly.

"An attack by the Green Wing, using their Leap spell! But that's some impressive footwork by the Blue Wing—he's avoided the hit and is passing the ball to a Blue Guard!"

"Aw, he missed it," Clara said with disappointment.

"Green takes the ball mid-pass!" the announcer crowed. "They're moving well, clearly been practicing, and they're advancing on the Blue goal! Green is on the attack! Their Guard, Sarah, is making a run towards the goal. This could get interesting!"

One of the Green Wings is coming up fast, and I think we're going to see them use the old one-two—yes! Kick spell activated, and the ball is—no! They've hit a trap!"

A visible concussion wave blasted out from the trap, knocking the ball off-trajectory and slamming half the players to the ground. "The Blue Goalie has reacted quickly, running out of the net and grabbing the ball. They're fielding it to their Center, who passes to a Guard. Green is moving in for an intercept—Earth attack! That'll be her only spell for this period, but she's got the Blue team off their feet and she's taken possession, heading toward the Red goal!"

"Look over there!" Clara pointed.

Everyone followed and saw the Blue player hauling themselves upright, less than a foot from where the Ender was buried. They took off running and passed directly over it.

"ENDER!" screamed the announcer, echoed by dozens of fans.

The ball burst from the field, scattering dirt that just as quickly re-formed to fill in the hole. The hapless Blue who'd triggered it was tossed out of bounds, where they'd have to stay until play stopped.

The Ender abruptly halted its upward flight, spun crazily for a split second, and then shot off perpendicular to the bounds line it had been buried beside. Players dove out of its way, even briefly abandoning the game ball. The ball stopped abruptly against the opposing boundary line, reoriented, and careened off in a new direction.

"Everyone's still trying to keep the game ball under control, but oh! Green Center down, and that looks like it hurt folks," the announcer said with glee. "But they've got the Ender moving toward the Blue goal now. That Goalie hasn't used their—Pop spell, folks! They've taken the Ender right on the chest and are down hard, but the Ender's back off in—Kick spell! That's a Blue Wing, and they've got the ball—goal! Point for Blue, goal in the Green net! But with the Ender out, play continues!"

The Green goalie, shaking their head, quickly grabbed the game ball and tossed it toward their Center—just as the Ender arrived, striking the Center in the back. He went down, and the Ender fired off at right angles, smacking directly into the Green goal.

The crowd went wild. "Game over, folks! Game over! With the Ender hitting the Green goal off a Green player, we look at the total score—and that's the Blue team! Congratulations, Tenth-years! Blue team wins!"

Clara and her friends were on their feet now, applauding wildly. The announcer continued reeling off a few statistics about the short game while the teams gathered to the middle of the field for fist-bumps.

"Well, at least it was over quickly," Elsie said, licking pretzel salt off her fingers. "What shall we do next?"

"Homework," Harriett sighed.

"You've got all day tomorrow," Elsie pointed out.

"Oh, you've forgotten, have you?" Harriett said, a wicked grin spreading over her face.

"Forgot—oh! I did!"

"What?" Clara asked.

""We're Tenth-years," Idalia said smugly. "We can go to Linginham on weekends!"

SATURDAY MORNING - LINGINHAM

"Good morning children, good morning!" Professor Maplethorpe chirped as Clara and her friends trooped out of the castle. Even Finlay had come along, although he'd jammed his hands into his trouser pockets, lowered his head, and slumped along with a despondent expression on his face. "We've a treat for you this term! Behold!" the professor added merrily.

Clara looked around, but didn't see anything in particular. Last term, transport to Linginham had been done either by the faculty or Twelfth-years, all of whom had been trained on the complexities of using translocation magic in Underhill. The distance between the school and the town was highly variable: it could be a five-minute walk one afternoon, and the journey of two or three days that same evening. Teleporting people across such variable distances required careful coordination between witches on both ends of the journey, instantaneous-communication crystals, and no small amount of sheer chutzpah.

But Maplethorpe was standing there alone, grinning wildly and pointing to a rock.

"Wait, is that an Anchor?" Elsie asked.

The professor's head bobbed emphatically. "It is! It is! One of the first to be successfully established out here in the wilds!"

Clara let her eyes slip out of focus, and she gasped at the swirls of lustrous magic packed into the white lump of limestone. She took a step closer, squinting to see.

"Is it safe?" Harriett asked dubiously.

Clara had never seen such complex magic. She'd seen what translocation magic looked like—she'd even cajoled a few senior students to teleport her around the mesa, a safe enough activity given the short distances, so she could scrutinize the spell. But this. . .

"Safe as tea!" Maplethorpe assured them. "And straight to the town square in Linginham! And back again!"

"What's an Anchor?" Clara asked as she continued to try and make sense of the magic. "Someone mentioned them before." The equations—all distended numbers and funhouse-mirror symbols, as usual—were impossibly tight, like the proverbial fine print on contracts that people were always telling about. The individual notations were smaller than her pinky-nails, and the lines of text packed so closely together that she could barely make out where one formula ended and the next one began.

"It's permanent translocation magic between two points," Ed said in awe. "I've used them in the Ordinary, but never here."

"Finlay said he used one coming in from the capital," Harriett recalled.

"Well, it's all thanks to this bright star, isn't it?" Maplethorpe gushed. Clara blushed as she realized the professor was talking about her. "It's these new Borders—they're making Underhill stable! You can get maps now, perfectly mundane ones, and they stay accurate! And this is the very first one on the castle mesa!"

Clara had picked out a couple of familiar-looking elements—that coefficient, for example, or that particular parenthetical expression. A derivative, there. That quotient. They looked a bit like—

"Let's go, Clara!" Ed said. Clara blinked and realized she and Ed were alone with Maplethorpe. "Everyone else is already through!" He reached down, touched the gleaming white rock, and vanished in a puff of light.

Maplethorpe waved Clara forward. "Just give it a pat, dear," she said excitedly. "Just a tap, right there on the—"

Clara's fingers brushed the rock and her world exploded.

Ribbons of rainbow-colored magic seared into life all around her twisting and curling happily off into the distance. Enormous geometric shapes, formed from the prismatic illumination, took shape: a shimmering octahedron, with facets of amaranth and zaffre, spun lazily before her. A delightfully complex icosahedron, this one glimmering in canary and periwinkle, bobbed gently in the distance.

We should have had these in geometry class, she giggled to herself.

Just as quickly as it had all flared into existence, it vanished, and Clara was standing in the middle of a large, grassy lawn.

"Finally!" Harriett said in exasperation. "C'mon!"

Clara blinked her eyes a few times and fell in behind her friends. "Where are we going?"

"We figure everyone gets to pick a place," Idalia said, hurrying after her sister. "Harriett insisted on going first. She wants chocolate. I'd like a new pair of jeans. Johanna's after a magic mirror—"

"I've saved for over a year for one!" Johanna said breathlessly.

"And then we're going to have lunch at The Eldritch Mare," Elsie announced.

"I have a couple of books I want to get, but you don't all have to come with me," Ed murmured. "What about you, Finlay?"

"New trading cards out," he said with a sigh. "M'brother's got one now, and I want to try and get a full set of his team. Clara?"

"I didn't know we were picking," she said as they hurried along. "And I was only here twice last term, I don't really—"

"You can hold your choice for later," Harriett announced. "We're here!"

All of Linginham was built in a very specific style that Ed had called "fantasy Tudor" last term. "It's basically what everyone thinks all of medieval England looked like," he'd explained, "but a lot sturdier and cleaner." The buildings were mostly two-story affairs with steeply pitched roofs, exposed beams stained dark brown, and spotless, whitewashed plaster walls. Harriett had led them to one that also featured large windows filled with trays of artful and delicate confections. A sign over the door proclaimed the shop as "Mrs. Efteling's Essential Enjoyments."

They all ducked in and Clara was instantly enchanted by the smell of the place. The strongest scent was that of rich, dark chocolate, layered over softer aromas of pastry and sweets. A display counter sat just inside, filled with brightly colored treats, while shelves along the two side walls were stuffed with gift boxes and assortments. Around the room, just below the ceiling, danced a line of magically levitating sweets, each wrapped in metallic foils and delicate ribbon.

"A Lemon Impossible, please," Harriett said, marching up to the counter. A kindly looking old lady stood behind the register, and she gave Harriet a smile and a knowing wink. She reached into the display cabinet, withdrawing what looked to be an ordinary, if somewhat large, lemon bar cradled in a paper-lace doily. A line of dark-colored berry was nestled into the top of the bar. "One dollar," she said, setting the treat on the counter.

Harriett paid, claimed her treat, and hustled everyone outside. As the shop door closed behind them, she said, "Stonna in the Eleventh year told me about these. Here, Clara, you try it first." Harriett broke off a piece, being careful to include a single berry. "Just nibble the edge, don't eat the berry yet. Be careful, they're supposed to be incredibly sour."

"I don't really like sour," Clara protested as she accepted her piece.

"Trust me," Harriett said with a grin.

Clara carefully nibbled off a tiny corner of the thick yellow curd. Her face immediately puckered, her eyes squeezing shut and her salivary glands suddenly going into hyperdrive. "Ow," she managed when her facial muscles relaxed a bit. "I told you I don't like—"

"Eat the berry," Harriett ordered.

Clara sighed, picked the berry off the top of the confection, and popped it in her mouth.

"Roll it around your tongue a lot as you chew," Harriett advised.

Everyone else was watching Clara intently.

"Okay," Clara said, swallowing the berry mash.

"Now take a big bite. The whole thing!"

"Harriett, I—"

"Trust me! But do it quick!"

Screwing up her courage and bracing herself for the onslaught, Clara shoved the remainder of the sour-lemon bar into her mouth.

Her eyes widened.

"Ish shweet," she mumbled as she chewed. And it was: what had at first been an almost indescribably sour flavor, something she'd been sure had been magically enhanced to be even more sour than possible, had suddenly become a wonderfully sweet, melt-in-your-mouth experience. It was still lemon, but now it was the silky lemon of a chiffon cake, or a fluffy lemon truffle filling. "Wow," she added, swallowing the last of it. "How is that possible?"

"It's not!" Harriett said with delight, breaking off pieces for everyone else. "That's why it's called a Lemon Impossible!"

Clara watched as everyone else repeated the experiment. Their faces scrunched as they nibbled a corner of the bar, looked speculative as they chewed the mostly flavorless dark berry, and then went all blissful as they ate the rest of the treat.

"What *is* that?" Ed asked dreamily as he swallowed the last of it.

"Magic berry," Harriett mumbled as she chewed. "Mrs. Efteling invented them. They turn anything sour into sweet, but only for a few seconds. Supposed to do the opposite if you eat something sweet, although I don't know why anyone would bother."

"That was *wonderful,*" Elsie sighed as she swallowed. "I'm coming back for another before we leave. Does she do other flavors?"

"Not yet," Harriett said, closing her eyes in satisfaction. "Mmm. But we'll check back. We can come down every weekend, now. Who was next?"

"Me," Idalia said. "Chwaraeon's is supposed to have a new stain-proof denim and I need a new pair of jeans anyway."

Clara and Finlay fell to the back of the pack, content to follow everyone on their errands. "You feeling better?" she asked quietly.

Finlay sighed and then shrugged. "I don't know. I really thought I'd get on the team, I guess."

"It's not the end of the—" Clara began.

"It is for me. My whole family is into football. Like, big. I'm the only one who's never made a team. Other than kiddies, which doesn't count."

"I'm glad to see you anyway," she ventured. After he didn't reply, she asked, "Is that all? You just seem. . . really down."

He sighed again. "It's. . . it's complicated." He shook his head. "I'll be fine. I just. . . there's nothing to talk about, is all." They walked a few more steps in silence. "Sorry."

"It's okay." It wasn't, though. Clara *liked* Finlay. She'd been mortified when she'd made him vomit by manipulating his magic to forcefully, but he'd eventually come around. She'd thought they'd grown close, and it hurt to see him like this. . . to see him aloof. Something was clearly bothering him and she couldn't imagine it was as simple as him not making a team.

They followed Idalia as she tried on and eventually purchased a new pair of jeans, and then Johanna as she claimed a small magic hand mirror. "You can tell it different makeup to try," she explained as the shop's clerk wrapped it for her. "And it'll show you what you'd look like. So you can try lots of things and not have to buy any makeup or clean it all off or anything."

"Makeup," Harriett had announced, "is stupid." It was the first time Clara had seen the triplets seriously disagree with each other.

The next stop was The Eldritch Mare, a sort of pub that apparently went all-out for student weekends. The school faculty and staff stayed out, along with most other adults who didn't work there, as the room was taken over almost entirely by students. Tenth-years and up were permitted unlimited visits to Linginham on weekends, and Eighth- and Ninth-years could obtain passes or come on designated weekends throughout the term. The Mare had decided to take as much of their business as it could.

Barrels of fizzycider were stacked along one wall, and the pub's owner's son stood guard, cheerfully accepting money for a mug full of the fall-flavored, foam-topped sparkling beverage. Clara had fallen in love with the stuff on her first trip through town with Professor Mycroft—she shuddered at the name—and hurried over to purchase a mug for herself. Another few dollars got a huge tray of snacks for their table. It was all food you might find in the Ordinary—hamburger sliders, chicken wings, nachos, cheese sticks, and the like—but each had been given a special twist from some unique Underhill intermediate or a bit of magic. The sauce on the sliders would fizz and pop as you ate them, tickling your tongue. The chicken wings worked in reverse: they were hot and spicy as you bit into them, but the fire faded quickly, leaving a pleasant sweetness behind. The nachos chips were in the school colors of gray and burgundy—Clara immediately wished the school had gone for something more appetizing—and covered in tiny red pearls. These would burst in your mouth as you chewed, releasing spicy, salsa-like flavors.

Lunch took well over an hour as they finished picking through the platter of snacks and bought two more rounds of fizzycider.

"I'm off to the bookstore," Ed said at last, draining the last from his mug. The triplets rolled their eyes and Elsie snorted. "I said you didn't have to go with me," Ed reminded them.

"I'll go," Clara offered at once. She knew the triplets would go off clothes shopping again, and she didn't really feel like tagging along.

"I'll go look at picture cards with you, Finlay," Elsie sighed.

"Trading cards," he mumbled.

"Whatever."

They agreed to regroup at the town square in an hour, with Harriett declaring her intention to buy another Lemon Impossible.

Everyone else handed her a dollar and asked for one for themselves, which she happily agreed to, before they broke off.

"What books are you after?" Clara asked.

"There's one called *Geotemporal Studies of Underhill in the Fae Era,*" he said. "There's supposed to be a copy in the school library, but nobody can find it. I know, I know," he said in a self-deprecating tone, "it's boring nerd stuff. I just—"

"It's actually not," Clara said firmly. "C'mon, Ed," she teased as he gave her side-eye, "I'm as much of a nerd as you are. And hey. . ." she continued thoughtfully, "do you think they might have books on mathemagic? Or at least other mathemagicians?"

"They might."

"The library doesn't have any. I asked."

"That's. . . kind of weird, actually. It's a well-known branch of magic, even if there aren't ever more than one of you at a time. We'll ask."

Bookenders' turned out to be a well-lit, non-musty shop with wide aisles between the neat, carefully ordered shelves—nothing like the kind of bookstore Clara had imagined. "I never came in here last term," she said.

"You spent most of your time at the Mare with Finlay and Elsie," Ed reminded her.

"I *do* like fizzycider," she admitted.

Ed approached the counter, where a tall, middle-aged man, dressed in a spotless button-up shirt under a trim black vest, waited for them. "Do you have any copies of *Geotemporal Studies of Underhill in the Fae Era* by any chance?"

The man frowned. "No. Wouldn't they have that up at your library?"

"They're supposed to," Ed said with a sad sigh, "but nobody can find it. Can you order a copy?"

"Oddly. . . no," the man said, shaking his head. "We *did* have a copy, maybe a month or so back. Only a third edition, but very well-bound and in excellent condition. We sold it, so I tried to place an order for another copy, only to find it's out of print. Nobody's making it anymore."

"Why?" Ed asked.

The man shrugged. "Beats me. Must not be moving enough copies to make it worth doing runs anymore."

"Huh," Ed said thoughtfully.

"What about mathemagic?" Clara asked. "Or something on mathemagicians?"

The man tilted his head, looking at her curiously, before recognition dawned. "You're her," he said in an excited whisper. "You're the witch—Clara, right? Clara Holdaway?"

"Clara *Thorn*," she corrected him firmly. "I was adopted."

"Y—yes, yes of course," he stammered. "Sorry. Um. Mathemagic. You know, I don't think I've ever run across a book on the subject. But. . . hmm. Oh! You know what. . ." he trailed off as he dashed from behind the counter and scurried down one of the aisles. Ed and Clara followed.

He stopped in front of a particular section and began running his index finger across the book spines. "Morrisy. . . Morrisey with an 'e,' no. . ." he reversed directions, moving to the next shelf up. "Morpendor, Morningstar, Mollifant, ah! Here we are, Moriarty." He withdrew a slim volume from the shelf and handed it to Clara. "A biography of Enola Weakman, by Talbot Moriarty. The most famous mathemagician of the Victorian age. She was the one who worked out the trick with the fairy rings, did you know that? First one to raise a witch-made Border. Led the way to the whole colonization of Underhill."

"Really?" Clara breathed as she ran a finger across the cover's embossed title. "How much?"

"For you? I insist," the man said firmly. "My treat. Most of my family lives in the Ordinary, you know," he added in a quieter voice. "In fact, most books on witches and magic are *written* in the Ordinary. There's only even one printer here in Underhill. So when the Borders went down last year. . ." He stopped, shuddering slightly at the memory. "So thank you."

"You're welcome. And thank you," she added, tucking the book into her bag. "Ed, what else did you need?"

"What?" Ed blinked, and Clara realized he'd been scanning the titles on the shelves. "Oh. Nothing. Thanks," he said to the shopkeeper before turning and hurrying out of the store.

"What's the rush?" Clara asked, scurrying to keep up. "We don't have to meet the others for at least another—"

"There's something weird," Ed said flatly. He led Clara a couple of blocks further before stopping next to a small art gallery. "So *Geotemporal Study* is gone, fine. So they're not printing anymore, fine. But you know what else he didn't have?"

"What?" Clara said, confused.

"*Translocational Basics* by Albus Mendocino. *Spatial Folding Techniques and Traps* by Elena Laciente. *Thirteen Rubrics for Anchoring and Staking* by Winfred McPherson."

"Why do you know all of those?" Clara asked.

"Because they were all on my list. They're all ones the school is supposed to have—Mendocino's used to be a *textbook,* for crying out loud!" Clara could tell Ed was stressed, as his normally undetectable Creole accent started getting stronger. "And all of them have to do with spatial and translocational magic. McPherson is the main authority on building Anchors!"

"I. . . what does that mean? The books, I mean?"

He shook his head. "I don't know. Maybe. . . maybe with all the new Anchors going up, he's just sold out. We'll check next week, I guess. It's just weird that they're *all* sold out. I mean, nobody from the government is going to be reading Mendocino as they wander around setting up new Anchors."

"The government does it?"

"Normally," Ed said. "They handle it in the Ordinary, at least, so that we can have a network of linkages between Borders. They've been running around like mad, setting them up since all the Borders have moved. So I assume they're the ones doing it Underhill, now that it's feasible. But," he said with some heat, "they're not reading Mendocino to do it."

"Could it. . ." Clara lowered her voice. "Oberherr still has supporters," she reminded him. "People who think we should all stay in Underhill, all the time. Would they have any reason to want those books?"

Ed thought about it. "McPherson covered Staking," he said at last.

"Which is?"

"It's how you take down an Anchored route. You have to take both Anchors at once or the magic will whiplash and cause a lot of damage. Staking is the process. It usually involves iron, so it's pretty dangerous in and of itself."

"So maybe," Clara said. "We need to keep an eye on this. And we're definitely checking back next weekend to see if he got more books."

"Okay."

"Now c'mon, let's go find the others. And I could use a fizzycider to go."

SATURDAY NIGHT - DREAM

After a light dinner in the school's dining hall, the Tenth-years retired to their common room to chat about their day. The football team, it turned out, had bought out the rest of Mrs. Efteling's Lemon Impossibles to celebrate their win on Friday. These they shared generously with their classmates, and everyone laughed at the pinched, pained expressions around the room as they dared each other to take ever-large bites before chewing the magical berries and blissfully enjoying the rest of the treats.

When lights-out was called, they all made their way out of the common room and down the hall that led to their individual rooms. This dorm had been two stories last year, but with their class so small the upper level had seemingly vanished, consolidating everyone into a single long corridor. Clara had again been assigned a room close to the shared lavatories, a luxury she very much appreciated. After cleaning up, and in a set of fresh pajamas, she snuggled into her comfortable, sturdy bed and closed her eyes.

Sleep came almost immediately, and with it came a dream.

"You're looking better," she said to the indigo-skinned elf.

And indeed it was. At the start of last term, as Borders were falling and magic failing throughout Underhill, the elf had been skinny, sickly, and barely able to support its own weight. Now, while it was still small in stature, it had filled out. Rather than stick-thin, it was lithe and healthy. Its face had filled out, and its eyes glowed a healthy blue-white. Its long blue-black hair was lustrous instead of limp, and it bounced gently on the balls of its feet as it smiled at her.

"Much better," it said, its voice strong and fluid. "More magic."

Clara had come to believe that magic originated in the Ordinary world, and flowed into Underhill through the Borders. That was a hotly contested theory, and therefore one that she'd never bothered to voice to others, but the connection seemed clear to her.

She was standing in the dream-forest, a stylized, even-more-magical representation of Underhill. Its trees glowed with a dim aqua light, no less than three moons moved lazily overhead, and thousands of brilliant yellow bugs drifted here and there through the high grass.

"It's been a while since I've seen you," she said after the elf remained silent for a time.

It nodded. "No need. Plenty of magic. Strong connections to the other. Everything fine." It nodded again.

"So . . . why now?"

"Almost done!" it said brightly, its face splitting into a wide, shining smile. "One more Border to go."

Clara frowned. "I thought we'd need at least a dozen more to—
"

It shook its head. "One," it said firmly. "But the most important one. Wrench pen."

"Wrench pin?" Clara asked, confused.

Its expression echoed her confusion. "Wrong words. Witch pen? No. Clench?" Now it frowned in frustration. "Most important. Holds the whole thing together. Lunch pen?"

"Do you mean *lynchpin?*"

Its expression lit up with delight. "Lynchpin! Yes. Lynchpin. Most important. Very important to get it in the right place."

"I'm pretty sure we already put one in Central Underhill," Clara said. "In fact, there's one right near the capital as well, and—"

"Nope nope," it said, wagging a finger at her. "Center not most important. Center just. . . center." It waved away any concerns about the center. "No, lynchpin *special*. Look."

Clara shrieked as her feet left the ground and she flew up *very rapidly*. Looking down, the dream-forest shrank away to nothing. She shrieked again as she came to a stop even faster than she'd left the ground, and another when she realized she and the elf were floating *next to one of the moons*.

"Sorry," the elf apologized. "Very fast. Much more magic."

"Is that the moon?" Clara shouted.

"A moon," it agreed.

Clara's heartbeat slowed as she grew accustomed to the new perspective. "It's smaller than I thought it would be."

"Underhill not so far apart," the elf said with a knowing nod. "But look."

Clara looked down again, and started picking out the few landmarks she knew. *There* was Linginbaum's, atop its tall mesa, out on a corner of Underhill where dangerous magics held by inexpert hands would do less damage. *There* was the capital, smack in the middle of the landmass.

"There," the elf whispered, pointing.

There was the upper edge of Underhill, a thick, ancient forest that glowed a gentle emerald green she could make out even up here.

"What is it?" she breathed.

"Forest," the elf said with a shrug. "But *important* forest. Greatest forest. Oldest forest. Older than the Fae. *Lynchpin,"* it added.

"So you want the last Border to go there?"

It nodded. "Need. Lynchpin. Most important, hold everything together."

"Anyplace specific?"

Now the elf frowned. "Yeeess," it said, drawing out the word uncertainly. Then it shook its head and flapped its hands gently. "But can't see exactly."

"That's okay," Clara said. "I'll have a team of—"

"NO!" the elf shouted. Clara would have taken a step back if she hadn't been floating in the air next to a glowing moon. "Sorry," it amended, flapping its hands in frustration. "No, no other witches. Not there. It wouldn't like it."

"It?"

"It likes to be left alone. One little girl, one who *sees,* okay. No more."

"You said 'it.'"

"Ask it where Border goes."

"Okaaay," Clara said uncertainly. "I'm not even sure how I'd get—"

"Look," the elf hissed.

Clara looked back at the forest. Then she squinted, as something caught her eye. Was it. . . moving? The gentle glow. . .

No. It wasn't moving. She was seeing *an equation.* Something clicked in her mind and she knew at once what it was: the magical equation that represented the forest itself. In fact, now that she looked, she could see similar dim equations looping everywhere, covering the landscape. And they weren't even different equations, she realized as her jaw fell open. They were *one gigantic equation.*

"But," the elf said, interrupting her thoughts. She looked back up at it. "Do not spend too much time there."

"I need people to feed me the magic," Clara pointed out. "I can't—"

"Plenty of magic there. More than you ever need."

"But I—"

"Do not spend too much time." It nodded gravely.

"But—"

"Remember."

CHAPTER 4

THE WOODS

Clara woke Sunday morning feeling refreshed, but it wasn't until she'd dressed and stepped into the common room that she realized how early she'd risen. The ancient mechanical clock indicated that the sun had barely risen outside, which meant the kitchens wouldn't even be serving a full breakfast yet. She considered sitting and reading for an hour or so, but something in her was. . . vibrating. *Resonating,* even, although she couldn't tell with what.

She left the dorm, descended the stairs to the main hall, and wandered into the dining hall. A sideboard just inside the entrance always offered steaming pots of water for tea, crunchy biscuits, and assorted snacks. This early in the morning, there were also pastries —croissants, danishes, and even glorious-smelling cinnamon rolls. She grabbed two and decided to head outside.

Her feeling of restlessness only grew as she wandered around the grounds, chewing the still-warm rolls. She let her feet take her where they wanted, and as she finished the last delicious bite, she found herself in the old football field, staring at the tall stone monolith of her first Border.

Lynchpin. Most important. Very important to get it in the right place.

Last night's dream roared back into her mind, and she gasped a bit at the. . . *reality* of it.

One gigantic equation.

A dim ribbon of magic, winding throughout and beneath Underhill, connecting it all. *Defining* it all.

A thick, ancient forest that glowed a gentle emerald green.

She'd seen its place in the equation, the exact parenthetical expression that marked the forest's place in this world.

Greatest forest. Oldest forest. Older than the Fae.

That's what she was resonating with, what was gently plucking the strings of her soul, even now.

Lynchpin.

She had to go.

But how? The elf had been clear: she wasn't to take anyone else with her.

No other witches. It wouldn't like it.

But she didn't *need* anyone else, did she? Not really. Not after all the translocation magic she'd seen, after all the teleports she'd been through. She *knew* the equations. She could picture them, even now, floating through the air like a distended trigonometry problem. Sines, cosines, tangents, cotangents. . . *the great circle equation.* Did that even have any meaning here? Underhill wasn't a globe. . . or at least it hadn't seemed like one last night. It was. . . flat. Rectangular.

But that didn't stop the equation from glowing brightly in her mind. Ballooned, pinched symbols—$\Delta\ \delta\ \phi\ \lambda$—danced just behind her retinas.

She knew how to teleport herself.

Her fingers were twitching by her side, eager to take up the magic and *do* something with it. She was bouncing gently on the balls of her feet, echoing the elf's nervous energy from last night's dream. The back of her neck itched. Her stomach was buzzing. A thrill ran up and down her spine.

In front of her, the tall stone pillar of the Border seemed to whisper *you built me.*

Quicker than thought, she reached out to the ambient magic of Underhill, twisted it gently into the shapes she needed, added the mathematical expression for the forest the elf had shown her, and wrapped the entire thing around herself.

It was like no teleport she'd yet experienced.

Although they were fast, nearly instantaneous, teleports had always bothered her. They'd stolen her breath, and their magic had always pressed uncomfortable against her eyes. But this. . . her own teleport, her first translocation magic, was effortless. A brush of wind against her skin, a blurring of the scenery around her, and she was *there.*

The forest was still dimly lit, its thick, ancient canopy blocking out most of the early morning sun. The *presence* of the place pressed down on her.

It's old, she thought. But no, that wasn't quite it. Old, yes, but older than that. Older than ancient. So old that the concept of age lost all meaning. *Eternal,* she thought, the word clicking neatly into place in her mind. *Timeless.* Even better.

But it wasn't just that. *It's quiet,* she realized, and then immediately understood that to be just as wrong a concept as *old.* It wasn't quiet: she could hear small animals waking and flitting through the treetops. A light morning breeze ruffled the broad leaves above her. And yet the silence of the place pressed against her eardrums, demanding her focus, insisting that she not only *listen* but *hear.*

Magic surrounded her, as it did everywhere in Underhill, but it was *thicker* here. She couldn't *not* see it, eddying slowly and confidently through the branches above, twisting around the thick, heavy tree trunks, undulating through the rich, loamy soil beneath her. It pulsed in mature, old-growth colors whose names flitted briefly through her mind. Frost. Fawn. Dandelion. Marigold. Then, in a rush: Garnet, rouge, iris, cobalt. She turned her head as another heavy ribbon of light passed by, glowing basil, carob, flint, and soot.

The mathematics of the forest were written in a heavy hand, Gothic letters slipping alongside Roman numerals, connected by traceries of Ionian symbols. She marveled at the weight of it all, the finality of it. Untold opportunities, unspeakable potential, writhed in these equations, yet they remained asleep. This forest held the possibilities of the infinite, and it kept them all quietly to itself.

Clara shook her head. Something about this place. . . *gets to you,* she thought. She forced herself to focus, unable to completely banish the equations drifting everywhere, but managing to relegate them to background noise for the moment.

Where do I put the Border?

She took a few steps forward, edged quietly around a tree whose trunk she couldn't have encircled had her arms been twice their length, and found herself in a small clearing. Overhead, the sky was the cobalt of a cloudless morning, and around her the breeze blew gently through the wood. Thick ropes of magic swirled here, forming a slow-moving vortex that spun and plunged into the earth.

Here. This is where a Border wants to be.

There was more ambient magic here than she'd ever seen before, anywhere, and she understood what the elf had said. She wouldn't need anyone's help. Not here. Even as she considered it, the magic orbiting around her seemed to bleach itself, magentas fading to coral and emeralds lightening to lemongrass, as if offering itself to her in the purest form it could manage.

This would do. She lifted her hands, feeling the magic dance across her fingertips, and—

"Girl!"

Clara's concentration shattered. The sharp, deep voice had come from across the clearing, but she couldn't see the source. Wait—was that a short tree? A tall stump?

It moved.

It was a woman, Clara realized, wearing heavy purple robes that had somehow provided a perfect camouflage. Her skin was darker than Clara's, her eyes flashing, and her hair a bouquet of salt-and-pepper dreadlocks that were loosely gathered behind her.

The woman's eyes narrowed as she stepped into the clearing. "Oh ho," she said softly. "I see, I see."

"I'm—I mean, hello. My name is Clara," Clara stammered.

"Yes," the woman whispered, nodding slowly.

"I, ah. . . I mean. . ." Clara attempted before falling silent, unsure of what to say or do.

"Raising Borders, are we?" the woman asked.

Clara nodded.

"Think this is the best place for one, do we?" Her tone was accusatory.

"Um. . . no?"

"No," the woman agreed, nodding emphatically. "What is it, then? Fairy rings, again? Rings of light?"

"They're. . . more like. . . um, stone pillars?"

The woman's eyes widened, the whites contrasting sharply with the midnight skin of her face. "Is it then already?" she said softly, so softly Clara barely heard her. Clara opened her mouth to ask what she meant, but realized the question hadn't been meant for her. "Well be it," the woman added, squaring her ample shoulders. "I am Ikwity," she announced in a louder, firm voice. "You will call me Aunt. I will answer both of your questions, but not here. Come."

"My—" Clara started to ask, but Aunt Ikwity had already turned and begun marching through the forest. Clara hurried to keep up.

No matter how long Clara extended her stride or how quickly she tried to move, the old woman managed to stay well ahead of her, maintaining and even increasing a speed that was completely belied by her notable girth. But within minutes, Ikwity came to a sudden stop, and Clara found herself practically on top of the woman. Backpedalling, Clara realized they were standing in front of a small cottage

"Inside," the woman invited—ordered?—Clara as she opened the door and stepped through.

Clara scurried in behind, and found herself in a small room. A cheery fire crackled in a fireplace along one wall, just a few steps away from a sturdy wooden table that showed decades—if not more—of use. Two equally sturdy chairs bracketed the table, and Ikwity had already sat heavily in one of them. "Sit," she ordered, and Clara slipped into the empty chair. "Tea?" she asked.

"Sure, I—" Clara started, when she realized that the empty table in fact contained an entire tea tray. Steam rose from two well-steeped cups, and a few hard biscuits were laid out on a simple plate in between them. "Oh."

"First question, where to put a Border in the Great Wood," Ikwity said with a heavy sigh. "Easy question of the two."

"Actually, I think I only—" Clara started.

"Aunt doesn't answer questions for free, you know. Never for free. Always a price. Didn't see you coming this morning." She frowned. "Who sent you?"

"The. . . I mean, in my dreams, sometime, there's—"

"Elf," Ikwity growled, her lips twisting into a frown. "No patience that one."

"I don't have much money," Clara began, "but I—"

"Money useless," Ikwity said, waving a hand in contempt. She picked up her tea cup and noisily slurped half of it down. "*Ahhh*. No, always rots and corrodes. Price not paid with money. You have everything you need to pay. More than enough for two questions, even the hard one."

"I actually. . . I just need to know where to put this Border, really. The elf said—"

"Lynchpin," Ikwity said, nodding. "True enough. Got to get it right. But two questions." She shrugged. "Sometimes I cheat, but I definitely see two." She frowned, seeming to reconsider. "Maybe not both here," she admitted, quirking one eyebrow. "But two."

Clara blinked as she processed that. She blinked again as the red-and-orange paisley pattern on Ikwity's robe seemed to shift and swim. "So how much—"

"Drink your tea, girl," Ikwity ordered, jerking her chin at Clara's cup. "Rooibos. Red tea, not black, not green. A favorite of Aunt's. Native to Africa. Also a favorite. Old people there, old ways. Old stories. Drink."

Clara obediently picked up her cup, blew on it a bit to cool the tea, and then sipped. Her eyes widened at the rich, herbal flavor, tinged with hints of vanilla. "It's very good."

"A favorite," the old woman repeated, nodding with satisfaction. She picked up a biscuit and crunched it in half. As she chewed, she brushed a few crumbs from the front of her red-and-white polka-dot robes.

Clara blinked again. Was it hot in here? She shivered a bit.

"Correct location easy question," Ikwity said as she chewed the second half of her biscuit. "But, wood full of dangerous beasts."

"Like direbunnies?" Clara asked. She'd had more than enough experience with those cute, fluffy, fanged menaces.

Ikwity scowled, brushing a few last crumbs from her black robes. "Pets of the Fae, those. Pets of Mab. Silly elf-queen. She's well-gone but left her pets behind."

Clara was struggling to keep track of the conversational thread, and the stuffy crispness of the small room wasn't helping. "Where did she go?" she asked gamely.

"Followed some dreamer boy into a place that never should have been," Ikwity said, a grim, satisfied smile settling on her face. "Forget her, even if she is your long-distant ancestor."

Wait, what? "What do you mean—"

"Wrong question," Ikwity snapped, pointing a finger at Clara. The woman's yellow-and-white striped robes seemed to bend and spin in Clara's vision. "Talking about the Border. New one. Last one, yes?"

"I, ah—yes, that's what the elf said," Clara stammered, once again hauling on the reins of her concentration to keep it on track. "Just this one last one."

"Last, last. . ." Ikwity said, her voice suddenly soft and contemplative. Then she nodded. "Yes. Last. Last for some time. Until the boy. Maybe after." She flicked her fingers toward Clara. "Neither now nor then. You have time, yes?"

Clara's mind was struggling to keep up. "I mean, yes. . . I need to be back by dinner, probably, but—"

"Dinner. Dinner *time,*" Ikwity said, suddenly grinning wickedly, her white teeth reflecting the flickering flames. "Done and done, then."

Clara stared at her, wondering how she managed to keep that pure-white robe clean all the way out here. "So you'll tell me where the Border should go?"

Ikwity's grin vanished. "Already did." Then she cocked her head, considering. "Maybe not yet, but definitely did."

The little white bunnies stitched into Ikwity's blue robe seemed to hop about, making Clara's eyes swim. "Oh, good," she managed. *Why* was it so chilly in here? She could feel warm sweat dripping down her back.

"Just the matter of payment for Aunt's answers," Ikwity said, her voice velvety and rough, filling every corner of the room to the point Clara could barely hear it.

"What about the second one?" Clara said muddily. Ikwity's linen robes, painted with rainbow-colored equations, seemed to glow in the blue firelight.

"Already answered," Ikwity assured her. "What's for dinner, Clara Thorn?"

Clara's brain gave up. "Hamburgers, I suppose," she said dreamily, her eyes drooping. "Or maybe gravy. It *is* Sunday, after all."

"Isn't it always?" Ikwity whispered.

CHAPTER 5
LEAP

"Clara, watch out!"

Clara blinked and snatched her hands back in the nick of time. A split-second later, a massive trunk crashed onto the table, its sides sliding up to reveal six plates of steaming food. Hands reach in to grab all but one plate.

"Hurry up!" someone said. Then: "Clara, what's the matter?" before a pair of hands reached in front of her and slid the last plate out, just a moment before the trunk's sides slid back into place and the entire contraption flew into the air, accompanied by various clanks and rattles.

Clara looked dumbly at the plate in front of her. "It's a hamburger," she said.

"Of course it's a hamburger," a deep voice to her left chuckled. "It's Sunday. It's always hamburgers for dinner on Sundays."

Clara looked to her left. "Ed?" she asked, confused. Her heart started beating faster. "Ed, you're huge." He'd. . . *grown*. And filled out. Clara blinked furiously, as if some piece of grit in her eyes was making everything look strange.

Ed frowned. "Clara, are you okay?"

The deep voice was coming from him. *Ed's voice isn't deep,* her brain insisted. *This is wrong.* Her heartbeat went even faster.

"Clara, what's the matter?" asked a more familiar voice from across the table. Clara slowly turned her head in that direction.

Her eyes flew open in alarm.

"Nononononononononono!" she cried, scrambling backwards off her bench. "Why do you look like that?" The triplets were. . . *wrong.* Their hair too neat. Their faces too trim. Their makeup. . . *they were wearing makeup.*

Dimly, Clara was aware that the room had been filled with a gentle background hubbub, and that a dozen conversations were going silent as heads turned to look at her outburst.

"Clara, don't—" another male voice said. It was the tall young man who'd been sitting to her right, the young man who was now looking at her with concern in his green eyes.

"WHAT'S HAPPENING?" Clara screamed as she recognized Finlay.

A *much older* Finlay. Much taller. Broader shoulders. A leaner jawline.

Ed stood and tried to take her elbow, his expression full of worry, but she twisted out of reach, almost stumbling into the students sitting behind her.

"Miss Thorn?"

Clara whirled to her right as one of the school's professors strode quickly toward her. "Professor Maplethorpe!" she cried as she recognized the familiar, *unchanged* face. "What's happening?"

"Clara, dear, what's wrong?" the professor said, quickly taking both of Clara's hands in her own. "What's the matter?"

Clara's eyes darted back to the table she'd been sitting at, the table where her four *clearly older* classmates still sat, their eyes wide with alarm, their dinners untouched. "I. . . what. . . no, no no no, something's wrong!"

"Clara," Maplethorpe said firmly, her usually bubbling voice now hard as a rock. "Tell me what you see. Tell me what's wrong."

Clara's eyes snapped back to the professor's. "Everyone's older," she whimpered.

The professor hesitated a minute, and then gave a quick nod. "I understand. I'm going to take you to my office now, all right?" Clara nodded mutely. "Children, please make your way there on your own."

A spin of rainbow-colored magic surrounded Clara and the professor, and with a breath of wind the dining hall vanished, replaced by the professor's cozily decorated office.

"Sit," Maplethorpe ordered, and Clara obeyed, sinking into one of the overstuffed chairs. *"Du thé pour une personne, immédiatement.,"* the professor added. Instantly, the small table next to Clara's chair contained a steaming mug of black tea. "Drink," she said.

Clara's brain was still running in mad circles, and so nearly on autopilot Clara picked up the cup, blew on it, and took a sip of tea. It calmed her immensely as its warm, gentle bitterness trickled down her throat.

"Breathe," Maplethorpe ordered.

Clara nodded, taking a deep breath, holding it, and letting it out.

"Again."

Clara obeyed.

"Tea."

Clara took another sip.

The office door burst open behind Clara. She started to turn, but the professor locked gazes with her. "Eyes on me. The rest of you stand where you are. Close the door, please."

A *click* as the door shut.

"Now, Clara, I want you to focus on me. Only me, understand?" Clara nodded, her eyes still latched to Maplethorpe's. "Sip the tea as we go." Another nod. "What's the very first thing you remember? Just now, in the dining hall, before I came up."

"The. . . food. The trunk. It had food in it. Hamburgers." Clara's eyes darted back and forth between the professor's, and her heart started beating faster.

"Tea," the professor advised, and Clara took another sip. "Now, before that, *immediately* before the trunk came down, what do you remember?"

Clara's mind struggled. "I. . ." she stammered. But it was like there was a wall of some kind, and trying to remember *before* kept throwing her against that wall. But no. . . no, she *did* remember. . . there was a face. . . "The woman," Clara blurted out.

Maplethorpe's eyebrows scrunched together. "What woman? Describe her?"

It was as if a floodgate opened, or as if the wall in her mind had been smashed. "The woman," Clara repeated, speaking quickly now as her heart hammered in her chest. "In the woods. Her cottage, the fire. . . hot, but cold. Her robes. . ." Clara's forehead creased as she struggled to get a firm image from the jumbled flood in her mind. "Aunt. Her name was. . . no, she said to call her Aunt." Clara frowned. "Ikwity?"

"What woods, Clara?" the professor said softly.

"In the. . . up. At the top." Clara struggled to find the word. "North? Where the new Border was to go. The last Border."

Now Maplethorpe's eyes flew wide. "The final Border?" she whispered.

Clara nodded.

"I see. And this woman. . . this Aunt. Did she help you raise the Border?"

Clara shook her head. "No, I didn't do it. She said. . . something about dinner. About Sundays. But then I was here. I never did it."

The professor leaned down, taking the tea from Clara's trembling hand and setting it gently back on the table. Then she took both of Clara's hands in her own again, holding them firmly. "Clara, I'm going to explain something to you. It may be alarming, but I want you to remain still, all right?" Clara nodded, and started trembling harder. "Breathe, dear. You'll be fine, all right? You *are* fine."

Clara took another deep breath, held it, and then released it.

The professor also took a deep breath before saying, "Dear, you raised the final Border almost four years ago."

Clara's eyes rolled up and everything went mercifully black.

~

SUNDAY EVE

"Maplethorpe said you should stay here," Ed protested as Clara tried to lever herself out of the sofa she'd been lying on. "At least for a few hours, to make sure you're okay."

"I'm just sitting up, Ed," Clara said wearily. "My head is throbbing."

"I'll get more tea," Idalia said quickly.

"Don't you all have. . . I don't know. Something? To do?" Clara asked.

Ed shook his head. "It's Sunday night. And Maplethorpe excused us all from classes tomorrow."

Clara had awoken to find herself lying on a sofa in the dorm's common room, surrounded by Finlay, Ed, and the triplets, all of whom shared the same expressions of fear and concern.

"Can someone tell me what's happening, then?" Clara asked. "I won't faint again, I promise."

Harriett chuckled. "You'd better not. Maplethorpe magicked the school nurse to her office so fast we thought *she'd* faint, the poor woman. You've 'suffered a nasty shock to the system,' she said. They made us promise to make you rest. Maplethorpe went off to consult with the rest of the faculty."

"But you mean why we're older," Ed said quietly.

Clara met his gaze and nodded slowly. "Yeah."

"It sounds like," Ed began, keeping his voice soft and steady, "that you've lost your memories of the past four years or so."

"Lost them like *that*," Harriett added, snapping her fingers.

"Stop it," Johanna chided her sister.

"When is it, then?" Clara asked, steeling herself.

"We're in the last month of our senior year," Ed said calmly. "We graduate soon."

Clara added up the years. "Four years," she breathed.

Ed nodded. "Three and a half, really. A bit more. But yeah."

"And I was here the whole time?"

"You were," Idalia said, returning with a mug of tea that she pressed gently into Clara's hands. "That's chamomile."

"Thanks," Clara said, taking a sip. "I don't remember any of it."

"So that last thing you remember. . ." Ed prompted.

Clara sighed. "So. Saturday. We went to the village. Harriett bought a Lemon Impossible."

"She always does," Idalia said with a grin.

"This was the first time. They were new."

Clara could see Idalia doing the math. "Tenth year, then. Start of the term, right?"

Clara nodded.

"Okay. Then what?" Ed asked.

"We came back. We sat up. . . we talked a lot. Did some homework, I guess. I went to bed and. . . I had a dream."

"A dream?" Johanna said, leaning over the back of the sofa.

"Yeah. The. . . it was the blue elf. The same one as before, when the Borders were coming down." Ed nodded. Clara had told them all about her panic-filled dreams back then. "But he looked good. Healthy. He said I needed to raise one more Border, and that it needed to go into the woods. We. . . flew, I think. He took me up, and I could see all of Underhill. He showed me where the woods were. At the top of the map, all the way on the edge."

"That Sunday," Ed said carefully, "you weren't around in the morning. Nobody could find you for breakfast. We started to worry —we told Headmaster Herrera. But then you showed up, right as meal service was ending. You went to the woods, somehow?"

Clara nodded. "I teleported myself."

"You did not," Harriett said, her tone a mix of awe and jealousy. "Back then?"

"I did. I knew how. . . I'd seen the magic so many times. And the elf. . . when we were up there, I could see everything. Underhill's magic, all of it. The math expressions for every place. I just had to add them to the base teleport spell."

"Okay," Ed said, glaring over Clara's head at Harriett. "You went to the woods. Then what?"

Clara's eyes narrowed as she struggled to remember. "It's fuzzy. There was a woman, in the woods. An Aunt. . . something. She said she would tell me where the Border should go." *And something else,* Clara thought, but it eluded her.

"The elf didn't tell you?" Idalia asked.

Clara shook her head. "No, he said he couldn't pinpoint it. That someone. . . something. . ." She trailed off, trying to focus.

Remember.

The elf's deep, melodious voice thrummed in her mind.

"Lynchpin. Most important, hold everything together," Clara recited softly. The common room had become less real, less *present.* She was back in the dream-forest, with the elf, as he told her what to do. "Can't see exactly. It likes to be left alone. One little girl, one who *sees,* okay. No more." She paused as the memory slowed, becoming sharper. "Ask it where Border goes."

"So you did," Idalia whispered.

"There was more," Clara said distantly, replaying the memory even slower. *"Do not spend too much time."*

Idalia's eyes widened. Clara refocused, the common room became real again, and the memory of the elf faded.

"So this woman. . . you said 'Aunt,'" Ed said.

Another memory clicked into place. "She said to call her that. Aunt Ikwity."

Ed's lips twitched into a half-smile. "You don't hear it, do you?"

Clara frowned. "Hear what?"

"What are you talking about, Ed?" Idalia asked.

"You're pronouncing it *aunt.* Like 'on.' Or 'font.'"

"So?" Clara asked.

"Pronounce it the other way. Like the insect."

"Aunt?" Clara asked, pronouncing it *ant*.

"With her name."

"Aunt Ikwity?" Clara's eyes widened. "Oh."

"I don't get it," Harriett said.

"Antiquity," Clara said, running the two words together.

"I think," Ed said carefully, "you encountered a Power. Something ancient. Obviously something capable of tampering with memories."

"Or time," Harriett said ominously.

Another nugget of memory surfaced. "She said something about paying her price," Clara said.

"Price for what?" Johanna asked.

Clara struggled to remember. "An answer. If she was the one who knew exactly where to put the final Border. . . maybe that. But she said there as a price."

"And you paid it," Ed said very softly. "I think possibly you did spend too much time."

"Cool," Harriett breathed.

SUNDAY NIGHT

"We brought burgers," Johanna announced as the triplets returned to the common room. "And fries."

"The fries are cold," Harriett grumbled.

"Duh," Idalia retorted. "We're witches. We'll heat them up. I'm just glad the kitchen saved some."

"Thanks guys," Clara said gratefully as she accepted a tray. She looked around. "Um, where's the dining table?" The round, battered old piece of furniture was nowhere to be seen.

"Ah, that's been replaced," Ed said, taking his tray. "You can use the worktable."

"The worktable" was an enormous, rectangular, glossy black

surface, supported on six stout wooden legs, pushed almost completely into one corner of the room.

"Ugh, why'd they replace the old table with this?" Clara asked as she slid her tray onto it and sat down. "And it's so dusty. Isn't there a spell or something to keep it clean?"

"Castle modernization," Finlay said as he sat down across from her. "They're tearing out all the steampunk stuff. Magic is a *lot* more abundant here now."

"A lot more reliable, too. They took out all the steam boards," Idalia added, gesturing to the wall where the persnickety, Edwardian-age substitute for a whiteboard had sat. Clara looked and saw that its hose hookups and valves were still in the wall.

"The dust is on purpose," Ed explained. "You can sketch whatever you like into it, and then the dust comes back when you're done."

"Gross," Clara said.

"Progress!" Harriett chirped sarcastically. "You remember Brinley Marsh?"

"Of course," Clara said. "I haven't been *gone.*"

"Right. Well, her dad started a company that got the contract for a lot of modernization. Apparently underbid the Witchers."

"Oh."

"And then," Idalia said ominously, "he just took Brinley out of school. Enrolled her somewhere else."

"Oh?"

Johanna sighed. "Phoebe was being. . . well, *extra* to Brinley. She was miserable."

"Yeah." Phoebe clearly took her social cues from her father's business priorities.

They ate in silence for a few minutes before Ed said, "Clara, if you want to talk any more about it. . . maybe see if anything else comes to mind. . . we're here for you."

"I'd very much like to take it from the top, if you're up to it."

Clara turned to see Headmaster Herrera slipping into the common room, closing the door quietly behind her. "Oh."

"Professor Maplethorpe filled me in," Herrera said as she slid into a chair next to Ed. "Do you think you'd be up to a retelling, Clara?"

Clara's friends looked at her, and Ed gave her an encouraging nod. "I guess so." She sighed. "Okay, so look, all my cards on the table, okay?" Herrera raised an eyebrow, but nodded silently. "I have dreams, sometimes."

"Yes," the Headmaster said. "With the elf, correct?"

Clara's eyebrows rose. "You. . . know?"

"You told me. Years ago. It's hardly unusual for someone in your position. With your unique abilities, I mean. And the Fae manipulated Underhill so often, it's not surprising that it developed a sentience. That it should express that to you as a blue elf is probably the least odd manifestation I could think of."

Clara blinked. "Oh. Well. . . okay. So Saturday night, after soccer practice—"

"Football," Finlay corrected automatically. He gave her a small grin.

"After football practice," Clara amended, smiling back, "I went to bed and had a dream. The elf told me I had only a single Border left to raise, and that I needed to do it in the woods."

Herrera tapped a long finger on the table and nodded slowly. "You'd shared that much. But you refused to say exactly where. You actually seemed. . . very vague about it. As if you didn't remember."

"You wouldn't even tell us," Idalia said softly.

"I guess the me you guys knew didn't remember?" Clara hazarded. "But the elf didn't know exactly where it needed to go. He said I'd find. . . he said *it*. It would know. And he said I wasn't to spend too much time there."

"And so you teleported yourself," Herrera said.

"I'd picked up the equations—the spell—from some of the older kids," Clara admitted. "And the elf showed me all of Underhill.

There's magic flowing through it all, and. . . to me, it's all parenthetical expressions. Each one identifies a place."

"Can you show me this place on a map? Now?" Herrera asked.

"Maybe?"

The Headmaster snapped her fingers and said, *"Kaart van de wereld, alstublieft."* A long scroll appeared in front of her, and she quickly rolled it out on an empty area of the table. Everyone pulled their trays back a bit to make room. She touched the corners and they adhered to the table, holding the scroll opened. "After you raised the last Border, Underhill's geography became absolutely static. People started making maps almost immediately."

Clara tilted her head. It was a map of Underhill, nearly exactly as she'd seen it with the elf. "Here," she said, tapping the great forest to the north. "It's in here someplace."

"Ah." Herrera frowned. "They've been calling that the Great Northern Wood. It is. . . inhospitable."

"Dangerous?" Idalia asked.

"You literally can't get in," the Headmaster said. "Anyone who tries gets no more than a few steps past the tree line, and they just stop. Magic stalls. People have had to be lassoed and hauled out. There are warning signs along the entire tree line now."

"She doesn't like visitors," Clara murmured.

"She?" Herrera asked sharply.

"Aunt Ikwity." This time, Clara pronounced it *ant.*

"Antiquity," Herrera said, getting it immediately. "Hmm."

"A Power?" Ed asked.

Herrera nodded. "Likely. More than a few of them loiter in Underhill, these days. And so she's the one who told you exactly where to put the Border?"

"I think so," Clara said. "I don't. . . I can't remember it. It was very hazy. But she said she'd answer both of my questions, and that I'd have to pay her price."

"What was the other question?" Ed asked.

Clara shook her head. "I don't know. She talked strange. She said she'd answered my questions already, or that she would have done."

"Whatever creature you met, I'm guessing it sits outside Time," Herrera said quietly. "That's. . . a Power indeed. Very dangerous. Clara, if you're ever tempted to go back there. . . don't."

Clara shuddered. "Wouldn't dream of it."

"So. Have your friends caught you up, otherwise?"

Clara sighed and took a small bite of her burger. "A little. I'm graduating soon, apparently. Magic is stronger." A thought occurred to her. "I should get a message to my parents."

Herrera exchanged quick glances with Clara's friends. "I. . . would suggest you consider that carefully before you do," the Headmaster said.

Clara frowned. "Why?"

"Your parents have been *getting* messages from you all this time," Idalia said gently. "You'll have to explain. . . all of *this*. It might be better in person."

"They'll be here for the graduation," Ed offered.

"Or I could go see them now," Clara countered.

Another round of glances passed between everyone. "Clara, we don't allow students to leave Underhill without armed escorts," Herrera said.

"What?"

"It's war out there, Clara," Ed said. "The Paladins are everywhere. They stake our Anchors whenever they find them, which makes us vulnerable when we emerge from a Border. And they're *good* at finding them, somehow."

"Oberherr?" Clara asked.

Ed shrugged. "Nobody's heard from him, so there's no way to tell."

"But you need to remain *here* unless you leave with an escort," Herrera repeated. "Your adoptive parents are well aware of the policy, and supportive of it."

"Oh." She thought for a moment. "Has anyone. . . have I seen my bio-mom?"

Her chest tightened as everyone's eyes flicked away.

"Oh dear," Herrera said. "I hadn't imagined we'd have to go through all this. Clara. . . oh, my poor girl." Herrera's expression was one of pain and sympathy now, all traces of the stern Headmaster vanished. "This may be difficult for you to hear. . . again. I'll just say it and go." She took a deep breath. "Two things. First, shortly after you raised the final Border, your mother. . . went rogue. She was determined to find your father, she wasn't interested in the government's help anymore. She took a small team of witches and they vanished. Nobody has heard from them since."

Clara blinked a few times as she processed that, but it wasn't really news. *Mom was never around anyway.* "Okay. You said two things."

Herrera bit her lower lip for a moment before speaking. "Another team was dispatched to find them. A team that had shown some success in mitigating the Paladin threat. That team was. . . killed. Their bodies were never recovered, but. . . there's a high level of certainty."

Clara's entire being went cold. "Who?"

"The team was led by Cecil Dimmick."

Clara's heart sank, and she felt hot tears trickling down her cheeks. Ed leaned over and wrapped an arm around her shoulders, and she leaned into him. "Sorry," she mumbled.

"It's okay," he whispered.

"I'm so sorry, Clara. Again. I'll. . . go. We'll speak again later. Try to rest."

Herrera stood and walked quietly out of the common room. Just as the door was about to close behind her, Clara said, "Wait!" She stood and hurried over, stepping out into the hallway and closing the door behind her.

"What is it?" the Headmaster asked.

"I didn't know you," Clara said. "The me now, I mean. I only saw you at dinners, and we only spoke that one time when the term started. You were. . ."

"Stern?" Herrera asked, her lips quirking into a wry grin.

"You seemed that way," Clara said, ducking her head in embarrassment.

Herrera sighed. "I was coming into an odd situation. A prodigy, a mathemagician—one per generation!—in my school. We were coming off the back of all that Oberherr nonsense. Cecil—Headmaster Dimmick—had briefed me on your role. Laudable, but also a bit of a wild cannon, no?" Clara nodded mutely. "Clara, over the past years, I'd like to think we've developed a wonderful working relationship. No more Borders to raise, obviously, but you've done more than just that. I think. . . again, I'd *like* to think, that we learned to trust each other." Clara raised her eyes to meet the Headmaster's. "I understand that we may need to start that process over, but I'm confident we'll get there again."

They held each other's gaze for a long moment. Then Clara stepped forward, gave the older woman a quick hug, and then ducked back into the common room.

"Everything okay?" Ed said, his voice thick with concern.

Clara nodded.

"You want. . . to just get some rest?"

She shook her head. "Would some of you stay up with me? For a while?" Her eyes met each of theirs in turn.

"Are you joking?" Harriett said at last. "We've got tomorrow off. I plan to stay up until then, if possible."

CHAPTER 6
BACK TO SCHOOL

Clara slept fitfully. She was half-afraid the elf would come to her in her dreams again—and half-afraid he wouldn't. In the end, she barely closed her eyes long enough for it to be a possibility anyway. As soon as the light in her room started to brighten, she dressed in sweats and made her way to the common room for tea.

"Morning," Ed yawned as she walked in.

"Hey. You didn't sleep?"

"Not much," he shrugged. "It's. . . weird, is all. Like, one minute you're *you*, and literally a second later you're you from years ago. I'm. . . worried."

"About?"

"You, obviously."

Clara sighed. "I guess I'll be fine. I'm more worried about graduating all of a sudden. We have like a zillion exams to get through, and we're missing class today."

"Class today is no big. It's just practicing for the finals, and today's all the soft stuff. Illusions, environmental effects, that kind of thing. You nailed those two years ago."

"I don't remember."

Ed considered. "Why don't you try one?"

"Try one what?" Idalia asked as she and her sisters stepped into the common room.

"A spell. She's worried she won't remember them."

Harriett snorted. "I'd like to see you *try* not remembering them. Everything we struggle with, you seem to do on autopilot. You got *superb* at it."

Clara blinked. Compliments from Harriett were rare. "What should I try?"

"Illusions are safest," Johanna said as she fixed herself a cup of tea. "But they're still complex. Are we going down to breakfast or ordering in?"

"Order in," Ed replied. "And I thought you guys were all going to stay up all night and into the morning?"

"You don't know we didn't," Harriett said with a sly grin.

"We didn't," Idalia said. "And I couldn't sleep."

"Which meant none of us could," Johanna sighed. "Egg sandwiches okay for everyone?"

"Fine by me if you're ordering," Finlay announced as he yawned his way into the common room. "Clara, you okay?"

"Okay enough. I was going to try some magic to see if. . ."

He nodded. "To see if you have to start over. Yeah. Hey, what about the one where you make a tree seem to grow out of the floor? Moving illusions are the hardest. I still get a headache with that one."

"Okay," Clara said dubiously. "Just. . . a tree?"

"Start there," Ed encouraged her. "A sprout, a sapling, work your way up from there. See if it comes back."

Clara nodded and let her. . .

She gasped.

"What?" Ed said, mildly alarmed.

"It's just. . . wow. I used to have to try a little, to see the magic. But it just *happened*."

"Yeah, you got good at that, too," Harriett sighed, stirring her tea. "No bacon on mine, Johanna."

"Mine, either," Idalia added. "Yeah, you said you'd gotten to a point where you blocked out the ambient magic most of the time, but whenever someone was actively casting, you'd just see it. I can still barely make out auras."

"Ours is too strong," Harriett said smugly. "Blocks everyone else out."

"Okay," Clara said nervously. "A tree, then."

She reached out, caressing the ambient magic in the room. She was surprised at how easily it responded to her, how quickly it assembled itself into a shape. . . she *remembered.* Or no, not *remembered.* . . she simply *knew.* A bright-green shoot popped out of the worn rug in front of her, quickly unfurling its first few leaves.

"That was quick," Ed said. "Keep going."

It was *effortless,* Clara realized. And her perception of the magic itself was more. . . sophisticated. The streams and ribbons of rainbow-colored mathematical equations had evolved into something else. Now, those ribbons took on shapes and structures, forming hexagons, dodecahedrons, arcs, and more. It all centered around, and converged upon, the illusory tree that was rapidly growing into a sapling in the middle of the common room.

"You've got it!" Finlay said approvingly.

Clara relaxed, letting the magic do the work. In moments, the sapling grew into a mighty oak, its upper branches disappearing into the ceiling, its leaves casting shadows across the room.

"Wow," Idalia said admiringly.

Clara held it there for a moment before letting the magic go. It sighed away from her, dispersing back into the air she'd summoned it from, and the tree faded away.

"See," Ed said, a broad smile on his face, "you still got it."

"It just *felt* right," Clara said happily.

"Our turn," Harriett said.

"Harriett—" Idalia started.

"No, we've been working hard on this one. C'mon."

"Oh, let's," Johanna said, clapping her hands.

Idalia sighed. "Fine."

Clara's eyes widened as all three triplets raised their right hands in unison, stopping them in the same position: shoulder-height, palm out, index finger bent slightly downward.

"This will be weird," Ed warned, but his tone was excited.

Magic burst to life.

In Clara's eyes, an almost searingly bright helix of equations sprang into existence, looping around the three girls. Their eyes began to glow, scintillating with colors so intense they were almost white.

««มีอยู่»**,** the triplets said in the eerie, three-in-one voice Clara had heard when they'd raised the first Border.

The common room became a lush rainforest. Vines and moss covered every surface, and the walls were hidden by thick, densely spaced tree trunks. Brightly colored birds flitted from branch to branch, and one even landed on Finlay's shoulder. Bugs large and small roamed around, and drops of water rolled off broad leaves and splashed to the ground.

Clara frowned. It was beautiful, but silent. She couldn't *feel* the humidity, couldn't *hear* the exotic birds. It ruined the illusion, showed it to be just a lie. Instinctively, her eyes darted around the room, examining the triplets' math. *There,* she thought, spotting an incomplete equation, and *there,* as she saw a missing parenthetical. Without thinking, she nudged the magic into what she *knew* was the proper place.

The air in the common room went hot and moist, and that heavy air was full of sounds: chirps, buzzing, and the *drip* of water everywhere. Aromas filled their noses as well, with scents of rotting vegetation, damp air, loamy earth, and perfumed flowers.

««???»**,** the triplets exclaimed in a wordless crash of emotion. Their magic splintered, and the entire display disappeared in a shower of golden sparks.

"What," Idalia said, the glow fading from her eyes,

"was that?" Harriett finished.

"I... think I nudged it," Clara said. "I'm sorry."

"Don't be!" Johanna said, her eyes wide. "It"

"was astonishing!" Idalia continued. "We didn't even"

"know you could do smells!" Johanna finished.

Clara's eyes darted between the three girls.

"That stops after a few minutes," Finlay said, rolling his eyes.

"They can't get out of each others' heads after they do synergistic stuff," Ed sighed. "Which is basically all they do these days. But they're right—I didn't know you could do smells with that spell."

Clara shrugged. "It just... fit. I haven't done that before?"

"You certainly," Johanna began.

"DID NOT," Harriett finished.

"I feel like you could *try* to finish your own sentences," Finlay said with a chuckle.

"When we first come out," Idalia explained.

"of it, it's hard to," Harriett continued.

"tell which ones are whose," Johanna finished.

"Sure, sure," Finlay said, laughing harder. "But Clara, that means you still got it. Nothing to worry about."

"I guess," Clara said with a smile. "I don't mind skipping today if this is what it all was."

"Wait until tomorrow," Ed said darkly.

"Wait, why? What's tomorrow?"

"Translocation," Idalia said.

"Licensing," Harriett finished. "It's—"

"I got it," Finely said, waving the girls down. "It's the government examination for our teleportation licenses."

"Wait," Clara said, holding up a hand. "What?"

"We're the last class to be taught teleportation," Ed said grimly.

"And anyone in Underhill using translocation magic has to pass a government test and get a license."

Clara stared at him for a long moment. "We are literally witches," she said. "And teleporting is *literally* magic. I don't get it."

Finlay sighed. "It's not all bad. The problem is that, after magic here got more available, and after the geography locked in place, *everyone* started teleporting *everwhere*."

"It's not like the Ordinary," Idalia said, and Clara held her breath to see if she'd finish. "Over there, you're careful where you teleport. You don't want to be seen. But here, it got out of hand a little."

"Some people teleported into a Governing Council session and thoroughly disrupted things," Ed said. "I'll admit it was too much. But now, if you don't have a license, you have to use the Anchor network, and if you *do* have a license, you have to file a flight plan if you're going anywhere but private property."

"Which means every town has Anchors *and* places who, for a fee, will let you teleport in and out without a plan," Harriett grumbled.

"Wait, fees?" Clara said, aghast.

"Three guesses who runs the Anchor network, and the first two don't count," Ed said.

Clara's mind raced, and then settled on the only possible answer. "The Witchers," she said with a grimace.

"Got it in one."

A knocking noise in the wall was followed by a section of bookshelf swinging open.

"Breakfast!" Harriett announced, diving for the food.

They ate in silence, focused entirely on the food. When they finished, the triplets put their heads together and began discussing improvements to their illusion, comparing notes to see if any of them had caught Clara's improvements. Ed began gathering the empty plates and napkins and bundling them back into the delivery niche in the wall.

Clara took the opportunity to walk over to Finlay. "Hey, you seem to be doing okay," she said quietly, laying a hand on his forearm. He looked down at it, then looked back up at her with an expression of mild panic. "Just, when I. . . I mean, two days ago you were really upset. I thought. . . I thought I'd done something wrong. But you seem happier now. Were we. . . I mean, did we eventually. . ." she trailed off, looking into his eyes.

She was vaguely aware that everyone else had frozen in place and was staring at her. She broke eye contact with Finlay, letting her hand fall from his arm. Ed was staring at her with a look of horror and. . . pain? Harriett had both hands over her mouth. Idalia's expression was blank and still. Johanna's eyes were wide.

"What?" Clara asked.

"Clara," Finlay started. His voice was gentle, but she could hear a tremble in it.

She looked back at him and he'd blushed slightly, and was clearly perspiring. "What?"

"Clara. . ." he stopped, shoved his hands into his pocket, and took a step backward. He seemed to have shrunk in on himself, and he refused to meet anyone's eyes. "We. . . I mean, I. . . it was. . . I. . ."

Harriett had turned deep red and looked like she might explode.

"I really like you," Finlay managed. His voice was shaking and he still refused to look in Clara's eyes. "But not. . . like that."

"Oh," Clara said softly. "I just. . . sure. I under—"

"No, it's not. . . ugh!" Finlay said in exasperation. "Okay, look. . ." He paused.

"What?" Clara said even more quietly, another tear trickling down one cheek.

Finlay took a deep breath, released it, looked directly into Clara's eyes, and said, "Clara, I'm gay."

"FINALLY!" Harriett screamed, leaping from her chair. Ed slumped against the wall, shaking his head. Idalia looked immensely relieved, and Johanna clapped her hands.

"Wait, what?" Finlay asked, his brow wrinkling in confusion.

"Oh, we've known for at least two years," Harriett said smugly.

"And when that Austrian boy, Wolfgang, transferred last year, that pretty much cemented it."

"Wh—wait, how. . . what did—" Finlay said, blushing a brilliant red.

"Oh, you thought you two were being discreet?" Harriett crowed. "Please."

Clara's heart was slamming against her chest. "I'm so sorry," she said hoarsely, a tear trickling down one cheek. "I didn't mean to—"

"No, no, it's fine!" Finlay insisted, grabbing her shoulders. "You're fine! It's fine!" he pulled her into a firm hug. "I'm the one who's sorry, I just didn't know how—I'm sorry!" he was crying as well now, and the two of them held each other and sobbed for a few moments.

"I thought. . . I just—" Clara began.

"Besides," Harriett said, "you and Ed make the much better couple."

Clara froze to the center of her soul. Finlay felt her stiffen, and he released her and stepped away. Clara turned to look at Ed, still leaning against the wall. He gave her a wan smile and a small wave. "Of course," she whispered. "I mean, were we—"

"You've been dating for two years," Harriett said with glee.

"Harriett, stop it," Idalia said harshly.

"Two years, six months, two weeks, and a day," Ed said quietly. "When we all stopped going to Ordinary school—"

"Wait, *what?*" Clara asked. "No, sorry. Later. So we—"

Ed nodded.

Clara rushed to him, wrapping her arms tightly around him. He'd grown more than she'd realized at first. At least a full head taller than her, as her head was pressed firmly into the top of his chest. "It makes so much sense," she whispered.

"You don't. . ." he began, his embrace more hesitant. "If you don't remember, I mean. . . we can—"

"I don't," Clara said, a sob threatening to strangle her words.

"But it *feels* right. Like the magic." And it did. Standing here, holding him. . .*fit.*

He tightened his arms around her. "We'll figure it out," he promised.

"I know," she sniffed.

They released each other. Clara heard Harriett start to say something, and heard the *thump* as one of her sisters hit her to shut her up. "You okay?" Ed asked, looking down into her eyes.

Clara nodded. "I'd. . . can we take a walk? I need some air."

Ed smiled. "Sure."

～

MONDAY LATE MORNING

"Wow, you weren't kidding," Clara said as she and Ed walked through the castle's main hall. Workers were everywhere, balancing on tall, magically steadied ladders as they cut the maze of brass and copper piping off the walls. "What're they doing instead of those?"

"More traditional magic," Ed replied. "Constructs, mainly. They're saving the dining hall until between terms, so we won't get to experience the new one. Unless you get accepted for advanced studies and stay on."

"What about the sphere that gets you up the mesa?"

Ed laughed. "Gone. That was the first thing to go, in fact. There's an Anchor down there now, and a matching one where the landing dock used to be. Not that anyone uses it—there are Anchors everywhere, now."

"Owned by Phoebe's father."

"Yup. It's a gigantic network. So for me, I have to Anchor to Linginham, which has an Anchor to Salthaven. That's a big town, so they've got a whole building full of Anchors where you connect. I connect out to a field near Maryshyre, which is where you put the Border that goes to New Orleans."

"Wow. Sorry."

Ed shrugged. "Not your fault. I mean, who knew, at the time? And besides, once I have my teleport license, I can just go direct."

"True."

They stepped out of the castle. "Which way?" Ed asked.

Clara considered it. To the right led to the new socc—football field, and its attendant concessions, locker rooms, stadiums, and so forth. To the left was the old field—and the Border she'd raised in the middle of it. "Did they ever finish the new team houses?"

"Oh yeah," Ed replied with a laugh. "Nobody could stand their teams being in the same dorms, waking up when it was still night out, banging and yelling as they ran out."

"Let's go see them."

They walked in silence. Clara noticed that the flower beds along the stone pathway had grown in considerably, providing attraction and shelter for all number of pretty creatures: flutterbyes, thrum-mingbirds, malachi bees, and more.

"Oh, this is nice," she said as they rounded the last curve.

The team houses—six in all—had been constructed in a loose circle, with her Border at the center. They stood well back from the stone monolith, making it seem a bit like a park. Stone pathways led everywhere, including to the Border itself. The houses were built as oversized stone cottages, two stories each, with false-thatch roofs.

Clara paused to look at the Border. "I never dreamed it would end this way," she said wistfully.

"End?" Ed said, concern in his voice.

"Not *end* end," she corrected herself hastily. "I just mean. . . the Borders. School. All this." She sighed and slipped her hand into Ed's. He gripped it firmly. "I missed it all." She continued staring at the giant pillar she'd raised. "Hey, did you ever figure out what was going on with the missing books?"

"The which?"

"The books on translocation magic."

"Oh, yeah. Yeah, I did. Witcher was behind it all, it turns out. He was already lobbying the government to license it and to stop teaching it in schools. You have to go to a government-run workshop to learn it now. Well, we still did, but all the years after us will have to, if they want to."

"Is it expensive?"

"Oddly, no. Or I guess oddly not. No, it doesn't cost much, but there's a massive amount of paperwork you have to fill out."

"Ah."

"Yeah. Anyone can do it, it's accessible to all, but *actually doing it* is essentially infeasible, if you're not a government agent with special orders."

They fell quiet again, listening to the *thrums* and *chirps* of the surrounding birds. Clara relaxed her mind a bit, and the magic of the Border itself, along with all the ambient magic around them, faded into sight.

"It's beautiful, you know," she murmured.

"What is?"

"The Border. They all are. For me it's. . . they're like fountains of light. All this magic, flowing out of them, spreading all over Underhill. It's stronger now." She tilted her head. "They're all connected now. All the Borders. I didn't expect that. I don't think Risewell's were." The previous generation's mathemagician had created the Borders that Oberherr had torn down just at the start of Clara's first year at Linginbaum's. "But these ones are talking to each other."

"What are they saying?"

Clara chuckled. "F equals G times M sub one times M sub two, divided by R to the second."

"Those cheeky devils," Ed said with a laugh.

"It's elegant, though. I'm betting that's how magic got so stable, though. The Borders hold everything in place, and they're spreading magic around evenly."

"But it comes from the Ordinary."

Clara nodded. "Somehow, yes. It's so clear, when you can see it. It's coming right out of them, and nothing's going back. Magic starts *there."* She paused in thought. "You know, for me it was only a year ago."

"What was?"

She nodded toward the monolith. "This. My first Border. We did it together, all of us. The triplets did their synergistic magic. For the first time, really. I was terrified Finlay would throw up again. And you, and. . ."

"What?" Ed asked when she didn't continue.

"Ed, where's Elsie?"

MONDAY BEFORE LUNCH

"I still don't understand *gone,*" Clara said loudly.

"Kidnapped," Finlay replied succinctly.

"We don't know that," Idalia countered.

"What else could it be, Idalia?" Ed demanded. "We've been over and over this. She didn't show up at the start of this term. Her moms sent her to the closest Border alone. They're torn up about it, but there hadn't been any Paladin sightings in Edinburgh at the time."

"Did anyone *look* for her?" Clara asked.

"Of course," Idalia said. "Our whole family was part of it, in fact. The entire faculty. She's *not* here, not in Underhill. They'd have found her. There are tracking spells that you just can't hide from here. And they tried the same ones—every one they could think of—in the Ordinary, too."

"And scrying. And communications. And summoning. You name it, some witch gave it a shot," Harriett said. Her tone was more subdued than usual. "You were dealing with so much, it just didn't cross our minds," she added apologetically. "Sorry."

"She's a *witch,*" Clara insisted. "She learned how to teleport, didn't she?"

"She was wonderful at it," Johanna mumbled.

"And fire—good grief, she could *blast* her way out of anything, couldn't she?"

"That's what I said," Finlay agreed.

"So how could—oh." Clara stopped and looked up at Ed.

He gave her hand a gentle squeeze. "Iron."

"An iron cage. Like a jail cell," Clara said as it dawned on her.

Ed nodded. "That would do it. Any magic she tried to use would be drained out. And it would work better than any ward. She'd show up as a blank to any magic, one of a billion blank spots in the Ordinary."

"Oh."

"Everyone's tried everything," Ed assured her. "Some of them still are."

"Abraham hasn't given up," Idalia said. Her oldest brother was well-known for his tracking abilities. "But we've run out of things to try."

Clara's heart continued to sink. How could she have not noticed that Elsie was gone? Because she'd always been the last one to speak. Because Clara's head was so full of *Clara's problems*. Because every time she turned around, something impossible was happening. Because—

She sighed. "I'm going to take a nap," she said quietly.

CHAPTER 7

LICENSING EXAM

"You okay?" Ed asked the next morning. Clara had missed both lunch and dinner, and when they'd knocked on her bedroom door she'd replied with "I'm fine, but not now, please." After a couple of attempts at coaxing her out, they'd given up.

"Yeah, I guess," she sighed. "Can we order breakfast? I'm not up to a crowd."

"Sure. The others already went down. Everyone's nervous about this morning."

"What—oh, right. The translocation exam. Yay."

Ed was already sending a food order down. It arrived quickly this time, clanking up into the delivery niche in just minutes.

"It's too much, isn't it?" he asked as they ate.

"The eggs?"

Ed laughed. "No. All of. . . this. All of it."

Clara sighed and pushed her eggs around on the plate. "It's a lot, yeah. Finlay has a boyfriend. The triplets can form some kind of witch Voltron. You and I are a thing. Elsie's gone. The Witchers have established a magic monopoly on travel. I have all these. . . *abilities* I don't remember getting. I'd say yeah, it's all too much, except I'm pretty sure there'll be something more, and then what?"

Ed chuckled softly. "Yeah."

"Am I going to be okay in this exam? Seriously?"

He nodded firmly. "You're better than any of us. Although. . ."

"What? Tell me."

He pushed back from the worktable with a sigh. "The examiner. She's been here twice before to check on our progress. They only agreed to let us continue learning translocation magic if we followed the government curriculum. She, uh. . ."

"What, she hates me?" Clara joked.

"A little bit, yeah."

Clara's eyes flew open. "Wait, *what?* Why?"

Ed spread his hands. "You're nontraditional. Everyone else struggles to learn this stuff. For us, getting the mental model right is really tricky. The words, the hand movements, all of that stuff helps force us to the right place, but personally, I still have to stumble around a bit before I find it. But not you. You just *see* it. It's like you could just write a spell down, read it back, and *boom,* you can do it perfectly the first time. Seriously, you nailed it the *second day.* And then you were *improving* it, which did not go down well."

"Great. Thanks so much, old me."

"Don't beat yourself up. You can't help it. The past couple of years, a little longer, you've been correcting magic before you even catch yourself doing it. *We* have all learned to pay attention to your little tweaks, so we can usually pick them up and we're fine. Mrs. Bumsteader, not so much."

"Her name is *not* Bumsteader."

Ed grinned. "It is."

"Fantastic."

"You're going to be fine. Just. . . play it by the book."

"I literally do not remember even seeing the book."

"I mean, keep it simple. Do exactly what she says. Tell you what, I'll volunteer to go first, if nobody else does. Watch what I do, and do *exactly* that. Don't tweak it, don't make the math more elegant, don't. . . do whatever you do."

"Okay," Clara sighed. "I get it."

"That's all we've got this morning. After that lunch, and after that is open workshop time for anyone who needs it."

"Okay." She sighed again and finished her breakfast. "Let's just get it over with."

~

TUESDAY MORNING

"Excellent, Mr. Langsdale. And thank you for volunteering to set us off to such a good start."

Clara took a breath, trying desperately to calm herself. Her mind may not have remembered Mrs. Bumsteader, but her *body* definitely did: the moment she'd walked into the classroom being used for the examination, her heart rate had increased, her hands had begun shaking, and she'd started sweating profusely. But, as promised, Ed had volunteered to go first, and Clara had watched him intently. His magic wasn't as elegant as hers; his equations were overly complex and redundant, and there was considerable leakage, even just in teleporting across the room.

But she could copy it.

"Miss Thorn, why don't you go next? I assume you can astonish us all with your unerring and superior grasp of the topic?"

Jeeze, Clara thought, nodding meekly as she stood. Ed had prepared her for this, though. As she approached the ancient-looking examiner, she kept her head down and murmured, "Actually, ma'am, I thought I'd try to do it like I'm supposed to."

She stole an upward glance and saw one of Bumsteader's eyebrows arch, and the woman's wrinkled lips seemed to relax an iota. "What a novel concept," she said drily. "This end of the room to the other, please."

Ed had taken a moment to breathe, centering himself before he invoked the magic. Clara did the same, and kept her hands tightly at her side as he'd done. She wiggled them in an approximation of the correct somatic sequence, and then whispered, *"Hic illic, non momentum inter,"* the utterly unnecessary-to-Clara, government-approved aural component of the spell. At the same time, she massaged the ambient magic into an exact replica of what Ed had done, and with a quick rush of wind, she was on the other side of the room.

"Sloppy but sufficient," Bumsteader announced. Clara clenched her jaw. "Now to the front steps of the castle. I shall go first, and you shall follow."

Clara nodded submissively as the woman vanished in a swirl of light. *Grossly inefficient,* Clara thought. With nobody there to watch her, she simply hauled the magic into the correct form and vanished.

"Mmm," Bumsteader hummed the moment she appeared. "You cheated there, didn't you?"

Clara's stomach clenched. "No ma'am, not at all, I—" *How could she possibly know?* Was she a mathemagician? Could she *see* the magic?

"Your aura didn't flare upon arrival," the woman pronounced. "I may not be a vaunted mathemagician, young lady, but I am certainly a *Dearthóir Aura.* Do it again. To the football field, and then back here. Directly."

Clara did the muttered cantrip and the fingers again, this time careful to exactly duplicate Ed's attempt, substituting only the coordinates for the different location. That was the tricky bit: regular witches *pictured* their destination in their minds, meaning they couldn't typically teleport to someplace they'd never seen. Even detailed photos were considered risky. But Clara's magic didn't work that way—she simply inserted the correct parenthetical expression for her destination.

But when she reappeared in front of Bumsteader, the woman gave a reluctant nod of approval this time, although her voice was still laden with disapproval. "Sufficient. I have a mind to put a companion restriction on your license—no, don't give me that look. I know perfectly well the friends you've made in high places. I won't."

Clara blinked. *I did?* she wondered. *I wonder who they are.*

"Back inside. You first," the woman ordered.

Clara repeated the whole rigamarole, and Bumsteader appeared beside her a moment later. "Acceptable," she said in a cold, flat voice. "Now, I'm told you three young ladies are capable of qualifying on your own? There's no three-way license, you know."

TUESDAY LUNCH

"I didn't see Phoebe or her lot there," Clara said as they pulled their trays of food out of the chest. A moment later, its sides slammed down and it rocketed upward.

"Oooh, salmon," Johanna cooed. "My favorite! And no, why would she be?"

"To get... a license?" Clara guessed.

"Phoebe never even took that class," Finlay said as he cut up his fish. "The upper-crust are saying that personal teleportation is beneath them. They can afford to use the Anchor network."

"You're joking," Clara said in disbelief. "Teleporting is. . . it's *magical.*"

"Yeah, well, not for that crew," Finlay shrugged.

"Did she ever. . . I mean, after the last Border went up. . ." Clara asked.

Ed laughed. "Oh, she went right back to disliking all of us po' folk," he said, deliberately leaning heavily into his accent. "Especially you, once Daddy had no use for you."

"She'll skip this afternoon's workshop, too," Idalia said. "Private tutors and all that. Truthfully, I don't even know why they came to school here."

"Oh!" Clara said, remembering something. "That reminds me. You said. . . did we stop going to Ordinary school?"

"Oh, yeah," Harriett said through a mouthful of food. "In fact, the last term of Ordinary you remember *was* the last one. Paladin activity picked up that whole year."

"They had an uncanny way of tracking down any kind of stationary magic," Idalia added. "Staking Anchors, monitoring Borders, it got really dangerous to go back and forth. Still is. So they decided to do the rest of our Ordinary classes here. Even brought in human teachers."

Clara's eyes goggled. "No way."

"Sure," Idalia said with a shrug. "Plenty of humans know we exist. Your par—your *adoptive* parents, for example. So they just scrounged up some who were good at math and history and whatever."

"It was nice," Johanna said with a fond sigh. "I like it here a lot better anyway."

"And this year and last were always full-time here on magic studies anyway," Ed added. "So I mean, you really only missed one term of Ordinary."

"Yeah," Clara said, deciding it wasn't that big a loss. "Okay, so what's this workshop this afternoon?"

"It's whatever we want to work on," Finlay said with a grin. "But it'll be Professor Charbrand coaching, and he's best at combat magics."

"Ahem," Ed said quickly.

"Sorry, *constructive elemental magic,*" Finlay corrected himself.

"And am I . . ." Clara ventured.

"You're *fantastic* at it," Finlay assured her.

~

TUESDAY EVENING

"I truly don't get the menu sometimes," Harriett groused as they filed back into the common room. "Salmon filets for lunch and bánh mì for dinner? That's completely backwards. And culturally inconsistent."

"You want, what, food themes?" Finlay teased. His mood the past day had been lighter and more sincere than Clara could remember. *Which is obviously not much,* she reminded herself.

"They did a German day last week," Wolfgang said. Now that Finlay was out, they'd insisted he bring his boyfriend along to meals, if nothing else. "Muesli, bratwurst, and schnitzel. It was like being at home."

"At home with lethal gas," Harriett added. "I don't know how you all do it. You must be genetically immune to cholesterol."

"So what's the plan for the evening?" Finlay asked. "No football tonight. We could play cards?"

"Actually," Clara said, "I was wondering if we could talk about Elsie."

The room got quiet.

"We've. . . done this," Finlay said, suddenly subdued.

"I know. And I know I have. But *I* haven't. And there's something. . . I don't know. Something's poking at me about it. Please?"

"Sure," Ed said immediately, drawing warning glances from the triplets. "Where do you want to start?"

"Start with how we can't find her. You said it's impossible to hide Underhill, so we know she's not here. Why is it impossible?"

"The network," Idalia said promptly.

"The who?"

"The network," Johanna said. "How we can all sense one another. Feel each other's presence."

"Like you couldn't when you were Lost," Harriett added.

Clara let her mind drift for a moment, and there it was: all the points of. . . *presence* in the back of her brain. Harriett, Idalia, Johanna, all of them. Even Wolfgang. But she had no sense of *where* they were, only that they *were.* "I can't locate any of you from that."

"No, but there are spells that ride on it," Idalia said. "What's the one, Harriett? That Mom always used when we were little?"

"Aurkitu nire jendea, aurkitu bere bidea," Harriett said promptly, enunciating perfectly. "She was always a fan of the Basque technique. Remember that. . ."

Harriett's voice faded in Clara's ears as she pictured the spell. She couldn't remember having heard it before, but she could see it now: loops of crocodile green, shot through with top-heavy equations in eggplant.

She shook herself as Harriett finished. ". . .why it won't work in the Ordinary."

"But will anything?" Clara asked.

"The Irish version does," Finlay said confidently. "Me Ma used it, too. *Aimsigh mo mhuintir, faigh a mbealach.* But they tried that one. A *lot,* Da says—he was in the search parties."

"And Elsie's moms tried *Dewch o hyd i'm pobl, dewch o hyd i'w ffordd,"* Wolfgang said. "I overheard them talking to the faculty about it."

"You can *pronounce* all that?" Finlay said in disbelief.

His boyfriend shrugged. "Once you get the hang of it, it's not so different from German."

"Whatever."

"And none of them worked," Clara said, dragging everyone back on track. "Fine. What could stop them from working?"

"A ward," Ed said promptly. "I know *Cachez-vous et couvrez-vous, ombragez et abritez-vous* would do it."

Harriett began debating the effectiveness of that spell, but Clara's attention wandered again as she pictured the warding spell. It was an icosagon, a twenty-sided polygon, rendered in periwinkle and daffodil. Its equations were gentle, its symbols loopy and elegant.

"But the Paladins wouldn't use magic," Idalia said, snapping Clara out of it.

"We don't know that," Ed objected. "They worked with Oberherr, after all."

"Okay, okay," Clara said, shaking her head. "What would Elsie use to get out?"

"Flame," Idalia said at once. "Obviously."

And again, Clara's mind filled with the spell, a simple pillar of equations in glowing fire colors of red and orange.

"Teleportation," Finlay added.

Clara's mind immediately switched to the more complex spell, variables highlighted in ochre amidst the shining colors of the spell.

"Concussion," Harriett suggested, "Although she doesn't. . ."

Clara lost the rest as a concussion spell, all carob and graphite, blazed in her mind, sullen-looking equations creeping slowly around a central core of lapis subexpressions.

"Communication," someone said—Clara's head was starting to spin and she was losing track of the conversation—"maybe something like *Dëgjo britmën time?*"

Again, Clara's brain snapped to the new spell.

"No, she'd have used *Clywch fy nghri,* her moms always taught her the Welsh—"

Snap.

"But they tried *Dewch allan dewch allan oen bach coll* and got—"

Snap.

"She might have—"

Snap

Clara's mind was chaos, now, full of blazing symbols, shining letters, radiant digits. The spells were all mixed up now, contorting themselves into strange lines, forming indistinct shapes.

No, Clara realized. *Not indistinct at all.*

She forced her brain to pull back a thousand feet, and a thousand more, and all the spells, and the lines of magic formed a *very* distinct shape.

Elsie Greene's.

"She's in Las Vegas," Clara announced, bringing the other conversations to a halt.

After a moment's silence, Ed asked, "How could you possibly know that?"

Clara's brain, having finally released its secret, was starting to cool. She fanned her face with one hand. "Aunt Ikwity. She said she'd answer *both* of my question. But I only wanted to know where to put the last Border. But I paid for *two* answers."

"So what was the second question?" Harriett asked with a frown.

"Isn't it obvious?" Clara said with conviction. *"Where is my friend?"*

CHAPTER 8

FORMING A PLAN

"It needs to be next week," Finlay said. "If you're going to do this."

Classes—more workshops, mostly, along with a mandated-at-the-last-minute lecture on translocation magic ethics—had gone well the next day. Clara's grasp of the spells was firm, and even facts and information bubbled up in her mind almost on-demand. She and her friends had enjoyed a quiet dinner of spaghetti and meatballs before retiring to the common room.

"Why next week?" Clara asked.

"Spring break," Ed said. "We get two weeks off, and then come back from that into two weeks of final exams."

Clara shook her head. "Duh. I'm still not back in my groove."

"You've been. . . well, not back, but whatever, for what, five days?" Idalia reassured her. "Give it a minute. But Finlay's right—if we're going to do something, it's next week or after graduation in June. Once finals start, they won't let us out of their sight. Even trips to Linginham are off for the rest of the term."

"Shouldn't you be telling someone?" Wolfgang asked. His brilliant blue eyes were tight with worry. "Like, adults or something?"

Clara hesitated before replying. "We should," she admitted slowly. "In fact, we shouldn't all go to Vegas. But. . . I don't know. I *need* to be there. There's something in my head telling me so. And if we tell someone, they'll stop me."

"More memories from Aunt?" Ed asked.

"I don't know. Maybe. But *I* need to go, at least."

"You're not going without me," he said in a tone that brooked no argument.

"Yeah, I figured," she acknowledged with a grin. "And frankly, Idalia, Johanna, and Harriett—you guys are the big guns, magic-wise. And your family is already in Vegas, right? So it'd make sense for you to visit on break, wouldn't it?"

"Mom and Dad are in Paris, but a bunch of the sibs are, yeah. We'd planned to go home anyway."

"Wolf and I were going to go meet my parents. . ." Finlay said hesitantly.

"Wait, as in *meet my parents?*" Harriett said gleefully. "As in, you're going to *tell* them?"

"Harriett," Idalia sighed.

"Yeah, yeah," Finlay countered. "But if you guys—"

"No, you should do that," Clara said firmly. "Five of us will be enough. If we all try to go to Vegas, someone will think something's up and try and stop us. It'd make sense for Ed to come with me, and the girls obviously have family there."

"How are we even going to find where they've got her?" Ed asked. "I mean, I know Vegas isn't New York City, but it's still a big place."

"I don't know," Clara said, doubt creeping into her voice. "I have a couple of ideas, but. . . I'm hoping something will happen when we get there. If it doesn't, we're no worse off than we are now."

"True," Ed admitted.

"What ideas?" Johanna asked.

"Well. . ." Clara said thoughtfully. "You guys mentioned a tracking spell that rides on top of our sense of each other."

"There are two that would be useful in the Ordinary," Wolfgang said at once. "The more precise is *Verlorenes kleines Kind,* but it is complex. Not that *you* might notice," he amended after a snort from Finlay. "The other is easier, and covers a wider area, but is less precise. *Hieraan zult u ze vinden,* a traditional Dutch spell."

"My Ma—" Finlay began.

Wolfgang shook his head. "Those family spells require a much closer connection. If that's all anyone has tried to find your friend, only the one her mothers used would have had a chance."

Clara blinked.

"I like this guy," Ed said with a chuckle. "He's right. Only *Dewch o hyd*— heck, I can't do Welsh. The Welsh one her moms tried. I didn't think of that," he added, giving Wolfgang a respectful nod. "But he's right on the family connection. There's a possessiveness built into those spells. It's why there's a variant in nearly every tradition."

"But iron would stop anything," Harriett pointed out.

"Well, maybe," Clara said before Wolfgang could reply. "I've been thinking about it. Remember, I can *see* magic draining into iron. I've seen it lots. And it goes in a trickle. Hit it with a spell, and I can almost. . . it's hard to describe. It's like the iron heats up, but it's not actual heat."

"You're thinking you could overwhelm it," Ed said, nodding slowly.

"Maybe," Clara said. "And Wolfgang's German spell—smaller area, more complex—might do it. Is it more complex because it's more powerful?"

Wolfgang nodded. "That's why it's more precise."

"So we make it even *more* powerful," Clara said with a thin smile.

"How?" he asked.

"Witch Voltron," she said, her smile widening. "If the triplets cast that in full synergy mode, and if I'm there to tweak it, reduce the equations, put every *erg* of power into the spell's core. . ."

"It could overwhelm the iron just long enough," Wolfgang finished, nodding again. "Yes. Yes, that might work."

"So we're going to need to learn that spell," Clara said.

"Fortunately, tomorrow's morning workshop is with Professor Durchdenwald," Ed said. "He's an expert at geographic spells."

~

"Clara, a word?"

Clara turned to see Headmaster Herrera waiting just down the hall. She nodded. "Be right there." Then, to her friends, "Head to lunch without me, guys. I'll catch up."

Her friends nodded and trooped off through the main hall to the dining room.

"What's up, Headmaster?" Clara said as she walked up to the older woman.

"Let's go to my office," she said enigmatically, leading Clara into the main hall. "We'll take the Stairs."

"Why not just—oh, right. Licensing." Clara fell in next to the Headmaster.

"Oh, I'm licensed," Herrera said cooly. "I just prefer to set a good example."

Clara remained silent. Something about Herrera's demeanor had changed.

"How are your graduation preparations going?" Herrera asked as they stepped onto the Stairs. "My office," she instructed.

"Um. Good? It's mostly coming back to me. The stuff I guess I learned. . . before. You know."

"Mmm." The Stairs wound them round and round its spiral, easing them up and up to the castle levels that didn't exist in real space. "Any plans for the upcoming break? I assume you're planning to spend the time preparing for your finals?"

Clara's heart beat faster and the Stairs seemed to speed up in sympathy. "I guess?"

"How noncommittal of you," Herrera said, nodding as if with approval. "Ah, we're here."

When Dimmick had been Headmaster, he'd kept his office fairly Spartan. The large, stone-walled room had been mostly empty, save for his enormous desk. Herrera had gone a different direction, lining the room's walls with bookcases and curio cabinets. Her actual desk was a tiny, spindly affair, barely wide enough for her large, comfortable chair to tuck under. She slid that chair out now, sitting down on its edge, her spine ramrod-straight, and gesturing for Clara to sit in the single low-backed chair that faced the desk.

Clara sank into it carefully, her mind racing.

"Now, what *do* you plan to do on your break? And you should assume I have eyes and ears everywhere." The Headmaster fixed Clara with a piercing stare.

"You. . . know?" Clara stammered.

"Know? Of course I don't *know.* I may *suspect,* but I suspect all manner of things, all the time, particularly from our seniors. Elder children, about to cross the invisible line into young adults, testing their boundaries, making the most *inadvisable* decisions."

Clara blinked.

"I understand you've been concerned about your classmate, Elsie Greene."

"She's my *friend,*" Clara corrected. "And of course I am."

"A small number of families have been similarly concerned about missing children." Herrera's stare hadn't changed, but Clara sensed something new behind those silver-gray eyes. The Headmaster wasn't *asking* anything.

"The government in Underhill has, of course, made every effort to keep that information private. As it should. I certainly wouldn't expect you students to know anything about it."

"Of. . . course," Clara said. *Where is she going with this?*

"And of course, the government *continues to look* for Elsie and the two other missing children," Herrera continued.

Clara frowned at the odd emphasis she'd placed on those words. "Good?"

The Headmaster nodded. "It's very good. It's among the

many *very good things* the government does, such as establishing the Anchor network so that we can all travel more safely and more conveniently, without all this unnecessary and dangerous popping about." One of Herrera's eyebrows slowly raised.

Clara's frown deepened.

"You have, of course, heard nothing from your biological mother, since you and I last spoke." A question, not a statement.

"No," Clara said truthfully.

"She's ever so missed. Quite irresponsible of her to leave you here. Particularly when she did. Imagine, haring off just when a Counter-Hunter of her skill and reputation was most needed."

"Imagine?" Clara asked, confused.

"Well, just when so many of those first children had been. . . *misplaced.*"

Understanding dawned. "Of course."

"In fact, the advice of the government is that all of you *should* remain here at the school, or at the very least in Underhill, until after graduation."

"Are they—"

A quick, tight shake of her head. "Properly approved parental requests for you to return home for your break will, of course, be honored. And you will provided with an appropriate escort. Naturally, an offer has been extended for parents—even yours—to visit here during the break. Which I'm sure would be very exciting for them."

"Um, yeah?"

"But I imagine your parents are quite hardworking."

"Oh? I mean, yes. Yes, they'd never be able to take the time off," Clara said, suddenly catching on.

"Which is why I've approved you and Mr. Langsdale returning to Las Vegas. And the triplets as well, although obviously they'll be visiting with their own family."

"Obviously." Clara and Ed hadn't even submitted a request, yet, and she knew for a fact Mom and Dad hadn't, because they'd have mentioned it.

"You know, I've always been impressed with your success with the new Borders. I understand they should last for generations."

"I guess?" The conversation had taken a hard right turn, leaving Clara bewildered again.

"Shows quite a strong grasp of your craft, at such a young age."

"Thank you?"

"It must have taken an immense amount of power. But then you had your friends, didn't you?"

"Um. . . yes?"

"Just so. Seems to be a real. . . *synergy* amongst you, I must say."

Ah. "Yeah. I mean, yes. That's very important."

A tight nod. "Of course. Well. It's been lovely speaking with you. I want to give you these." Still holding Clara's gaze, Herrera extended a hand over her desk, palm up.

Clara finally broke eye contact to look down, and saw two dime-sized, flat crystals, ringed in silver settings. "What are these?"

"For you and Mr. Langsdale. The triplets will receive their own set. Courtesy of the government. They're. . . emergency beacons, of a sort. Simply snap them, or even feed a small burst of magic into them, and they'll alert us. We'll be able to use them to determine your precise location."

Clara took the two crystals and pocketed them.

"Your *precise location,*" Herrera emphasized, once again locking eyes with Clara. "You understand? In case of an emergency?"

Oh. "Yes. Good idea, really. In an emergency."

Herrera gave her a tight smile. "I knew you'd understand the wisdom of it. Now," she continued, pushing back her chair and rising. "I'm very busy just now, and I assume you'll want to join your friends at lunch. In the *public* dining hall?"

What? "Yeah."

"Excellent. Of course, eating in your dorm's *public* common room is permitted still. Should you find the dining hall too. . . noisy."

Clara's mind went *click*. "Oh. Right. Um, thank you. Good to keep in mind."

"Of course. Good day, Miss Thorn."

Clara quickly left the office, her mind racing even faster. Thankfully, the Stairs deposited her in the main hall without incident.

"CLARA THORN, we just spent four hours practicing area-effect spells, and now you want us to to come *out here* and do *more?*" Harriett grumped.

After the afternoon workshop had ended, Clara had rounded up her friends and insisted they follow her out to the parklike area between the football team houses, just to one side of the enormous Border stone. Harriett had immediately demanded explanations and ignored the *look* Clara had given her, but Idalia had repeatedly told her sister to "suck it up and come along."

"I couldn't tell you in the castle," Clara said at once, gathering everyone into a tight circle.

"Is this about—" Idalia started.

"Don't say her name," Clara interrupted quickly. "But yes. She. . . it was really weird. I think her office is bugged. Or she thinks it is."

Six sets of eyes widened. "What?" Ed asked.

"She. . . wants us to find Elsie. And two other kids. But she didn't say so. Not exactly. She actually. . . like I said, her office must be bugged. She was talking all around it, saying exactly the opposite. About how the Anchor network is all good, and how the government is doing all the right stuff, things like that."

Everyone simply stared at her.

"She implied that we can't talk privately anywhere. Not even in the common room. It's all bugged."

"She *said* that?" Idalia asked.

Clara shook her head. "Not in so many words. But. . . yeah. That's what she was getting at."

"Wow," Finlay said.

"She's going to let us go to Vegas, the five of us," Clara continued, nodding to Ed and the triplets. "The government isn't doing anything. Either they've given up, or. . ."

Idalia frowned. "Or *someone's father* has told them to stop."

"He has that much influence?" Wolfgang asked.

Harriett snorted. "Are you kidding? Dad says he has the entire Council in his pocket. They all get kickbacks whenever his businesses make money. Half the witches who live in Underhill permanently work for him."

"All I care about right now is finding Elsie," Clara said. "Her—I mean, *she* implied that Mom—my bio-Mom—had gone off looking after the first kids disappeared, that she wasn't happy with what the government was doing."

"But your Mom vanished," Johanna said.

Clara nodded. "I know. I'm betting we find her with Elsie and the others. Maybe even Dimmick and my old Border team."

Johanna frowned. "But they said Dimmick and the others had— oh," she breathed, suddenly understanding. "So maybe not."

"Dimmick was *super* forceful with. . . *her* dad when he kept trying to force me to put Borders where *he* wanted," Clara said, waggling her eyebrows with each pronoun. "So it makes sense that, if he's that influential, he'd make up a story. So maybe. But," she emphasized, looking at each of her friends in turn, "Elsie is the priority. That's what we're after. Anything else is a bonus and we'll figure out the rest once she's back."

"Agreed," Ed said.

"I feel like we should be doing something," Finlay muttered.

"You can," Clara said firmly, drawing a curious look from the boy. "You and Wolfgang are going to Ireland, right?" Finlay nodded. "Does Brinley Marsh live anywhere nearby?"

Finlay's eyebrows rose. "Oh. Yeah, actually. They were permanently here, but they moved back to Ireland. They're about half an hour away, I think. Easy enough to teleport to, I know the town square really well."

"Her dad worked for. . . *him* while they lived here, but he's left. And Brinley got friendlier and stopped hanging out with. . . *her* crowd," Clara said. "Go get some dish. Find out what you can about what's going on. We may need to know."

"Okay," Finlay said with a firm nod. "I got you."

"So we have a plan?" Idalia asked.

Clara nodded. "We do. We're going to let them escort us to the Ordinary. Your parents will pick you up, mine will get Ed and me. Once the escorts are gone, we'll reconnect. Get one of your sibs to bring you Downtown for dinner—there's a place called Bacon Nation at the D hotel. Plan around six o'clock. Oh, you're going to be given these," she added, reaching into her pocket and withdrawing the two crystals. "Ed, this one's yours," she said as she handed one over. Ed took it, turning it over and looking at it curiously. "I'm pretty sure it's a location tracker. Supposedly if we break it or poke it with magic, it'll summon help, but I'm betting it tracks us the whole time regardless."

"So we'll leave these at home," Ed said.

"Yeah, and—"

"How do you know it isn't listening to us?" Wolfgang asked, eyeing the crystal uncomfortably.

"I looked at it," Clara said confidently. "There's nothing in its magic that picks up sound. And it's definitely sending information somewhere. I can see it doing it right now. We'll put ours in Mom's purse, so they'll just see us going from home to her work and back, always with her."

"They have to have thought of that," Ed pointed out.

"Probably, but the Head—she put on a big scary show. We're probably supposed to be terrified of being outside alone, and from what I can see these *would* send an alarm if we cracked them or something."

"Okay," Ed said dubiously. "I guess we don't really have a choice."

"So we play it cool until Sunday. We leave first thing, as early as they'll take us. They're sending messages to our parents on where to meet us with our escorts. Once we're there, we're going to narrow down where Elsie is, and then we'll take it from there. You two," she said, nodding to Wolfgang and Finlay, "will find out what you can and we'll sync up when we're back from break. Everyone got it?"

Six heads nodded.

Clara gave them all a tight smile. "Let's go find our friend."

CHAPTER 9

RECONNAISSANCE

"You all left those crystals at home, right?" Clara asked.

The triplets nodded. "They're attached to the cat's collar," Idalia confirmed. "She moves around a lot, but she stays inside or in the yard. We don't know how precise they are on location."

"Good idea." Clara had gathered them in the social lounge of her parent's condo building. The lounge was empty this early on a Monday morning. Clara unfolded a map of Las Vegas on the large, glossy white table in the middle of the room, and Ed helped her smooth out the creases until it lay perfectly flat. "Okay. You guys ready to do this?"

The triplets nodded, this time in an uncanny, simultaneous motion. Their eyes were already starting to spark eerily with white energy, and Clara recognized the signs of them slipping into what she'd named their "Voltron mode."

"The power of three shall set us free," they whispered in precise unison.

"Do not," Ed said in a firm voice, "do that."

Harriett grinned, and her sisters' lips twitched in near-unison.

"Go," Clara ordered.

The room filled with rainbow, neon-bright light as the sisters recited the spell:

"In mondhellem Schein und sternenklarer Umarmung,
    Verlorenes Kind, finde Trost, kehre in diesen Raum zurück.
    Flüstern webt durch tiefe Schatten,
    Von Magie geführt, sicher und gesund."

Clara translated in her mind:

In moonlit glow and starry embrace,
    Lost child, find solace, return to this space.
    Whispers weave through shadows profound,
    Guided by magic, safe and sound.

It was an ancient spell, and Professor Durchdenwald had been delighted that they'd asked to learn it. "It's nowhere on your finals," he'd cautioned, "but it's so nice to see young people taking an interest in these old spells," he'd said.

Helices of magic looped around and between the triplets, glowing ivory, buttermilk, marigold, and rose, shot through with delicate equations rendered in iris and lapis. Questing tendrils of shimmering lime shot out, hovering over the map, waving slowly as if in a soft breeze.

Clara and Ed concentrated on their sense of witches, small motes of presence appearing as bright lights in their minds. The green tendrils moved throughout this network, pushing and seeking as they pulsed with energy.

The spell was indeed complex—Clara's eyes darted back and forth as she tracked the many equations, each with intricately scribed subexpressions, parenthetical clauses, and divisors.

Too complex, she thought at once. *Just as I suspected.* Almost on autopilot, Clara's brain began simplifying the expressions, eliminating redundancies and focusing more and more of the triplets' power into the core of the spell. Glowing icosahedrons collapsed into pyramids, and then into even simpler two-dimensional triangles. Convoluted splines reduced to simple arcs, each one burning more intensely, more purely, and the girls' magic condensed and coalesced.

Elsewhere in Clara's mind, the bright pinpoints that represented the rest of the world's witches grew more brilliant, drowning out all the dark spaces between them.

But suddenly, one of the tendrils stabbed into one of those dark places, a place where there was no sense of any witch, no luminous point of light. At the same time, another tendril jabbed onto the map, piercing it in a single, precise location. Still holding her sense of other witches firmly in her mind, Clara hurried to mark the glowing point of light on the map with a pen. "Got it," she said victoriously.

The triplets relaxed their hold on the magic, and it dissipated slowly, the room's light returning to normal.

"Where," Johanna began.

"Is she?" Idalia finished.

"Right here," Clara said, pointing at the map. Her ink dot was smack in the middle of an unremarkable residential subdivision cul-de-sac.

"Well," Ed said, a bit of surprise in his voice, "I honestly didn't expect that to work. How are we getting there?"

Clara grinned. "It's walking distance."

"Huh," Ed said quietly. "Didn't see that coming."

They'd made the twenty-minute walk into the historic John S. Park neighborhood, Clara and Ed strolling casually together down one street, while the triplets took another route. The houses here we mostly single-story ranch-style affairs, many with vague mid-century elements. Clara had scanned constantly, looking for any signs of magic and more or less ignoring Ed's small talk.

They'd stopped dead across the street from their target cul-de-sac, and Clara heard the triplets arrive two blocks further down at almost the same time.

This cul-de-sac *had* been part of the larger neighborhood at one point, but a developer had recently purchased the smaller homes on this lot, razed them to the ground and started over. The new homes were *very* modern in style, and in Clara's vision each of them burned a low, sullen red as they gradually drew ambient magic from around them and fed it slowly into the earth below.

"Concrete houses with steel rebar rods?" Ed asked.

"Yeah," Clara said, her voice a mix of disappointment and finality. "At least we know why we can't sense anyone."

"But we don't know which one they're in," Ed pointed out.

"Yeah."

Clara made a shooing motion with one hand, and watched as the triplets retreated back the way they'd come.

"So what do we do next?"

"We need to keep an eye on it. On them." Clara's head swiveled as she scanned the rest of the neighborhood, the other houses' wood construction providing no obstacle to her vision. "I have an idea. Let's go meet the girls."

They turned and walked back two blocks before following the curving road back west toward the triplets.

"Poured concrete?" Idalia asked at once.

Clara nodded. "With iron rebar. The roofs, too, and even the foundation slab, as near as I can tell. As good as a jail cell, but prettier."

"They couldn't just bust a window?" Harriett muttered.

"They could be sedated," Ed pointed out. "Or the windows could be blocked from the inside. Or made of polycarbonate or something shatterproof. And they're probably under guard."

"We need to keep an eye on things," Clara said. "In one of the workshops last week, there was—" She paused as her time-lagged brain took a moment to surface the answer. "—I think it was *Fís Charm chun Daoine a Rialú?*"

Ed nodded. "An old Fae spell, one of the few we can fully replicate. It's a combination of illusion, glamour, and mild hypnosis. But —oh, I get it."

"Sharing is caring," Idalia said.

"She wants to charm someone in one of the adjacent houses so we can use their place as a lookout."

"Exactly," Clara confirmed.

"Needs to be one with no pets," Ed cautioned. "Especially cats. Cats hated the Fae."

"I have a better idea," Idalia said slowly. "There's one called *eaba'at fireawn,* the Pharaoh's Cloak. Much more modern, and it's easier to keep running in the background for a long time. And cats should fall for it."

Ed smiled. "Since when did you three get into Egyptian magic?"

"They make the best air conditioning spells," Harriett said primly.

Clara chuckled. "Okay. So we go back, pick a house that has a view of the cul-de-sac's entrance, charm whoever's home, and take up a watch."

"We'll do that," Idalia said confidently as her sisters nodded agreement. "We can. . . sort of take turns. Stand watches. But if we're in the right headspace, whatever one of us sees, we'll all know about. We can do a sending to you two whenever something comes up. You can stay out of sight somewhere nearby, or even back at your parents' condo."

"Deal," Clara said.

"What exactly are we looking for?" Johanna asked.

"Any activity. They have to be bringing them food now and then, at the very least. Anyone dressed like a Paladin, obviously. We just need to figure out which house has Elsie in it."

"What if," Ed said cautiously, "they're using more than one house?"

Clara blinked. "I didn't think of that," she admitted. "So obviously you'll have to watch them all, but yeah, it might be more than one. We'll... I guess figure that out when the time comes."

"Okay. Leave it to us," Idalia said. The three of them walked confidently down the street, back toward the cul-de-sac of concrete homes, leaving Ed and Clara on their own.

"We should think about disguises," Ed said as he and Clara turned back north toward her parents' condo. "And we promised your mom we'd check in every couple of hours." Clara's parents hadn't been enthused about their proposed rescue mission, but they'd contented themselves with periodic check-ins. Dad had insisted they simply call the police, but Ed had pointed out that the Paladins usually arranged tight connections with local law enforcement, making that a dangerous option.

"Okay," Clara agreed as they began walking. "I'm betting we'll have at least a few hours to kill."

WEEK ONE WEDNESDAY AFTERNOON

"Okay, I didn't think it would be *two days,*" Clara groused. She and Ed had taken up a spot at a bookshop-slash-coffee-shop not far from her parents' condo, and on the way to where the triplets had been hiding. The girls had done a sending every hour on the hour, with no news to report, and Clara was started to get anxious. "What if the spell didn't work? What if—"

‹*Clara! Ed!*› the triplets' weird, three-in-one voice echoed in their minds. ‹*We've got something!* ›

An image of a Paladin, wearing the customary black trenchcoat but without a hat or goggles, filled their minds. He was carrying a half-dozen plastic grocery bags marked with "Smith's" logos, approaching... house 1307. They could clearly make out the large metal house numbers. The Paladin sat the bags down on the front step, knocked twice, and then took several steps back. After a moment, the door opened, swinging inward and revealing a second Paladin, this one wearing their full outfit, including the heavy goggles slung around his neck. He picked up the bags and stepped back inside, the door quickly closing behind him.

Clara and Ed blinked as the image faded from their mind. "Well there we are," Ed said hesitantly.

"Should we have been able to sense them when the door opened?" Clara asked.

"Not necessarily," Ed said uncertainly. "If the interior walls are concrete, or if they used steel studs. . . probably not. And it was really fast. I wasn't paying attention to my sense of everyone."

"Me either," Clara frowned. "But I guess at least now we know—
"

‹*More!*› the girls' mental voice called.

Another set of images arrived: the same Paladin, carrying another load of groceries. The girls had pulled their perspective back, and Ed and Clara could now see the white, nearly windowless Ford Transit van the man was pulling the bags out of. This time he walked to another house, 1321, and delivered the bags. This time, Ed and Clara quickly focused on their Witch-Radar, as Clara had begun calling it. When the house's front door opened, a few faint flickers glimmered into life, cutting off just as quickly when the groceries were taken inside and the door closed.

"So it's a metal door as well," Ed mused as the vision faded. "And we've got two houses to worry about."

"At least," Clara muttered darkly.

But after a few minutes, ‹*He drove off,*› the triplets sent. ‹*We think that must be it, just those two.*›

"Okay," Ed said. "Now what? Do we just pick one?"

Clara thought about it for several minutes. "We could try the Girl Scout Cookie bit," she said dubiously.

"I'm pretty sure they'd recognize us. And that close to all that metal I wouldn't trust an illusion spell."

"What if we—"

‹*HARRIETT!*› came a scream in their minds. With it, another vision: Harriett was marching across 8th Street toward the second house. Clara and Ed also sensed more: Johanna, holding Idalia back even as hot tears began pouring from her eyes. Idalia, struggling against one sister's viselike grip as the other strode confidently up to the door of 1321, rapped smartly, and waited for the door to open.

"Clara," Ed said quietly, gripping her forearm.

"I see it," she replied. She began pulling ambient magic around her in a teleport spell.

"No!" Ed said firmly, somehow sensing her intention.

"Ed, I have to—"

"We don't know what they'll **do**, and they'll recognize you," he said urgently. "Just—"

They watched in horror as, almost in slow-motion, the front door of 1321 opened. Harriett was saying something, waving her hands energetically.

Then she took a step backward—

Or tried to.

A black-sleeved hand reached out, grabbed the front of Harriett's shirt, and dragged her into the house.

The door slammed shut behind her.

‹*HARRIETT!!!!*› the other two triplets screamed in anguish.

CHAPTER 10

ATTACK!

"This is a bad idea," Ed cautioned.

Ignoring his protests, Clara had teleported them both into the house the triplets had used for their stakeout. Idalia and Johanna, sitting on a sofa and hugging each other, were nearly catatonic with grief and confusion. The elderly residents of the home puttered about, doing their business as if the four teens were their own children.

"Lemonade?" the woman asked, setting a tray of glasses on the coffee table.

Clara ignored them. "It's the *only* idea, Ed," she insisted. "Look at them."

"We could at least call their siblings," he shot back.

"Can't," Johanna moaned softly. "They all went off with Mom and Dad."

"Whom we *could* get in touch with," Ed said firmly. "And they *can* teleport directly here. For that matter, we could go get those crystals they gave us, and break them," he added sensibly.

"Which would take time," Clara argued. "Ed, we need to do this. Now. We're going to break in there and get our friends."

"We have no idea how many Paladins are even in there!" he said heatedly.

"I'll tear the door off its hinges," Clara growled. "I'll pull the whole wall down, if I have to." Her heart was hammering in her chest, and while she was dimly aware of a tiny voice telling her to listen to Ed, she ruthlessly ignored it.

"Clara, this isn't like you," Ed said, shifting to a pleading tone.

"It's *exactly* like me. *This* me," she insisted. "Idalia, Johanna, once the door is open, find Harriett. You can do your synergy thing. Teleport *everyone* out. Into the field next to the school."

"Your parents, Clara—" Ed begged.

"At work, too long," Clara snapped. "We'll deal with the second house later, after—"

"We can *try* the police. They—"

"Too risky, you're the one who told us the Paladins always get to them to cover kidnappings anyway. We're going in *now*. You two with me?" Idalia and Johanna nodded quickly, each helping the other stand from the sofa.

"What about your mother?" Ed asked desperately, standing as well. "Couldn't she. . . I don't know, get someone from her hotel's security? Maybe they'd know someone, like a private security firm or something?"

"Ed," Clara said, forcing herself to be patient, "no private security firm is going to bust in there. They'd call the police. And if I call Mom, she's going to tell me not to do anything. And I'll tell her okay, which will be a lie." She glared at Ed, daring him to raise another objection.

"Please," Johanna whimpered softly.

Clara clenched her fists. "Ed, you can stay here if you want and—"

"Don't be stupid," he growled. "I mean, if you're going to be stupid, and this *is* stupid, I'm going to be stupid with you."

Clara blinked at the vehemence in his voice. "Okay," she said more quietly. "Here we go."

"How exactly are you going to do this?" Ed asked as he followed her out the front door.

"You're going to feed me magic," Clara said with a calm she didn't feel. "And I'm going to tear the door off its hinges, like I said."

«Here,» Johanna and Idalia said together, their voices oddly dissonant without their sister's. A wave of magic crashed into Clara from behind, its colors jittering nervously between amaranth and celadon. As it poured over and around her, Clara noticed its equations were equally unstable, letters ballooning crazily in one direction before suddenly contracting and then expanding in another. She wrestled it under control, exactly as she'd done every time she raised a Border, forcing the letters, numbers, and symbols into the shape she wanted. Another flow of magic joined: Ed's, smaller but more stable, glowing a steady, calming azure.

But Clara was in no mood for calm.

She knitted the magic into a massive hectagon, poured raw energy into its middle, and flung it at the door of 1321.

As she'd anticipated, it shattered on contact, but Clara continued to pour power into it and to shape it, reforming the hectagon into five pentadecagons, assigning one each to the door's corners and the fifth toward its middle. In her mind's eye, the door began glowing an angry, hot chili powder-red as it siphoned off more magic than it was capable of handling.

Still, Clara pounded magic into her mathematical structures, the torrent of energy from Johanna, Idalia, and Ed not letting up for a moment. Her pentadecagons began to merge, the two on the left connecting at their extreme vertices, while the two on the right did the same. Those connections merged into the central polygon, forming a complex, multi-faceted set of pincers. These grabbed at the door, sinking into it as the doorframe began glowing marigold.

With a sudden, loud *crack,* the door flew out of the doorframe. Clara quickly waved her left arm, and the door instantly shifted vectors and flew off down the street, sliding to a clattering halt a dozen yards away and setting off two car alarms.

A trenchcoat-covered Paladin leapt out of 1321's now-gaping front entrance.

Clara refocused her magic into a single, densely colored torus, and sent it driving into the man's chest. The leading edge of magic sparked against the iron plates in the trenchcoat, but like the door, those plates weren't designed to deflect or absorb this much energy. Clara could feel Ed and the girls finally starting to flag, but she continued driving the torus forward until it smacked into the man with brutal physical force, slamming him back into the house with a loud crash.

The magic began faltering in Clara's mental hands, and even the ambient energy was roiling and uncontrollable at this point. Clara gathered as much of it as she could into a shield, holding it in front of them as the four teens stepped into the house—

—and fell into a deep pit.

CHAPTER II
TRAPPED

"Hey, you okay?"

Clara opened her eyes groggily, struggling to focus in the dim light. "Harriett?"

"Thanks for coming to get me," the triplet said with a wan smile.

Clara's eyes finally locked into focus as Harriett arose and was embraced by her sisters. "I don't suppose you called for help before you crashed in here?" Harriett said, tears running down her face.

"We did not," Ed grimaced as he pulled himself upright and started massaging the shoulder he'd landed on.

"Sorry," Clara mumbled. "This is all my fault. We should have—"

"You probably should have, but if you're as hot-headed as I can be, I suppose it's no surprise," an older voice said.

Clara's head whipped around. "Mom?" she said quietly.

"Hey, baby," Jessamine Holdaway said, walking over and gathering her daughter into a tight hug. They held each other for several moments. "Any chance Arlene or Theo know you're here?" Clara buried her face in her mother's chest and shook her head, sniffling. "Ah well."

"This was a trap," Ed said flatly.

Jessamine nodded, wrapping her arms around Clara. "Yeah. They've been moving us around since they caught me and my team, every three or four weeks or so. They'll fill our room with sleep gas, and we wake up in a new one. This is the first basement. Are we still in New Orleans?"

"Vegas," came Clara's muffled reply.

"Oh," Jessamine said with false levity. "My favorite. Convenient for you guys, huh? Close to home and all?"

"I'm sorry, Mom," Clara repeated, choking back more tears.

"Baby, baby, it's okay," Jessamine assured her, patting her back. She pulled back, looking into Clara's eyes. "They fooled all of us. Although I'm pretty sure you're the prize, baby."

Clara's eyes widened and she sniffed again. "Me?"

"Yeah, I think this jerk told them all about you." Jessamine cocked a thumb over one shoulder.

Clara looked past her mother to the basement wall, where a small iron cage had been erected. In it crouched a bald-headed man clad in dingy, torn black clothing. Clara gasped. "Oberherr?"

"Aldworth will do," the man rasped. "My movement is dead, thanks to you."

"Why Clara?" Ed asked.

Jessamine sighed. "They've got the impression she's some kind of super-witch. That if they can control her, they can get to the rest of us. *He,*" she repeated, making a rude gesture toward Aldworth, "told them she created the new Borders."

"They're trying to get into Underhill," Ed said, nodding slowly.

"The Borders won't activate for anyone but a witch," Clara said.

"They have more than a few of us," another voice said. Clara peered into the dim corner of the basement and saw three other adults there.

"My team," Jessamine said. "And I believe you've met Elsie Greene?"

"Hey, Clara," Elsie said, stepping out from another dark corner. "What's up?"

"Elsie!" Clara sobbed, freeing herself from her mother's arms and dashing over to embrace her friend. "Oh, I'm so glad we found you!" She pulled back. "Are the other kids here, too?"

"Trevor Hill and Latoya Immelson," Elsie said, nodding in their direction.

"What about Dimmick? And his team?" Clara asked, looking to her mother.

Clara's heart fell at her mother's expression. "As far as I know, they didn't make it," Jessamine said quietly. "They found us in Austin, but they put up too good a fight. The Paladins couldn't capture them, so they were—well. Like I said, as far as I know..."

Fresh, hot tears streamed down Clara's face. "This is my fault," she said, trying not to start sobbing again. "We should have called the cops, or—"

"No good," Jessamine said firmly, shaking her head. "First thing the Paladins do when they move into an area is buy off the cops. They'll have had people in Vegas *years* ago, starting with dispatch. All you'd have done is told them where to find you."

"Our sibs?" Harriett said.

"Girls, much as I respect your family, you're no fighters. Cecil Dimmick *was,* and it wasn't enough. No."

"What do they want with us? With Clara?" Ed asked quietly.

Jessamine sighed. "To kill us all, in the end. Like I said, I'm pretty sure they think Clara is some kind of key to—"

"To your secret hideaways?" A cold voice, dripping with contempt, sliced its way through the room. A light *clicked* on. It was an iron-barred window, set in what Clara had thought was just a basement wall. It was low, almost at the height for a seated person. A slim figure at the window was backlit, showing just a dark silhouette. "That's precisely what we think you are, child."

"Who are you?" Clara asked hotly.

"Our hostess, Laura Deuxm," Jessamine said, rolling her eyes.

She pronounced the woman's last name *doom,* and Clara shuddered a bit at the word.

"I have to say," their captor continued cooly, "it feels like poetic justice for us to use you to access your fellow witches, given how *you* tried to use *us.*"

"What's she talking about?" Idalia whispered.

"Aldworth," Jessamine said with contempt. "They didn't know he was a witch when he was running their West coast operation. When they realized, he told them everything they wanted to know in hopes they'd free him. Which was *stupid,*" she snapped toward the caged man. "But he was always nine-tenths stupid and one-tenth crazy, so there you go."

"So you, what, bought these two houses to trap us?" Ed said, trying to mimic Jessamine's bored tone.

"Two? Child, please. We bought all of them. Concrete and rebar construction? Yes, please. Basements? Absolutely—and now we've connected them all. Every one modified to be a trap specifically for witches. Our most promising city, especially given the number of times you've been spotted here. We knew it would be a matter of time. And the fact that you found them all even through all that steel and iron—well, it just proves my point."

"I didn't—" Clara started, but clicked her mouth shut when Elsie pinched her.

"We'll begin planning the next phase of our operation right away," Deuxm continued as if Clara hadn't spoken. "It will take a few days for us to move sufficient forces into Las Vegas. But then you'll show us where your local portal is, and you'll activate it for us, and then we'll begin moving to finally end the blight of magic in this world." The light clicked off, and Clara heard a soft *chunk* as a metal panel closed shut over the barred opening.

"She's a delight," Jessamine said, shaking her head. "She's practically a cartoon character. But she runs the whole North American operation."

"She can't seriously think she can just march into Underhill with, what? Even a hundred Paladins wouldn't be enough."

"It would if they carried enough iron," one of Jessamine's teammates pointed out.

"It'd collapse the Border," Idalia said.

"It wouldn't," Clara countered quietly.

"But they—wait, what?" Jessamine said, looking closely at Clara. "Did you say iron *wouldn't* collapse the Borders?"

"Not mine," Clara replied. "They're anchored in the Earth. Iron is part of what keeps them stable. The. . . it's hard to explain. The roots of this world connect to the roots of Underhill. It's iron threaded in, all the way through. It holds the magic that keeps them both connected to each other."

Jessamine blinked a few times. "Oh."

"So if they go marching into Underhill with iron. . ." Elsie said.

"The Fae called it the Rot," another of Jessamine's teammates said, his voice flat. "In the legends, Underhill came too close to the Ordinary, and started breaking down the magic that held it all together."

"I'm not going to show them where it is," Clara said firmly.

"They don't need you to, baby," Jessamine sighed. She lowered herself, cross-legged, to the dusty concrete floor. "They have a lodestar."

"A what?" Clara asked.

"A lodestar," the man who'd spoken of the Rot said, stepping forward. "Reuben Jameson. I've worked with your mother for a long, long time."

"What's a lodestar?" Ed asked.

"A magical device for detecting static magic," Reuben said. "Except the Paladins fancy it a holy relic of some kind. No idea where they found it, but we've seen them using it. It's *old*."

"So they can find static magic," Clara said. "Like Anchors?"

"Which they stake with iron as soon as they can," Jessamine said, nodding. "Which is tactically a little stupid, since if they left them alone they'd be able to predict where we were going a lot more easily, but like I said—cartoon character. She's obsessed with destroying any magic she finds. But yes, anything static. They've not managed to find your Border yet, but I think that's only because she's been so focused on finding *you. He* did tell them that they can't activate the Border on their own. And I think she half-plans to try and force you to stand up a new one that's more advantageously positioned."

"I can't," Clara said at once. "I can only open them from the other side, and I've almost no control over where they come out in the Ordinary."

"I doubt she'll much care," Reuben sighed.

"I don't think the lodestar works with Borders," said Jessamine's other teammate. She stepped forward. "Sandy Strong. I'm the new one on the team. But I specialize in magical devices, and I don't think their lodestone can see Clara's new Borders."

"Why not?" Clara asked.

"They're not. . . *magic* in the same way an Anchor is. And I know there are Borders in New Orleans, Austin, and Columbus, and they've never given any suggestion they could find them. I think Clara's Borders are somehow more. . . I don't know, *fundamental* in how they work. Like, a direct connection between the worlds. They even feel different than the old ones."

"I still won't show them where they are," Clara insisted.

"You might, baby," Jessamine said, shaking her head sadly. "They've plenty of your friends here to threaten. And me."

Clara's heart skipped a beat. "Then we have to get out of here," she said.

Reuben chuckled. "Your Mom here says you're special, that your magic works differently, and I believe it. I've used your Borders. But in case you hadn't noticed, we are quite literally surrounded by steel and concrete. And steel might not absorb magic as efficiently as raw iron, there's a *lot* of it all around us. They've been good enough about feeding our bodies these past months, but we haven't felt so much as a trace of magic in our souls since we were captured."

"I don't absorb magic," Clara said distractedly as she unfocused her eyes and examined the environment. "I manipulate it directly." Reuben was right in that not a single glimmer of magic was present in the basement. Even so, Clara could see the telltale, dim glow that meant magic was being absorbed from *outside,* and anchored into the ground through the metal rods in the walls, floor, and ceiling. "Do they ever let you upstairs?" If she could make it to a window...

"Not here," Elsie said. "But this is the first basement they've put us in."

"Hmm," Clara murmured, her eyes still slowly scanning the structure. "What's this?" she asked, pointing to the wall.

"That's the wall," Harriett said.

"It's different," Clara insisted.

"It isn't really," Johanna said apologetically.

Clara shifted her vision. "Well, no, not like this. But magically," she continued, letting her eyes slip a bit out of focus, "it's not absorbing magic the same. It's like there's a piece of metal missing."

"Plumbing," Ed supplied. "There's probably a drain there, probably the main drain to the sewer connection. But I didn't think that'd normally be *in* the wall," he said, craning his neck back to look at the ceiling.

"True," Reuben said. "I've built more than a few homes in the Ordinary, over the years. But normally you'd have all the plumbing running overhead, down here." He, too, was looking up at the basement ceiling. "And there's nothing here. So it must go up through the walls."

"Well, there's no metal in *this* section," Clara said confidently. "Idalia, what's it like when you guys absorb magic? Like, how do you do it?"

"We just do," Idalia shrugged. "You kind of just... let it happen."

"You can't force it?"

"Not that I know of."

"You can," Jessamine countered, standing. "It's a combat witch technique. We draw more power than we'd absorb naturally, and do it a lot faster. Helps to keep you powered up when you're fighting."

"Could you teach the triplets?" Clara asked.

Jessamine shook her head. "Not down here. Not with no magic at all. What is it you're trying to do?"

Clara sighed and returned to staring at the wall. "I'm going to coax magic in. I need someone to suck it in. Ideally, the triplets. They can multiply the effect of whatever they take in. Synergistic magic."

Jessamine frowned. "I don't know if we could—"

"We could," for first teammate said. "Sorry, Chuck Bishop. We could, Jess. The old Latin rite, remember? *Hic est sanguis meus bibens gratis.*"

"Gross," Harriett said, translating the spell's name.

"It's not literal," Chuck said. "But all four of us can pull magic—we all know the technique. And we can feed it to another witch. Or witches. They don't need to do anything special, and it'll go a little faster than absorbing it naturally. But down here—the magic will just be drawn to all the metal."

"I'll sort that out," Clara said confidently.

"You can't just—" Chuck started.

"I bet she can," Jessamine interrupted, patting Clara on the back. "Okay then, baby. Where do we start?"

"Stand here," Clara said, pointing at a spot on the floor next to the wall she'd been studying. "I'm hoping when you start your—whatever it is you do, it'll start attracting magic. I'm going to keep it tight, keep it away from the metal in the walls. Then you draw it in, and feed it to the triplets. I'll keep that tight, too."

"Okay," Bishop said doubtfully.

"You're going to *feel* me doing it," Clara said, turning to look at him. "You'll feel me messing with your magic. I'm improving it, trust me. Don't fight me on it. Just. . . let it do what it wants to do, even if it feels wrong to you, okay?"

"Feel?" Sandy asked uncertainly.

"If you fight it," Harriett promised solemnly, "you'll throw up. So don't."

"She's done this to you?" Reuben asked.

"Lots," Idalia assured him.

"Okay," Chuck said dubiously.

"Here we go," Clara said, motioning for everyone to take their place.

"Clara," Idalia said quietly, "once we have the magic. . ."

"Teleport," Clara said just as softly. "Me and Mom, if you can't handle everyone. Mom alone, if that's all you can manage."

"But—"

"She's the best fighter we've got," Clara assured them. "And now she knows what's up there. Or at least has an idea. She can get the rest of us out, or even get help."

Jessamine had walked silently up to the two girls. "It's a good plan, baby," she said gently. "And you're right. I'd be the best shot. Once I'm out I'll only need a second or two to gather enough magic to teleport a short hop. From there, I can get help, come back, whatever is needed."

Idalia nodded, turned, and began whispering urgently to her sisters.

"Okay," Clara announced. "Everyone else, stand back." Ed joined Elsie and the other two kids on the opposite side of the basement. Clara sank deeply into her magical view of the world, concentrating intently on the dim magical symbols she could see vanishing into the wall's steel bars. "We begin."

Reaching out with her mind and her will, Clara yanked the nearest symbols away from the rebar, grunting at the unexpected resistance she felt. She clenched her fists and ground her molars together, *forcing* the magic to obey. The first few symbols slipped through the concrete and were vacuumed into Jessamine and her teammates, who inhaled sharply with surprise.

Clara formed the magic into a tight cylinder, holding it in the precise middle of the "dead" area she'd noticed. She pushed her awareness through it, sweat beginning to trickle down her back. More magic lay outside, all of it lazily eddying toward the grounding steel rods in the walls, but Clara cajoled them into her cylinder, drawing more and more magic into the basement. Magic tended to stick together when it was flowing with purpose, and the more Clara convinced to come through, the more that wanted to join it. Before long, her cylinder—no bigger than the cardboard core of a roll of paper towels—was shimmering white-hot with compressed, rapidly flowing magical power.

"Get ready, girls," Jessamine said tightly.

Clara split her attention, one half holding the almost-self-sustaining cylinder in the wall, and the other now catching the magic pouring out of Jessamine and her team. She quickly tweaked the equations coming from them, and heard a couple of uncomfortable grunts as the adults adapted to the changes she was making to their spell. The magic now stayed in a tight line between the four older witches and the triplets, splashing into the girls' bodies and sinking into their skin.

«Ah,» the girls said as their eyes started to glow. *«That's more like it.»*

"Weird," Latoya whispered from the corner.

"You haven't seen the half of it," Ed assured her.

"I can't hold all of this long!" Clara said as she realized her hold on the wall cylinder was wavering. "Mom, stop sending to the girls and save some!"

«It's enough. Here we go,» the triplets said. «我们送你走。»

Jessamine vanished with a *pop* as air rushed to fill the space she'd been occupying.

"Oooh," Chuck said, bending over and putting his hands on his knees. As Clara watched, most of the magic he'd absorbed starting leaching out into the walls again. "I hope that was enough."

"Chinese—" Idalia said.

"—travel—" Johanna continued.

"—spell," Harriett added. "Best for—"

"—accurately moving—" Johanna added.

"—other people," Idalia finished. The glow in the triplets' eyes was fading faster as the metal around them accelerated the comedown from the synergistic state.

"You're right," Latoya said to Ed.

Above, they could hear crashing noises, and then silence. A moment later, the trap door that Clara, Ed, Idalia, and Johanna had fallen through swung down, admitting a bright swath of light. A chain ladder rattled down a moment later, and the adults began helping the teenagers clamber up.

"Mom," Clara said as she emerged, stepping out onto the house's concrete front step. "What happened?"

"Two Paladins, didn't see it coming," Jessamine said, giving her daughter a satisfied grin. "Tight, fast blast of sleepy magic to the eyes, followed up by a frying pan concussion once they went down."

"That Deuxm lady?" Ed asked.

Jessamine shook her head. "Already gone, I think. We can check next door, but—"

"But let's not push our luck," Reuben said as he hauled himself out of the basement prison. "What about Aldworth?"

"Let him rot," Jessamine said firmly. "I want to get everyone out of here as soon as possible, and we'll get the kids home from there. Draw in enough magic to teleport us all a short distance, Reuben. Chuck, Sandy, you too."

"Already on it," Chuck said, breathing deeply.

"Where to, boss?" Sandy asked.

"Pickleball courts at the Plaza," Jessamine said immediately. "We can charm anyone who sees us arrive, and it's usually empty anyway."

Clara gasped as four swirls of magic surrounded them all and whisked them away.

CHAPTER 12

CATCHING UP

"This is a really nice place, Arlene," Jessamine said, looking appreciatively around the condo. "It must be such a relief not to have to move. . ." she stopped and frowned.

Arlene Thorn snorted. "Don't think for a moment that Theo and I would have wished for anything different. This young lady has been all the love in our lives," she added, smiling at Clara. "We're just so happy she's finally found her people. And *you.*"

The Thorns had caught up with Jessamine when she'd first reappeared, just as Clara had been starting her first term at Linginbaum's. But it had been a short reunion, with Jessamine soon vanishing again as she tried to track down Clara's biological father.

"And I'm sorry I've been around so infrequently these past few years," Jessamine sighed, giving Clara a sad smile. "But at least we had fun those few times, yeah?"

Clara heaved a sigh of her own. "Actually, that's one of the things I need to tell you guys." All three adults frowned. "So, you remember when I raised the last Border?"

Arlene nodded slowly. "Three. . . four years ago, now?"

"Close enough. But the thing is. . . *I* don't remember it. And I don't remember anything since then, until like a couple of weeks ago." Clara's eyes darted between her parents', gauging their reaction.

Her adoptive father's eyebrows beetled together in confusion. "Come again?"

"So, I had one of my dreams. Did I tell you all about them?"

"The elf," Jessamine said.

"Yeah. He told me where the last Border would go. *Roughly.* But he said I had to go alone, because something in the woods there wouldn't want other witches coming in. And that something would tell me exactly where the Border would go."

"Okay," Arlene said. "And then?"

"I met a woman. An old woman. Or. . . I guess she *looked* like a woman."

"We think she was a Power," Ed said quietly.

"What's that?" Theo asked.

"Fae leftovers," Jessamine snorted.

"Not exactly," Ed corrected her. "They're. . . so, the Fae did muck around with major forces. Entire seasons. Life and death, fate, you name it. Time," he said, looking at Clara. "After a while, those things started to get concentrated. They developed personalities. They say most of them have dissipated since the Fae left, but I guess some of them didn't."

Time, Clara thought. *Don't spend too much time.* Well, they'd rescued Elsie, and Mom, and all the others. Clara would happily pay the price again, even if she'd had a choice.

And. . . maybe Aunt Ikwity had known that. Maybe Clara *had* made the choice.

"And they're. . . friendly?" Arlene asked.

"They're not *inimical,*" Ed said carefully. "But they're not human. They have their own values, their own concerns. It was always better to stay away from them, if you could."

"And so you found one," Theo said to Clara.

"Yeah. And she told me she'd answer two questions. Or that she. .

. *had* answered two questions. Like, before I asked them. And that I had to pay her price, but she never told me what it was. It's really hazy. I. . . blacked out, maybe. And I came to in the dining hall at school, at the end of my senior year."

"*Two* questions," Jessamine said sharply. "Not just where to put the Border, then."

Clara nodded. "The other was where to find my friend. Although I didn't know it at the time. I mean, I didn't even ask, I don't think. But when I found out Elsie was gone, and we started talking through it. . . I just *knew.*"

"So *that's* how you found us?" Jessamine asked incredulously. "On a. . . *hunch?*"

"No, Mom," Clara insisted. "I *knew.* I. . . don't know how to explain it."

All three of Clara's parents gave her long, searching looks. Ed, sitting next to her on the sofa, slipped his hand around hers. "The triplets already know all this," he added, slowly making eye contact with each of the adults. "And Finlay and Wolfgang. So does the Headmaster, and at least a couple of the professors. They all agreed that there's something in the forest, something that doesn't want witches in. But that's where the final Border was raised."

"Did this woman have a name?" Arlene asked.

Clara sighed. "She said to call her Aunt. Aunt Ikwity."

Jessamine barked a laugh. "Yeah, that tracks with one of the Powers. All cleverness, from what the legends say. Still. . . my own baby, meeting one." She shook her head. "And you paid in time."

"Yeah."

"So. . . *nothing,* from these past few years?" Theo asked softly.

Clara hesitated. "I have the *knowledge.* All the spells I learned, all the facts, they're all in my head. They come up when I need them. Like a. . . almost a reflex, I guess." She shook her head. "But no, none of the actual experiences."

"So *you* think you've only seen me, what, once or twice since I made my way back?" Jessamine asked in a very low, pained voice.

Clara nodded, a single tear trickling down her cheek. "Oh, baby." Jessamine rose from her chair, wedged herself onto the sofa on Clara's other side, and hugged her daughter tight. "Then I guess we have a little catching up to do."

"Yeah," Clara said. It all flooded her, then: missing her mother, missing the years of experiences she'd lost, being worried about Elsie, feeling helpless. She choked back a sob.

"Well," Jessamine said, sitting up and patting Clara's knee. "No time like the present. Arlene and Theo can keep me honest if I miss anything. You and I—the four of us, really, and Ed here most of those times—spent every Christmas and New Year together. And all but one Easter. I made it for. . . two summers, was it?"

Theo nodded. "Including the trip to Disneyland."

"Oh, man," Clara moaned. "I went to Disneyland?"

"It was epic," Ed teased. "You almost barfed on the teacups."

"Did I really?"

"You'd eaten an entire funnel cake and we *did* warn you," Arlene chuckled.

"So. . . we did see each other," Clara said, wiping her eyes.

"As much as I could. Whenever a lead on your Dad played out, I'd come back. And the holidays. Never long, baby. Never as long as I wanted." She paused, and leaned into Clara. "I'm so sorry."

"The Headmaster said you'd gone rogue," Clara said.

Jessamine straightened again. "From their perspective, yes. I did. Me and a few others. Not many. The government—I tell you, Aaron Witcher has far too much control over that council, and he's got far too many votes in his pocket—they wanted to spin down the counter-hunter program. Defund us. Wanted to stop fighting back."

"Wanted all witches to just live in Underhill," Ed said. "The pressure's been. . . a lot, for anyone who wants to be in the Ordinary."

"They offered to let us go there, last week, so you wouldn't have to come here," Arlene added.

"Although we do have to talk about you running off on rescue missions alone," Theo said sharply.

"I wasn't alone," Clara protested. "I had my friends."

"Still, it's—"

"Theo," Arlene said softly, giving him a *look*.

He sighed. "Fine."

"Like Mother, like daughter," Jessamine said with a smile. "Although. . . look, I'll make sure you have ways to contact the team. And the others who've 'gone rogue.' Next time, ask for help."

"Okay," Clara agreed in a small voice.

"And you've still no leads on Mr. Holdaway?" Ed asked.

"No," Jessamine said tightly. "But now that I've been a guest of the Paladins myself, I'm starting to see why. They're likely moving him around all the time. I had some *solid* leads, now and then. And if they're keeping him in steel and iron. . ." She shook her head. "It makes sense that I wouldn't find him." Then she tilted her head and looked at Clara. "But *you* found *me* anyway."

"Technically," Clara said, "we found *Elsie*. We didn't know to look for you."

"But how?"

"The triplets," Ed replied. "They have a synergistic effect on each other. Their magic multiplies. They fed that to a locator spell, the German general-purpose one. *Verlorenes kleines Kind.* Clara supercharged it. We all felt it—we were able to poke through the iron, just for a moment, and pinpoint that row of houses in the cul-de-sac."

Jessamine nodded thoughtfully. "But you already knew Las Vegas. You had a starting point."

"Yeah."

"So that's not going to work for finding Alex."

Ed shook his head. "That spell is precise, but it can't cover a huge area. Frankly, I think we got lucky trying to cover all of Las Vegas."

"You did," Jessamine agreed.

"Most of the spells I've learned," Clara said slowly, "aren't very efficient. Not from my perspective. A lot of your magic is wasted in them." She shrugged. "So I fix them. It didn't seem like the locator spell was straining."

"Hmm." Jessamine looked fondly at her daughter. "My baby, the mathemagician," she said with a loving grin. "Although you know, I could sure see that coming in handy."

"How so?" Ed asked.

Jessamine chewed her lower lip for a moment before answering, a habit they all recognized from Clara. "We've been pretty sure the Paladins have had help. Not just these so-called holy relics, but actual *assistance.* They know too much about how magic works, and we've even run into pretty sophisticated magical traps. But they *don't* know how you work, Clara."

"But you said I was the one they were trying to trap," Clara reminded her.

"I'm sorry, *what?*" Arlene demanded.

"Well, that's kind of my point," Jessamine said, shooting Arlene a look. "They can't possibly know what your. . . what mathemagic is, unless someone's told them."

"It's pretty well-known all over Underhill, what with the new Borders and all," Ed said.

"But someone *told* the Paladins," Jessamine emphasized. "That almost proves they've got inside help. But how many people actually know what Clara *does?*"

Ed considered it. "The professors at school. The Headmaster, I assume. Me, Finlay, Wolfgang—he's new, though—and Elsie. The triplets. Some of the older guys. They've graduated now, but Clara tweaked their spells when the old Borders were coming down."

"I don't think they know *what* I do, or how, just that I *do* it," Clara said.

Ed nodded. "Maybe. Probably. I mean, you've told me, and I still can't really picture it."

"So that gives us a secret weapon," Jessamine said. "They don't know the limit of what Clara can do, just that she's special."

"But still," Ed said, "why would any witch help the Paladins? I mean, I get Oberherr, he was using them, but—"

"Oh, it happens," Jessamine said darkly. She paused a moment.

"Alex and I . . ." she trailed off, shaking her head and pressing her lips tightly together.

"You're talking about when you brought Clara to us," Arlene said softly.

Jessamine nodded.

"You know, I've always wondered," Arlene said. "If you're up to it, Jess. And . . . we understand if you aren't."

"Yeah. Wow," Jessamine said, leaning back an running her hands through her thick hair.

"Like I said, you don't have—"

"No, no, it's fine. It was. . . a long time ago, now." Jessamine took a deep breath, held it, and then exhaled slowly.

"I'd like to know too," Clara said, putting her free hand on her mother's knee.

"Of course you do, baby. Of course you do." She took another deep breath. "Okay.

"Your father and I were tracking down some unusual Paladin activity. They'd started recruiting—twenty years ago, they never did that, not openly, it was all just family lines and stuff. But they'd started bringing in people. Really playing up the religious angle. And they'd started developing an absolutely uncanny record for finding witches' homes. There'd been. . . I think it must have been a dozen families just vanished overnight. Never seen again."

"Oberherr," Ed said, nodding.

"No," Jessamine said. "No, he was just a minor functionary, back then. Not even connected with the counter-hunting effort." She paused, thinking. "I think they had him in charge of the archives or something, and he'd never been much with magic, to be honest. His brother was the star of the family.

"But we *did* suspect that the Paladins had magical help. *Fealltóirí* weren't unheard-of. Really, there have always been—"

"Translation?" Theo said with a soft smile.

"Roughly, 'traitor,'" Ed supplied. "But it's an old Fae word. *Fealltóir Fola* is the whole thing. 'Blood traitor.'"

"Witches who stand against other witches. Goes back further than the Salem trials," Jessamine agreed. "Ones who'd turn in a neighbor to distract attention from themselves. Or who'd testify against someone in exchange for being left in peace. So that's what Alex and I figured was happening."

"I'm guessing that wasn't it," Arlene said.

"Well, it may have been a *fealltóirí,* but certainly not some low-level snitch," Jessamine said, heat rising in her tone. "Three of the homes that had been attacked didn't have any known Paladin cells in the region. And two of the most recent ones had clear signs of combat magic."

"Maybe the family defending themselves?" Clara asked.

"Oh, absolutely," Jessamine said, nodding emphatically. "But more than that. There were *battles.* And in the last home, they'd gotten sloppy. The Paladins, that is. They dropped a map."

"Targets?" Theo guessed.

"Targets," Jessamine said grimly. "And our home was marked."

"Ah," Arlene said. "So that's why—"

"We brought Clara to you. Yes. At her age, nobody would have been able to tell she was really a witch. We figured we could run, lay low, get to a Border and back to Underhill. Pull together some help. We never imagined we'd be gone for more than a few months at the outside."

"You couldn't have just teleported to a Border?" Ed asked.

"Well, yes. But no. Alex and I had a number of magical constructs that wouldn't have survived a teleport. Like, explosively so. And we couldn't leave those behind. And we'd started to suspect that the Paladins could track us somehow. Track teleports, I mean. We didn't want to give away the location of the Border, and if we had Clara and they *could* track us. . ."

"You did the right thing," Arlene assured her softly.

"Do you still think they can track teleports?" Ed said, anxiety creeping into his voice.

Jessamine shook her head. "We—I mean, none of us have found

any evidence, no. If they're using one of their artifacts we know they can detect the teleport, both leaving and arriving, but that's not exactly *tracking* the person teleporting."

"So what happened?" Clara asked.

Jessamine took another deep breath. "They definitely had magic working for them. Alex and I had opened a portal, one big enough for us to drive the car through. Not easy, moving that much sheet metal through a portal, but Alex is a master. But we barely got the portal established. . ." She trailed off, staring out the window.

"Mom?" Clara whispered.

Jessamine shook her head. "Sorry. Even after all this time. . . it's still fresh." She shook her head again. "They sent a *qonli hayvon* after us. A blood beast. Practically mythical, something you have to raise with actual Blood Magic. It. . . grabbed the car." Her gaze returned to the window. "Pulled us backward. And then something, something magical, hit us. I blacked out." She shivered, and looked Clara in the eyes. "When I came to, I was alone. Strapped to a table."

"How did you—" Theo started.

"I can't right now," Jessamine snapped. "Sorry," she added, her tone relaxing a bit. "Sorry. Someday. Not now."

"We understand," Clara said, rubbing her mother's knee.

"It seems pretty clear that the Paladins still have magical help," Ed said. "You mentioned an artifact?"

Jessamine nodded, gathering her thoughts. "Their 'holy relics,' yeah. But I've seen a few. They're definitely magical constructs. Basic token-magic, although the spells on the ones I've seen are incredibly complex. Way beyond me. But yes. . . they may also have a *Cailleach Fola* working with them. A Blood Witch."

Everyone was quiet for a long moment.

"We learned about them," Ed said hesitantly. "But it felt like there was a lot they weren't telling us."

"No legitimate school will tell you much," Jessamine said. "Just that they use blood sacrifices to enhance their energy and their spells. And to cast darker spells that can *only* be accomplished that way."

"What more do you need to know?" Arlene asked, disgust written on her face.

"A good bit, unfortunately," Jessamine grimaced. "For one, once you have the taint of Blood Magic on you, Underhill will try to repel you. Quite energetically. It's actually the basis for the exile spell Alex developed."

"Energetically is an understatement," Clara said wryly. She'd had that exact spell on her the first time she stepped through a Border.

"We wanted you away from there," Jessamine explained. "The further you were from magic, the safer you were going to be. And again, we didn't think it was going to be for so—"

"It's fine, Mom," Clara assured her. "Really. But it *is* really energetic."

Jessamine smiled. "Yeah. Anyway, the other big thing to know is that Blood Magic can wreak havoc on normal magic. Disrupt spells, but even worse. Some spells will go out of control, run amok."

"Amok, amok, amok!" Clara and Arlene chanted at once.

"Very funny," Jessamine said as Ed chuckled. "Although I do love that movie. But yeah, if the Paladins have a Blood Witch working with them, it would explain a lot. And if that witch is in contact with anyone in Underhill, they'd certainly know about you, baby."

"Then maybe staying in Underhill *is* best," Arlene ventured. "Especially—"

"I don't accept that," Jessamine said firmly. "This is our world, too. Our home. You know, it's convenient not to speak of it, but witches can't conceive children in Underhill." Arlene's eyes widened. "Honeymoon trips to the Ordinary aren't unusual. It's said the Fae used up all the creative magic ages ago. So no, I'm not relinquishing our right to be in this world."

"Me either," Clara seconded. "This is where you guys are."

"My family lives here too," Ed added.

"So you'll. . . keep fighting these Paladins?" Arlene asked.

Jessamine sighed again. "I want to say yes. But I don't know how. There are so few of us willing to do it. Most witches who live in the Ordinary have moved to out of the way places, made themselves hard to find. They watch themselves. They try to be careful. But the Paladins found us before. They'll keep doing it."

"What's the allure of living here?" Theo asked. "I mean, I understand about the conceiving thing, but—"

"It *feels* better here," Ed replied. "It's richer. I don't know how to explain it, just—"

"It's the magic," Clara said. Ed and Jessamine looked at her. "Magic comes from here. It gets into Underhill through the Borders, but magic starts here. I mean, *I* don't feel any different, but you guys actually absorb the stuff. It's probably. . . fresher. Or something."

Jessamine tilted her head. "'Fresher' isn't a bad description. I always feel slightly stifled in Underhill, to be honest."

"It's like it's too dry," Ed agreed.

"But if these Paladins have all these weapons. . ." Theo said.

"Well, they don't, exactly. They can use magic to find us, and we know they do. But constructs like that are hard to make, trust me, and most of the time a trained witch can defend themselves, or just escape."

"So why are they such a threat?" Theo asked.

"It's the iron," Jessamine said with a shrug. "They know it's our weakness."

"Is it really that bad?" Theo asked.

Jessamine grimaced. "It is. Honestly, even being in this condo is a little uncomfortable. Your windows are big enough, but I can *feel* the rebar in the walls, the steel studs. It'd be a struggle to do any complex magic in here."

"So finding Dad isn't going to be easy," Clara said. "Not if they've got him jailed up like they did with you. Unless you've got me helping."

Jessamine chuckled. "Let's get you graduated, first, baby. But no. It isn't going to be easy. Although. . ." she fell silent, thinking.

"What?" Clara asked after a moment.

"Well. . . you were so precise with the magic. You were able to draw it through the wall, through a space where there was no rebar. Have you learned token magic in school?"

"Learned it? She's *aces* at it," Ed said proudly.

"I do okay," Clara temporized.

"There's a type of crystal in Underhill. *Cíoch Draíocht,* it's called," Jessamine said thoughtfully. "The lower quality stuff is good for adhering spells to. The—"

"Like these?" Arlene said, withdrawing the two locator crystals from her pocket.

Jessamine examined them and nodded. "Like those. But the better quality stuff can actually store raw magic. And—this is the important bit—it's locked into the crystal structure until you actively draw it out. And you have to touch it to do that. Iron can't pull it out."

"So. . . like batteries?" Clara asked.

"Batteries," Jessamine confirmed. "But it's really tricky."

"Clara *specializes* in tricky," Ed bragged.

Clara grinned. "I kind of do."

"I had the team take the other kids back to their parents," Jessamine said. "Oberherr can rot with the Paladins, for all I care, but if we take a little trip back, look the places over for clues. . . maybe we can find another cell of them. And if we can carry enough magic— enough batteries—with us, maybe we can find the artifact they're using to find *us.*"

"This artifact," Ed said thoughtfully. "Are you thinking it's a *Triangulierende Kraftquellen?*"

Jessamine nodded. "It'd have to be. And they can't have more than one. You can't make them using Blood Magic, and even a specialist takes years to make those things. I doubt anyone's made one for a century, possibly longer. And if it is a *Triangulierende Kraftquellen—*"

Theo laughed. "Translation?"

"It's a German spell-construct," Ed explained. "It's the perfect tradition for that kind of magic. Very precise. It's designed to locate concentrations of specific types of magical energy. It triangulates—you'd drive it around in circles until it starts homing in on something in particular."

"Theirs will be old," Jessamine added. "Or at least look old, if they're pitching it as a holy relic. But like I said, nobody makes those things anymore."

"Second Epoch, then," Ed said with a nod. "Late 1600s. That kind of thing got made more often, back then. They had a whole theory of ley-lines and power concentrations and stuff."

"Interesting," Jessamine said, narrowing her eyes. "That'd correspond with the rise of the Paladin movement in North America, too. They could easily have brought something over on the ships from Europe."

"But wouldn't they have taken everything, at this point? I mean, we busted up their hideout," Clara said.

Jessamine shook her head. "We busted up their *jail*. That house definitely wasn't their hideout."

"They were delivering groceries to the one next door, as well," Clara said.

Jessamine cocked an eyebrow. "Oh? Well. *That* they may have evacuated, given all the fuss you made. But no, they'll have something in town. That Deuxm woman won't give up so easily. Alex and I crossed with her a few times, back in the day. She's stubborn."

"I'm not sure if I'm comfortable with Clara participating in this," Arlene spoke up. "And Ed, I'm sure your parents—"

"I'm not suggesting the kids confront the Paladins," Jessamine said firmly. Clara's face fell. "Sorry, kiddo. You're not ready yet. But you *can* help me make some batteries, so that *I* can see what I can find. At the very least, taking that relic out of action would help us all be safer."

"Well. . ." Arlene said doubtfully. "If it's just that. . ."

"Just that," Jessamine insisted. "Although we're running out of break time. We should get back to Underhill and get some high-quality crystals. I can show you how they're meant to be charged, although again, I'm not good at it."

"Once I see it, I can figure it out," Clara assured her.

"Well. Seems like we have a plan," Jessamine said with a grin.

"But first," Arlene said in a tone that brooked no discussion, "we have dinner."

CHAPTER 13

FORAGING

"Welcome," Jessamine said, "to *Réimsí an Athraonta.*"

"The Fields of Refraction," Ed supplied. "I'm still vaguely uncomfortable with the two of you going in alone."

"Why, brave sir knight," Jessamine teased, "your concern is so touching!"

Ed blushed. "It's not like that. It's just. . . there are stories about this place."

Jessamine snorted. "Tales, you mean. The Fields aren't dangerous, exactly. They're not. . . what was your word? *Inimical.* If you know what you're doing, you're safe. And smaller groups are actually safer. You attract less attention. And more importantly, it's safer because I only have one neophyte to keep track of."

"Gee, thanks," Clara said.

"Don't take it personal, baby."

"You won't even take a guide?" Ed asked.

"Those guys? Heck, no. I know the Fields as well as any of them, and half of 'em are just here to extract as much money from tourists as possible."

"Tourists?" Clara asked.

"Witches who decide to go on some kind of journey. Or quest. They come tramping in to find 'just the right crystal' for whatever lame spell they're trying to cast." Jessamine snorted again. "In reality, those same guides are the ones who go in and get all the low-grade stuff that's suitable for constructs and tokens. They're strongly incentivized to take tourists to the truly useless stuff. Too small, full of flaws, you name it. So no, we will guide ourselves, thank you so much."

"How long will it take?" Ed asked, bowing to the inevitable.

"A full day, maybe a day and a half," Jessamine said confidently. "And that's at the outside. You planning to wait here?"

It was Ed's turn to snort. "It's cheaper to get a place at one of the inns than to pay the Anchor fees to go anywhere else."

Jessamine frowned. "The Witcher family has gumption, I'll give them that. Do you know that when I was young, maybe thirty-five years ago, we didn't even have money in Underhill? Witcher and his cronies created an entire *economy*. I can't believe what we had to pay just to get here."

Clara nodded agreement. They'd returned to Underhill through the Las Vegas Border, and then taken an Anchor from the school to Linginham. From there, they'd had to take another to a larger town, and then changed again to get to the little village that sat on the edge of the Fields. And they'd been charged, per person, for each leg. "We should have just teleported," she muttered.

Jessamine shook her head. "We don't need that kind of visibility right now. And honestly, I'm the shoddiest at translocation magic. Just terrible. Your Dad always handled that. I can move myself, but it gives me a migraine to move anyone else."

"We both can," Clara pointed out.

"And we're not licensed, yet," Ed reminded her. "And it's *very* easy to monitor for that kind of magic here. It creates ripples you can detect from almost anywhere."

"But we're here now," Jessamine said. "And we need to get going if we're going to get this done quickly. Ed, I recommend the Mended Bear. Friendly family runs it, reasonable prices. You have money?"

Ed stuck a hand in one pocket and rattled his collection of the copper tokens that served as currency in Underhill. "Plenty."

"All right. Let's go, baby."

Jessamine set off, and Clara fell in beside her. They walked quickly down the packed-earth road that led out of the village and into the Fields. The road narrowed to a footpath as they crossed the tree line.

"Not really field so much as forest," Clara noted.

"It's actually bands of dense forest surrounding pocket meadows," Jessamine said. "This outer ring is safe enough. Very normal. But once we get to the first meadow, stick close. Do not, under any circumstances, touch the. . . vegetation. Not even a brush of your sleeve." Before they'd left Las Vegas, Jessamine had made Clara don a long-sleeved pullover hoodie. It had been sweltering in the Vegas heat, but she'd insisted.

"So," Clara said as they ambled along the footpath, "are you going to tell me what you found at the houses?" Mom had spent a couple of hours there after dinner, and upon returning had pleaded exhaustion and gone straight to Clara's room to sleep. Clara, Ed, and Clara's adoptive parents had stayed up a while longer, chatting quietly. When Clara had crawled in bed next to Mom, she'd been snoring lightly.

Jessamine sighed. "More than I'd feared, less than I'd hoped. The house they had us in was just a jail. I'm guessing they had one, maybe two Paladins in with us. They'd been making simple meals for us—sandwiches, pasta, canned stuff, that kind of thing. I had to be a little careful—someone obviously called the cops at some point. There was nobody there when I went, but they had police tape everywhere. Kind of hard to keep people out entirely when your daughter clawed the entire doorframe off, though." She grinned at Clara. "I'd love to know how you did that to a steel door."

Clara shrugged. "Metal can only ground so much magic. I can

only manipulate what's around me, but the triplets can pull together a *lot*. So I just kind of shaped it directly. I didn't realize I'd pulled the whole doorframe out." She felt a brief rush of pride.

"You did indeed. So, nothing there. Watch, don't step on that." Jessamine made an exaggerated step around a red-and-white polka-dotted mushroom that had sprung up in the middle of the path. "You'll have a pack of *Fuath Leanaí* on you in a moment."

Clara frowned. "I don't know that one."

"You only find them here. Little crystalline pixies, almost. Full of ire. Friendly enough to chat with, but don't touch their things or cross them, or they'll attack. Mind you, they can't do much more than give you paper cuts, but they can give you a hundred of them."

"Gross."

"Yeah. Anyway, the second house was more useful. Empty of course, but the police hadn't been in. I'm guessing they had four, maybe five Paladins staying there. Do you know what this is?" Jessamine asked, withdrawing a small amulet from her pocket and holding it out for Clara's inspection.

Clara took it and carefully unfocused her eyes, slowing a bit as she examined the brass medallion. Tight equations spiraled around its edge, glowing a soft vermillion. *Inefficient,* she thought, noting several redundancies in the math. "It's a magic detector," she said as she recognized the core equation. She handed it back to her mother.

"Very short-range, but yes. And there *was* residual magic in the house. So whatever artifact they've been using, it was there. Which means I'm guessing it's still in Vegas someplace. And they left in a bit of a hurry, and they were fairly sloppy about it."

"How so?"

"'Fridge full of food. Half-full bottles of whiskey and vodka. An Uno deck, a couple of board games. Someone left an iPhone charger. And," she added with a wide grin, "a piece of paper taped to the 'fridge with two phone numbers on it."

"How's that useful?" Clara asked. "You're not going to just call them?"

"No, but Paladins are huge believers in landlines. They know magic messes with cell phones, but landlines are pretty simple, especially if you can get an old-school plug-in phone. So I looked around a bit more, and they'd left the phone cord plugged in. Took the phone, but that's fine."

"So. . .?" Clara asked.

"So, those phone numbers are probably at their main locations in town. And they're landlines, so they're traceable. I did a Sending to the team. Sandy's an expert at tracking that kind of thing. She's got human friends who do it, I think. So she's running that down. We'll have addresses by the time we get back."

"Wow."

"Yeah. And—oh, we're here. Hold up."

"Wow," Clara breathed.

The meadow that rolled away from the tree line could have been one from the Ordinary world. Emerald, calf-high grass waved in a gentle breeze. Multicolored wildflowers poked their blooms through that thick carpet, and gentle swells of earth undulated into the distance. Far off, Clara could see where the trees picked up again.

What an Ordinary meadow wouldn't have contained were the tall, shining *Eascraíonngem.* Clara's memory supplied the name as soon as she laid eyes on them, along with a diagram from some textbook she must have read. Their crystalline stalks were as high as she was, and they were covered with thin, multifaceted glass leaves, each plant sporting a different jewel color. Ruby, topaz, sapphire, peridot, hauyne, and emerald were all represented, and they caught the early morning sun in a cascade of glimmers and sparkles.

Clara shifted her vision, and marveled at the slow, graceful ballet of shining equations. These were the simpler, natural expressions of Underhill's ambient magic, far less complex than that of the Ordinary. They drifted in long ribbons, swaying alongside the grass as the morning breeze tickled its way through the meadow. Whenever the magic brushed against one of the crystalline *Eascraíonngem* it would swirl into playful eddies, some of it settling into the plants' translucent leaves for a moment, until another breeze kicked them loose and sent them on their way.

"They're beautiful," Clara said.

"That they are. Although this pocket, close as it is to the village, will be picked clean of anything useful."

"We're after the gemstone plants?"

Jessamine shook her head. "Not the plants themselves. What we want grows right at their bases. The ones here will be small, and relatively fresh—which means they'll have internal flaws. Let them grow a few years and those flaws will heal as the crystal matures. So these would be fine for—well, like that locator token the school gave you. Simple magic, doesn't need to last a long time, doesn't need to do anything complex. But as batteries, they wouldn't hold much, they wouldn't maintain the purity of the magic, and they'd be likely to shatter when you drew the magic out. So we'll go deeper in. I just wanted—oh! There they are! See them?"

Clara's eyes swept across the meadow until she spotted a gleam of movement that wasn't from one of the tall plants. "What is it?"

"A *féileacán criostail*," Jessamine answered. "Pretty much like your basic Ordinary butterfly, but they're made out of living crystal. They're a good example of what we have to watch out for."

"Why for?"

"Well, like Ed said, they're not *inimical*. Like, they're not going to come after us or attack us. But their wings are sharper than the sharpest knife you've ever seen. If they so much as brush your skin, you won't even know you've been cut until you feel the blood start to run. These sweatshirts won't provide a lot of protection, but they're thick and baggy, so they'll give us a little room for error."

"Wow," Clara said in a subdued tone. "Is that all?"

"Oh, no," Jessamine said off, turning back into the trees. Clara hurried to follow. "That's not all."

They walked a way in silence, Jessamine's eyes carefully taking in the path ahead of them. "You know," she said, breaking the silence as she stepped around another polka-dotted mushroom, "I worried you would hate me, when I made it back."

Clara's jaw dropped, and it took her a moment to recover. "Hate you? Why?"

Her mother shrugged. "We abandoned you. I mean, we'd hoped you'd never notice, that we'd come for you after a few months at most, but. . . if I'm being honest, we knew there was a risk we'd get caught. That's why we couldn't take you with us. And if we did get caught. . ."

"It's okay, Mom," Clara assured her.

"And even then I haven't been around much, have I?" Jessamine's voice dripped with regret. "Not much of a Mom."

"You've been looking for Dad," Clara said. "I understand that."

"Alex and I are best friends, you know," Jessamine said softly. "We've been together since we were kids. I can't imagine. . ."

"We'll find him," Clara assured her.

They walked a few more steps in silence. "You were a surprise, you know," Jessamine said softly. "A wonderful, miraculous surprise."

"What do you mean?"

"Counter-hunters aren't exactly the best parental choice," she said wryly. "It's a dangerous job. A dangerous life. We'd planned to retire. In fact, we'd already made arrangements with another pair to turn over our equipment, all our information that we hadn't already reported back. We were going to settle down in Colorado. Raise you properly." She shook her head. "Keep clear of that tree," she said, nodding toward it.

Clara gave the indicated tree a wide berth, and noted the thin glasslike shards that protruded from the creases of its thick, gnarled bark. "Do those shoot out at you?"

"They do, and they'll disrupt your—well, they'd disrupt *my* magic. But they hurt like the devil regardless."

"Yikes."

"Clara baby, what was your childhood like?" Jessamine suddenly asked.

Clara sighed. "It was okay. I mean, we moved around a lot. You knew that. Anytime my magic got. . . out of control, I guess. We had to. And it meant Mom and Dad—the Thorns, I mean—couldn't always get good jobs. Dad—Alex—was working in construction when we moved to Vegas, and it wasn't steady. So we didn't live fancy. But it was good. We never starved."

"It's ironic."

"What is?"

"Witch families in the Ordinary live however they want. Rich, poor, in between, doesn't matter. We don't *need* money. We can magic up food, magic up repairs to a house, anything. If you do need money, you can magic that up, too." She sighed. "But my little witch didn't have that option."

"It's what it was," Clara said, trying to sound reassuring. "Like I said, we didn't starve. I got ice cream sometimes. We went to see movies. It just wasn't fancy, is all."

"We owe the Thorns everything."

"I know."

They kept up a brisk pace through midday, passing four more pocket meadows on the way. "Better, but not what we need," Jessamine commented each time. She conjured iced tea and fruit for them to snack on as they walked, and regaled Clara with tales of taking on Paladins.

As they were leaving their sixth meadow behind, Jessamine stopped suddenly. Clara came to a halt beside her. Her mother was stock-still, barely even breathing, and Clara tried to mimic her stillness.

The footpath here has barely visible beneath the short, dark, blue-green grass that managed to survive under the tree canopy. The trees themselves were gigantic this far in, with trunks Clara couldn't have wrapped her arms around. The soared fifty feet and more overhead, taller than Clara's old school back in Las Vegas.

It was eerily silent.

Their entire journey so far had been accompanied by the cheeky chirps of birds as they flitted through the leaves overhead, by the titters of wild pixies that tracked their progress from meadow to meadow, and the buzzing of the huge, gentle bees that fed on the meadows' floral bounty. They'd even spotted a few direbunnies hopping through the undergrowth, eyeing them greedily until a lance of magic from Mom sent them scampering away.

All that was gone.

"Mom," Clara said in the barest whisper.

Jessamine twitched a hand, but said nothing.

Clara's heart began beating faster. She could feel the adrenaline trickling into her blood stream as she became more alert. She let her vision shift, and—

One hand flicked out to tap her mother.

Her mother began slowly raising her arms, fingers twitching in a complex somatic pattern. Magic gathered at her fingertips, building slowly.

Ahead of them, shining darkly in Clara's eyes, was a mass of bleak equations, roiling slowly over the path. They were more complex than the ambient magic, glowing sullen grays and blacks, shot through with the blues and purples of a day-old bruise. The mass of them were low to the ground, centered on a particular point. Clara's eyes picked out odd redundancies in the math, unnecessary expressions that should have cancelled themselves out. But there they sat, seeming to eye her with—

The ground exploded in a shower of dirt and grass, and a mass of teeth and fur shot toward them.

"Onaanvaarbaar!" Jessamine shouted, and a blast of orange-red light flashed from her hands, smashing into their attacker and sending it skidding backward.

When the air cleared, Clara could see it, not twenty steps away. It was vaguely human-shaped, although at the moment it was crouched on all fours. It was covered in matted blue-black fur. It had no head, only two large, intelligent eyes perched on its shoulders. It reared back slightly, and to Clara's horror she realized that its mouth —a gaping, slavering maw filled with wicked-looking teeth—was centered in its torso.

"Anthropophagi," Jessamine said, breathing heavily as her fingers twitched another spell to the ready. "Cannibals. Dark Fae pets. There shouldn't be one here."

The thing's eyes narrowed as it crept forward a step.

"Pragaro šviesos ugnis!" Jessamine snapped, and this time a thick lance of green-gold power shot from her hands.

The monster executed a standing backflip, somersaulting over the deadly magic. Jessamine's attack shot beneath it, shattering into one of the enormous trees and leaving a smoking hole in the ancient bark.

The Dark Fae creature landed on its feet, its knees flexing easily. The corners of its dripping mouth twitched into a horrible caricature of a grin. It reared back, then jerked forward, a horrific glob of spittle flying their way.

Jessamine's fingers were still crafting a new spell.

Clara hauled the ambient magic in front of them, dragging some of the creature's own magic with it. Blue-black merged with emerald-amber, equations simplifying and coalescing instantly. The monster's wet projectile turned itself inside out, all of its momentum reversed at once, and it collided with its source, splattering in a crash of magic against the thing's upper chest.

It shrieked, spinning in place as its hands batted the vile fluid from its body.

"Tra-tehaka mahery vaika!" Jessamine growled. This time, her attack was a purple-orange sphere, and it shot directly into the creature's left leg. A *crunch* of breaking bone was accompanied by an even louder, higher shriek as the beast fell.

"It'll heal quickly," Jessamine panted, stepping back and grabbing Clara's arm. "It's magic—"

"No, it won't," Clara said firmly.

She reached out with her will, grappling with the creature's dank magic. This time, rather than trying to simplify the magical equations and make them more pure and concentrated, she did the opposite. The ugly vortex of magic bloated as she added duplicate expressions, unnecessary expansions, and redundant divisors. The creature shrieked again as its magic ballooned and brightened, slapping its hands over its eyes.

"Shield, Mom," Clara ordered.

Jessamine complied at once. *"Aegis!"* she barked.

The monster exploded.

Wet lumps of flesh and a spray of black blood splattered everywhere, smacking damply into Jessamine's shield, eliciting glowing, golden motes as the debris slid to the ground.

"Gross," Clara said, wrinkling her nose as Jessamine dropped the shield.

"No kidding."

"Are there more?"

Jessamine shook her head. "You'd probably see them better than I, but no. They're lone hunters. Although again, I don't even know what this one was doing out here. Maybe pushed into the woods? I know they've been building more villages along the forest edge."

"Immigration?" Clara asked.

"Basically. Witches who don't feel safe in the Ordinary anymore. We'll tell the headwoman at the village when we go back. They'll send in hunting parties to look for any other Fae nasties."

"I'll keep my eyes open from now on," Clara said.

"You could see it?"

"Once I looked. I have to make a little effort to see ambient magic. It wasn't doing anything active so I didn't notice it."

"Interesting."

"Do we keep going?"

Jessamine nodded firmly. "We do. We should find what we need in the next meadow. Even the crystal gatherers don't usually come this far in."

They set off, picking their way carefully through the stinking remains of the Fae monster.

"So what did you do, exactly?" Mom asked as they moved on.

"I overcomplicated its magic," Clara replied. "Almost every spell I've ever seen has a lot of redundancy in it, right?"

"You've mentioned."

"So I can tweak them, remove the redundancies, simplify the equations. It makes the spell tighter, more powerful. When I do them myself, I just kind of naturally do that more efficient version."

"Okay," Jessamine mused. "I mean, you've said that, but if I'm being honest, I don't really understand it."

"It's mostly algebra," Clara explained. She stopped, and dragged a bit of the local magic into a glowing equation that her mother could see. "So this is a simple example."

$$x = a\left(\frac{8}{16}\right) \cdot b\left(\frac{20}{100}\right)$$

"Okay," Jessamine said, nodding slowly. "Eight-sixteenths is really just one-half."

"Right. So the first step is to just simplify all that." Clara wriggled the magic around a bit, and the glowing equation shifted.

$$x = a\left(\frac{1}{2}\right) \cdot b\left(\frac{1}{5}\right)$$

"Sure."

"But even that's kind of unnecessary, right? I mean, you're saying take half of *a* and multiply it by a fifth of *b*. And I prefer decimals to fractions." The equation shifted again.

$$x = .5a \cdot .2b$$

"Okay," Jessamine said, following the logic.

"But *magic* can go even further. It's harder to draw, because the actual symbols, even the letters and numbers, they're not normal-shaped for me. Like, I'd remove the point-five and just bloat the lower half of *a,* and get rid of the point-two and kind of distance the *b* like this, maybe." As she spoke, the glowing symbols in front of them twisted themselves into odd shapes.

"That's weird, baby," Jessamine chuckled.

"But it *works,*" Clara said. "And so now you've got an equation with just three terms. So the actual energy can focus right there."

"So for that critter," Jessamine said, resuming walking as Clara let the diagram fade, "you did the opposite."

"Right. I added a whole bunch of redundancies until the magic couldn't hold itself together anymore. I mean, I could *see* it was a magic creature, so I figured no magic, no creature."

"Explosively."

"I mean, it wasn't until the end that I realized it was going to do that."

"What a *mess,*" Jessamine laughed. "But you'd do the same thing to take apart a magical construct? Like a token or something?"

"Mmmm," Clara mused. "Maybe. I mean, I guess that would work. But most of the time I just have to break the math on those, and they all fall apart. Like, right before first term, Professor Mycroft locked us in our dorm. But it was a magic lock, and so I just had to find the weak spot in the equation and break it." She considered. "Actually, that was kind of explosive, too. The doorknob shot off and almost clocked one of the triplets."

"Duly noted," Jessamine grinned. "Keep well back when you're tinkering. Ah, we're here."

Here was another wide meadow, this one contoured into a kind of lazily winding, shallow valley. The high grass was tinted with teal and lime, and small points of azure light bobbed above. The crystalline stalks were a bit taller here, with far thicker bases. Their multicolored leaves were sturdier as well, with the ones just above the grass tips almost as thick as one of Clara's fingers. The glasslike butterflies were more numerous was well, flitting from leaf to leaf with bright tinkling sounds.

"Now, a meadow this old, this unvisited, we've got a couple of things to worry about," Jessamine instructed. "One, the butterflies. Two, even those thick leaves are razor-sharp at their edges. Three, there are going to be direbunnies and *fuath cats*. Four—"

"Wait," Clara said with a frown. "Did you say *hate cats?*"

Jessamine nodded. "Slinky, evil little things. Great for wiping out a rodent population, except the direbunnies have a real taste for them."

"But *hate* cats?"

Jessamine shrugged. "Basically normal cats, I guess. But with magic."

"Got it."

"All of those are easy enough to take care of. In fact, I know a handy repellant spell we can use that will make most of them very interested in being somewhere other than right near us. *Alde infernua nigandik.* The Basque have the best pest-control magic."

"So what *do* we have to worry about?"

"*Dhá Nathair,*" she answered grimly. "Snakes with heads at each end. They're hot-blooded, so they prefer the shade of being deep in the grass, and they do *not* like to be disturbed. Their bite is incredibly toxic, disruptive to magic, and if you actually hit them with enough magic, they absorb it and use it to bud off a clone of themselves. Takes seconds, and then you've got double the problem."

"Snakes," Clara muttered. "Why'd it have to be snakes?"

"Hah!" Jessamine laughed approvingly. "I love that movie. So does Alex. But yeah."

"So what do we do about them?"

"The crystal gatherers came up with a spell. *Acima das dicas.*"

Clara frowned as she translated. "On top of the tops?" she guessed.

"Close. 'Atop the tips.' It'll let us walk on top of the grass, where we won't bother the snakes. But it's *stupidly* delicate. You need to go *very* slowly and *extra* carefully. No sudden movements or the whole thing collapses."

"I mean, I know we're not supposed to teleport," Clara said slowly. "But—"

"Absolutely not," Jessamine said firmly. "Those crystal plants will one hundred percent disrupt any magic like that. You can only use stuff that basically sits right on your skin. Which is why *you* are going to wait here."

"But—" Clara protested.

"No buts," Jessamine insisted. "And there's a good reason for it. I know what I'm doing, first off. I can reach down and pull up crystals. I can maintain the pest repellant, the walking spell, and *Handschuhe aus Stahl* to protect my hands from cuts. But if something goes wrong, I need *you* out here to cast a *Ligne de grappin sacrée* spell to haul me back."

Clara's memory obligingly detailed the spell, along with its deceptively simple equations. "Okay. I know that one."

"You'd better, I insisted they teach you the entire book it came from. Including *Pincez-le hors de l'air.*"

Again, Clara's mind pulled up the reference. "Pincer spell?"

"When I get a good crystal, I'm going to toss it into the air. You pinch it and haul it back over here. Lay them in the dirt, but don't let them touch each other. We'll need to bundle them up a bit before we can carry them, and if we let them sit on the earth for a few minutes they'll be less volatile."

"Okay," Clara said confidently. "I can do all that."

"Then we begin," Jessamine said with a broad grin.

Clara held her breath as her mother cast the spells, and she called up the formula for her two spells, holding them ready.

Jessamine stepped out of the trees, lifting one foot to step atop the thin blades of grass.

They held.

More confidently, she raised her other foot and was standing atop the gently waving stalks. She took one step. . . and then another. . . and then a third. Clara exhaled as the grass held.

Jessamine paused as a cluster of scintillating butterflies cavorted past, slowly ducking and leaning to avoid their sharp-edged wings. Then she continued.

Clara held the grappling spell in her mind.

Jessamine reached the first translucent stalk, which soared easily six feet above her head. She knelt carefully, ever so slowly, and then reached down through the grass to the stalk's base. A moment later, she straightened. "First one, baby," she called softly, tossing a two-inch, perfectly clear spear of crystal into the air.

Clara was so flustered she almost cast the grappling spell, but she caught herself at the last moment, and magic pinched the shaft out of the air and drew it toward her. Mindful of its sharp edges, Clara let it land in the clear soil where the forest's grassy underground ended. She nudged it to one side with her sneaker, and looked up to see Mom already withdrawing a second one from the grass.

Within minutes, they'd landed a half-dozen crystals, ranging from two to four inches in length and almost as thick as Clara's wrist. Clara lined them up on the dirt, maintaining a few inches of space between them.

Jessamine stood. "About that many more, I think," she called softly as she took a few slow, tentatively steps toward another tall stalk.

They repeated their routine three more times when Clara saw the grass move in an odd pattern, maybe sixty feet away from her mother. "Mom."

Jessamine looked up. "What, baby?"

"There's. . . something. In the grass."

Jessamine scanned the meadow ahead of her, but the grass had stopped—

And then a black triangle thrust through the grass and began cutting toward Clara's mother.

"Meadowshark," Jessamine said, and Clara could tell she was forcing herself to sound calm. Rather than standing, she reached down and plucked one more crystal free, tossing it into the air.

Clara almost let it fall, focused as she was on the black fin that was weaving left and right, drawing inexorably closer. But she cast the pinching spell in time, and a tenth crystal landed at her feet. "Mom!" she hissed urgently.

"Now's good, Clara," Mom said cooly.

Clara unleashed the grappling spell, twisting the pastel-toned ambient magic into a bright, concentrated equation of power and elegance. Ropes of viridian and celadon lashed out, wrapping around Jessamine's torso and under her arms. They went taut at once and then *jerked.* The magic flashed gamboge as Clara's mother was hauled back to the treeline at speed. Clara barely leapt out of the way as her mother zoomed toward her and crashed into the soft, deep-blue grass amongst the trees.

"Back, baby," Jessamine ordered as she scrambled to her feet. Clara saw falu-tinged lines of light leap from her mother's hands, grabbing the crystals they'd harvested and dragging them back from the meadow's edge.

A moment later a black *something* leaped from the tall grass. Clara made out a cylindrical body, far too many short, scuttling legs than any creature should own, and wide, snapping jaws. It arced four feet into the air, twisting madly as it sought prey, before slipping back into the grass. A ripple of movement betrayed its location and then faded as the creature slunk low and away.

"That was close," Jessamine said, breathing heavily. But her eyes were bright with excitement. "Ten will do us. These ones are good." She used magic to gather the crystal up into a bundle, keeping a thin veneer of energy between each one. "We'll let them rest when we get back, and they'll be fine." She slung the bundle over her back, the crystals tinkling softly in their magical cocoons. Then she stretched, looked at Clara, and said, "Ready to head back?"

"Jeez, Mom," Clara said, her heart finally slowing. "That was close."

"Nah," Jessamine said, waving away the concern. "You had me."

"You didn't mention meadowsharks," Clara said.

Her mother shrugged. "They're kinda rare, actually. I mean, this far out, I guess I should have figured. But we're good."

Clara opened her mouth to retort, but decided against it. She fell in alongside her mother as they began retracing their steps. The dappled sunlight that filtered through the forest canopy was growing dimmer as the sun made its way across Underhill's sky in an approximation of the Ordinary sun.

"Now," Jessamine said cheerfully, "we just need to worry about the dusk-monkeys."

FORTUNATELY, their return journey was free of dusk-monkeys, and they found Ed finishing a meal at the Mended Bear.

"Two more of those, please," Jessamine asked the innkeeper. "And do you have another room for the night?"

"Indeed I do," she said with a smile, accepting Jessamine's payment.

"Mom, we could Anchor back tonight," Clara said.

"I'm inclined not to give the Witchers any more coin than necessary," Jessamine growled. "Besides, if we're going to work these crystals, we'll do better in the Ordinary. The magic is. . ."

"Fresher," Ed supplied.

"Yeah, you said that earlier. Good as any other word, I guess," Jessamine said. "And I've got a small row house I rent in Philadelphia. The basement is set up as a workshop, and I've spare cots, but it'll be the middle of the night if we go now."

"Philly. . ." Clara mused. "There's a Border there, now. It's in Penn's Landing, I think."

"It is," Jessamine agreed. "It's a haul to my place from there, but we can get a taxi. I'd rather not teleport with these beauties until they're settled and charged. Speaking of which—" she turned her attention to the innkeeper "—would you have some kind of canvas or burlap or something? I need to wrap some crystals." She pointed to the glowing parcel.

"Oh, easily. I can go you one better, in fact," the woman said. "I've padding you can use to keep them apart. Be right back."

"Thank you."

"So how long will it take to charge them?" Clara asked.

Jessamine chewed her lower lip a bit as she thought. "A couple of days. Figure all day Friday, most of Saturday, if Ed here helps."

Ed frowned. "Of course. But that's still pretty fast. These things are huge."

"I'm thinking Clara may be able to help accelerate the process."

"I can try," Clara offered.

"And the workshop is just a couple of blocks from what I swear is one of the best cheesesteak places in all of Philly," Jessamine promised with a smile.

"For cheesesteaks," Ed smiled, "I will make this work."

CHAPTER 14

GATHERING AND CHARGING

"C'mon, baby, you're doing fine."

"Am not," Clara said crossly.

They'd spent the morning charging—or in Clara's case *attempting* to charge—some of the crystals they'd gathered. Jessamine had managed two full ones, while Ed was just behind her with one full one and one mostly full. Clara, on the other hand, had struggled to fill one crystal even halfway.

"I just don't *get* it," she added, aware that she was pouting a little. "I can see you guys moving the magic around, but. . . you're not *doing* anything. I mean, I can shove it here and there too, but it just doesn't take."

"We'll try some more after lunch," Ed said, patting her on the shoulder.

They'd decided to make the short walk to Philip's Steaks, with Jessamine declaring that the fresh air and sunshine would be good for them. It was a mild Spring day, and even the humidity was fairly low. "Clara, did you decide what you want? We'll probably get it to go, it'll be packed right now."

Clara frowned. "I've never actually had a cheesesteak," she

admitted.

Her mother stopped in her tracks, turned, and glared at her. "You blaspheme, child," she said sternly. Then she smiled. "Although, I'm definitely going to have to talk to Arlene and Theo next time I see them. Cheesesteak is a basic food group. Philip's does it right, your options are basically 'wit' or 'witout.'"

"Which means what?" Clara asked.

"With our without grilled onions. And you can choose American, Provolone, or Wiz cheese."

"Wiz?"

"Cheez Wiz," Ed supplied with a smile.

Clara wrinkled her nose. "Canned cheese? Gross."

"It's traditional," Mom shrugged. "You can add stuff like pickles and mushrooms and even pizza sauce, but you're risking life and limb from some folks. Best to keep it simple."

"Do they have turkey?"

Jessamine let out a long-suffering sigh. "My own flesh and blood. Saints and ministers of mercy defend us. No, baby, they do not. It's a cheese *steak.*"

"You can get chicken," Ed pointed out.

"You *can* just get plain bread with nothing on it," Jessamine said mock-seriously. "But if you've never had a proper Philly cheesesteak before, you are getting the proper model first."

"Witout, then," Clara said.

"So mote it be. Vinegar fries with it?"

"Vinegar on *fries?*" Clara asked, aghast.

"I swear to all the baby angels, I am going to file a lawsuit against the Thorns," Jessamine complained, shaking her head and clearly trying not to chuckle. "Yes, baby, vinegar on fries. It's wonderful. A special treat when you visit the shore in the summer, in fact."

"Okay," Clara said dubiously.

"And now let me show you an adulting trick." Jessamine rubbed her hands together in front of her, as if trying to warm them in front of a fire. *"Lucre,"* she said softly. Clara saw a flash of magic, but it came and went too quickly for her to analyze it. But when Jessamine pulled her hands apart, a few crisp twenty-dollar bills lay in one palm. "Better than human ATM machines," she grinned.

Clara's jaw dropped. She immediately thought of all the time she and the Thorns had struggled to make rent, to pay for groceries, to even maintain a cell phone line. How Mom had cleaned other people's homes for less than twenty an hour, despite having an advanced college degree. "Can I do that?" Clara asked hopefully.

"Of course," Mom shrugged.

"I've never picked up the trick of it," Ed admitted.

"I need to see it again," Clara insisted. "A bit slower, if you can."

Jessamine stopped short of the intersection and repeated the spell, another half-dozen perfectly crisp twenties appearing in one palm.

Clara frowned as she ran the spell's equations back in her mind, simplifying and reducing them. "That's translocation magic," she said sharply. "Where'd those come from?"

Jessamine copied Clara's frown. "No, it isn't," she insisted.

"Yes, it is," Clara insisted right back. "It's a teleportation spell. I just don't recognize the subexpressions."

Ed's eyes had widened. "It has to be from a bank or something," he said. "They're like brand-new."

"That spell *creates* them," Jessamine said, but a bit of doubt was creeping into her voice.

Ed took the bills and examined them. "Serial numbers are different, and they're not sequential. That seems like a lot of detail for such a quick spell."

"Mom, when we got to the house this morning, you summoned a flashlight before you went into the basement," Clara said. "Can you do that now? Summon the same flashlight?"

"Of course," Jessamine said, holding out her hands as if cupping water. *"Það sem er mitt er mitt."* In Clara's mind's eye, a more complex set of equations flashed across Jessamine's hands just before the flashlight appeared in them.

Clara closed her eyes and pictured the spell, once again simplifying and reducing it. "It's basically the same," she said slowly.

"Impossible," Jessamine protested. "The second one is Icelandic. I learned it when Alex and I—"

"Once you simplify it, it's basically the same," Clara said. "In fact, it's almost exactly the same as the summoning spell we learned in school."

"The Irish one?" Ed asked. *"Go tapa go tapa, isteach i mo lámha?"*

Clara nodded. "That one flips two subexpressions, but they're being multiplied, so it doesn't matter. Basically the same. I'd need to see it a couple more times, maybe, but I can probably figure out—"

"Maybe not right now, out here on the street," Jessamine said, looking troubled. "Let's perhaps put a pin in it?"

Clara opened her eyes. "Okay. But Mom. . . that's *stealing.*"

Jessamine nodded slowly. "We'll be. . . more careful, in the future."

"Is this how witches pay for everything?" Clara said as they began crossing the street.

"No, that's just usually for pocket change when you're caught out," Jessamine said. "Most families have a pretty substantial fortune in human banks, which they fund with gold from Underhill. The place is lousy with gold and gems, so much that they're practically valueless there. So they bring it out, invest it, and then live off the interest."

"I guess that's okay," Clara allowed. "Do you have one of those accounts?"

"Alex and I did, but we were gone long enough that I need to do some paperwork to get access to most of it, and I need him to do that."

"Oh."

They walked the rest of the way in silence, stepped into the tiny restaurant, placed their orders, and waited a few minutes for them to be made. The owner stepped out from behind the counter and exchanged a few pleasantries with Jessamine, introducing himself to

Clara and Ed and shaking their hands before returning to the grill. "He's a good one," Jessamine said quietly after he'd left. "He's in on it."

"He is?" Ed asked in surprise.

Jessamine nodded. "The family who rented my place before me were. . . *family,* if you know what I mean." She nodded significantly, glancing from side to side to ensure they weren't being overheard. "Came here all the time and apparently got to be really good friends. The neighbors on either side are in on it, too. They keep an eye on the place when I'm not around and don't make a fuss when I somehow come and go without any visible means of transportation."

As they waited for their order, Jessamine continued chatting with the staff over the counter. "Ed," Clara said, "do you remember Ordinary physics?"

He shook his head. "Honestly, most of us are lazy about Ordinary school. You didn't know you were. . . you know. So."

"I hated History, for what it's worth. But I liked Math, and Physics, because it's basically Math."

"Okay."

"So in physics, there's the rule that nothing is ever created or destroyed. Everything just changes shape. Matter can become energy, energy can become matter."

He shrugged.

"Do you think magic is the same? That it's just another way of making things. . . change shape?"

He considered it. "Maybe? I've never really thought about it, I guess. Why?"

"With the money," Clara said more quietly. "I mean, it's got to be harder to *make* money than to just move it around, right?"

"I. . . maybe?"

"I want to look into it."

"Possibly once the current mission is over?" he suggested.

"Yeah."

Their order came up wrapped and bagged, and they set off back home. "Let's eat outside," Jessamine suggested as they arrived back at her row house. "Before we have to head back into the basement."

They perched on the concrete steps and dug in.

"Wow," Clara mumbled through a mouth full of hot, cheese-laden steak, "thimf im umuzing."

"I told you," Jessamine said, delighted. "And nearly everyplace else in the country who pretends to make these gets them wrong. You have to have the right rolls, the steak has to be chopped nice and thin on the grill, and just. . . it's everything."

They attacked the rest of their lunch in silence, using copious paper napkins to wipe their fingers and faces afterwards.

"All right," Jessamine sighed contentedly as she stuffed the trash into the bag. "Back at it."

They descended into the basement workshop. The single street-level window admitted a small amount of natural light, but the rest of the room's illumination was supplied by bright floodlights screwed into fixtures on the low ceiling. Given the home's narrow, long footprint, the basement was surprisingly roomy. Jessamine had lined the walls with shelves full of books, equipment, and cupboards, and positioned a long, heavy worktable down the middle. That left plenty of room to maneuver down either side to the worktable. She'd taken one side, while Ed and Clara took the other, and spread the empty crystals between them. Three of those were now lying to one side on a thick blue bath towel. "They'll need to rest a few hours," Jessamine had explained, "and then they'll be fine to carry around."

Ed had already picked up his nearly full crystal, while Jessamine grabbed one of the five empties. She closed her eyes and smiled faintly as she started working.

"So what's holding you back?" Ed whispered as Clara picked up her own crystal.

"I think it's that you guys can actually *absorb* magic," she said, letting her eyes slip into magic-mode. "I mean, I can see it settling into you through your skin. And I can see it pulsing down into the crystal, right through your palms and fingertips. And didn't Mom say that you had to touch these to draw magic out again?" Ed nodded. "I think that's it. I can't actually do that. I *see* the magic, and I can push it around, but when I push it up against the crystal most of it just kind of bounces back."

"Maybe try going slower? More gently?" he suggested. He closed his own eyes and began concentrating.

And humming.

Ed hummed while he charged crystals, and Clara was starting to find it supremely annoying.

She spent another hour trying. Taking Ed's advice, she tried coaxing the magic more slowly, letting it gently loop around the crystal rather than shoving it right up against it. That *did* seem to help: the strangely misshapen ambient equations would fracture slightly as they slid along the crystal's surface, slipping into its microscopic lattice-like structure. *I wonder if Mom has a microscope,* Clara wondered. Maybe if she could *see* how the magic inserted itself into the crystal's actual physical makeup, she could make this go faster.

She finally managed to fill her crystal, and laid it gently on the bath towel. "I need some air," she announced, heading back upstairs by herself. She stepped outside and sank onto the steps, planting her elbows on her knees and letting her chin sink into her hands. *This is depressing,* she thought. *Although I guess it makes up for how quickly I pick up regular magic.*

"Hey, there!" a bright, young male voice said. Clara looked up to see a pale, dark-haired, lanky-limbed boy about her age grinning at her from the sidewalk. "Are you Jess' daughter?"

Clara nodded. "I'm Clara."

"I'm Benas." He jerked a thumb over his shoulder. "I live next door."

He had an accent Clara couldn't quite place. "Are you Russian?"

He snorted. "You joke. No, we're Lithuanian. We come here four years ago. Are you from Philly?"

"No, I'm kind of. . . from everywhere. We moved around a lot until recently."

"Not far as Lithuania," he grinned. "May I join?"

"Sure," Clara said, scooting over on the step to make room.

"So you live here now?"

"No. I mostly live. . ." she trailed off, trying to come up with an acceptable answer.

"Under the hill?" he asked, nodding knowingly.

Ah, right. "Yeah," she grinned. "Mom told me you guys knew, but I didn't make the connection. I'm still in school there. Graduating in a few weeks, actually."

"I also am graduating in a few weeks," he said proudly. "St. Monica, a few blocks from here."

"Congratulations," Clara said. "What will you do after school?"

"University," he said. "Already have letters from two here. Scholarship for at least first year." He bumped his knee against hers, and she felt herself flush slightly at the contact. "You go to university?"

"I actually don't know," she admitted.

"They *have* university, under the hill?"

"It's just *Underhill*," she corrected. "And sort of. We can stay on for advanced studies for another three years. You have to be accepted. I haven't. . . thought about it. I don't think." She paused to see if her brain would surface up anything to the contrary, but nothing came. "I don't know what I'll do."

"Maybe move to Philly?" he suggested with a grin. "Not so many pretty girls our age in this neighborhood."

Clara flushed again and smiled uncomfortably. "Maybe. But hey, I have to get back inside and help with. . . chores." She stood. "Nice talking to you."

Benas stood and extended a hand. "Nice meeting you, Clara," he said as they shook.

Clara hurried back inside, all but running into her mother as she closed the door behind her.

"Meeting the neighbors?" Jessamine asked. Clara nodded. "Mmmm. Step into the kitchen."

They stepped out of the narrow hallway, and Jessamine leaned against the fridge. "Now, I don't know how much Arlene and Theo told you about the facts of life—"

Clara's face grew hot. "We talked, Mom—"

Jessamine smiled and shook her head. "That's not what I meant. I mean between. . . us. Witches and humans."

Clara managed to blush even harder. "Mom, I wasn't—"

Her mother chuckled. "Oh, I know, baby. Benas is a terrible flirt, always has been."

"And Ed and I—"

"I know, I know," Mom said soothingly. "But you're a young woman, and I want to make sure you know a couple of things Arlene and Theo wouldn't have known. Just. . . well, seeing you talking to a boy reminded me, is all."

"Okay," Clara allowed, her flush fading a bit.

"Witches and humans. . . can't. Romantically, I mean." Clara's flush returned. "It's unsafe. *Very* unsafe, actually. Magic gets involved." Jessamine frowned. "It might be different for you, since you don't gather magic into yourself, but. . . I wouldn't risk it, baby."

"I mean, I wouldn't," Clara said at once. "Ed and I. . ."

Jessamine tilted her head. "Is it that serious?"

Clara sighed. "I don't know." When her mother raised a single eyebrow, she repeated, "I don't *know*. Like, I literally don't know. It. . . *feels* right. Like, when I need to remember something we learned in school, it just bubbles up in my head, but I don't remember learning it. Ed feels that way. It's right. We're supposed to be together, I *know* it, just like I know all those spells. But I wasn't *there* for it, and it's different than just knowing."

Her mother nodded slowly. "I think I understand. But you really do. . . you feel sure? That it's serious?"

Clara nodded.

"Hmmm. Well. I assume you're still having trouble with the crystals?"

"Ugh."

"Then let's try something."

Jessamine had led Clara back into the basement, where Ed had just begun his third crystal. She'd repositioned them on opposite sides of the table, laying the crystal on a small rubber mat between them.

"Take each other's hands," she instructed. "Now, I want you to both close your eyes. Ed, start loading that crystal. Clara, don't *look*. I know that's how you experience magic, baby, but for now just don't. Try to *feel* it. Try to feel what Ed's doing. What *he's* feeling."

"Okay," Clara said dubiously.

She closed her eyes and tried to just *feel*. With nothing to see, there wasn't much sensation other than the smooth table top under her hands, and the warm skin of Ed's hands atop her. She became acutely aware of her own breathing, of the gentle sound of her own heart beating. Then she noticed Ed's pulse, thumping quietly in his palms. After a few minutes, she realized her own heartbeat was starting to synchronize with his, thumping more firmly in time.

Her breath began to slow, flowing in and out of her in time with her pulse.

She felt...

...something.

It was like she was underwater, floating, with warm, silky water brushing against every inch of her skin. The water was thin enough to breathe, almost like liquid air, and it filled her with warmth. She breathed it in, and it trickled gently through her, sliding through arteries and capillaries, making her heart glow. It filled her and filled her, slowing and surely, almost like she was gently drifting into a deep sleep, surrounded by that supportive, almost imperceptible water.

Then, when she was so full she thought she'd burst, that warmth began flowing out of her. Distantly, she felt her hands draw closer together, felt a smooth sharpness settle between them. And that sharpness grew even more distant as it shared in the warmth that was gently spilling from her. It absorbed that liquid heat, but not greedily: instead, it was almost entirely passive, taking whatever she fed it and demanding no more. But it accepted *so much.*

Then, in what seemed like mere minutes, it too was full. It was the satisfied, satiated fullness of a comforting meal with her parents, sleepy and safe all at once. Her hands moved apart a bit, releasing it to let it settle into a well-deserved nap.

She opened her eyes.

Ed opened his in the same moment, and they widened as he released Clara's hands. "Wow." His voice was soft with amazement.

Jessamine reached between them, gently laying a finger on the crystal that lay between them. Her own eyes widened. "My goodness." Her voice, too, was laced with awe.

"Did we do it?" Clara asked, blinking as her eyes readjusted to the harsh floodlights.

"You filled that in under ten minutes," Jessamine breathed.

"Oh," Clara said softly. Then she smiled. "Can we do it again?"

THEY MANAGED the rest of the crystals before dinnertime, and although Clara was starting to feel physically tired when they started the final one, she couldn't imagine not sinking into that same not-place, experiencing the same sensations of tranquility and comfort.

"Is that what magic feels like to you?" she asked Ed as they set the last crystal aside to rest.

He shook his head. "No. Never even close. That's. . . I don't know what that is."

"That," Jessamine said with a happy sigh. "Is love, my dears. That's what magic feels like between two perfectly matched souls."

Her expression grew slightly said. "It's what Alex and I had. Have," she corrected herself at once. "It's what we'll have again."

"I wonder if that's what the triplets feel when they do their Voltron thing," Clara murmured.

"You guys down there?" a female voice called from the top of the stairs.

"Ah," Jessamine said, a satisfied grin settling onto her expression. "That's Sandy. Let's see if she's found our Paladins. We're down here!" she called.

Sandy clattered down the steps. "We got it. Both lines go to the same house, in fact."

"Perfect," Jessamine said. "Now. . . look, kids, we need to go into this carefully, right?"

"Right, Mom," Clara agreed.

"The team and I will lead the way, of course. But Paladins usually lay some traps for us. So. . . baby, would you mind trying something for me? It shouldn't hurt, but it may be uncomfortable."

"Okay," Clara said hesitantly.

Jessamine gestured. "That little crate in the corner, under the shelves. With the red stamp on it. Would you pull that out, and pull the lid off?"

Clara complied. "It's heavy," she remarked as she slid the box across the concrete floor. The lid was hinged, so she flipped it back. "Is this chain mail?"

"Old-school," Mom confirmed as she, Sandy, and Ed took involuntary steps backwards. "The crate is lined with silk, which insulates the metal."

"Now that the lid is open, of course. . . " Sandy muttered.

"You'll live. So baby, what I want you to do is pull that out and kind of drape it over yourself. Be careful it doesn't snag in your hair. Actually, just around your shoulders should do it, even."

Clara didn't look convinced. "But iron drains magic."

"Yes, baby, but you don't *have* any magic in you. If it feels bad, even for a moment, just drop it back in the crate. Ed, Sandy, here."

Jessamine reached into a drawer and pulled out thick, slick-looking gloves. "These are silk, and they're insulated with spun silk. We can help her if needed."

"I guess," Clara said dubiously. "Here goes."

She reached into the crate slowly, as if expecting to be shocked. When her fingers touched the heaps of small metal rings, she jerked her hand back on reflex. "Huh," she mused as nothing happened.

She reached in more confidently, pulling one edge of the chain mail out. It was a wide sheet, composed of half-inch metal rings that all interlinked. "It's *really* heavy."

"Knights did it all the time?" Ed offered.

"I think they had squires to help," Clara countered.

"I thought you were bad at History," Ed teased.

"I didn't *like* History," she clarified. "I wasn't *bad* at anything." She wrapped the heavy chain mail around her like a shawl. "Okay, now what?"

"Well, that's more than I was hoping for, actually," Jessamine said. "But can you still manipulate magic?"

"It's fuzzier," Clara said, shifting her vision. "But yeah." A multi-colored shower of sparkling lights filled the room, dimming quickly as Clara released the ambient power. "Not really any harder."

"Excellent," Jessamine said, collecting the gloves and stowing them in the drawer. "Back in the crate, then. And close the lid."

"So what's this for?" Ed asked.

"A common Paladin trick is to set traps that drop iron chain mail on us," Sandy said, her tone full of awe. "I think we just found a counter-weapon."

CHAPTER 15

COUNTERATTACK

"This spell is amazing," Jessamine murmured as they are peered out the window.

Clara's mother had assembled her entire team, and Sandy had shown them the target house on a map. They'd identified another house—across the street and down two doors—and used the *Fís Charm chun Daoine a Rialú* spell to glamour the couple who inhabited it. Now, the seven of them were in for a visit with Aunt Evelyn and Uncle Jeff.

"I'm surprised we never thought of it," Reuben remarked.

"You've done this before?" Ed asked. "Taken over people's houses for a stakeout?"

Trevor chuckled as Jessamine replied, "I mean, maybe I wouldn't have put it *that* way, but yeah. Not very often, though. Usually when we have to recon their bolt-holes it's a combination of hiding in the shrubs, maybe finding an empty home. This is actually safer for us, and it doesn't really create any danger for Evelyn and Jeff."

"Wish they'd taught us this one in school," Reuben agreed.

"They didn't," Ed said. "I. . . like to read a lot."

"Well, cheers for reading a lot," Trevor said cheerfully. "Shall I?"

he asked, gesturing to the large front window, through which they could see their target.

"By all means," Jessamine said, stepping back from the window.

Trevor stepped forward and laid one hand on the window. "*Magnify. Enhance. Monitor.*" Clara saw the spell form at his fingertips and sink into the glass. A moment later, the target house zoomed in, and began glowing gently around the corners.

"Did you just," Clara said, her voice full of surprise, "just cast a spell in *English?*"

Trevor chuckled. "Technically in American," he replied with a smile. "Not many of them around, and almost all of them relate to combat magic or surveillance."

"The Anglo-Saxons didn't have a strong magic tradition," Ed added from the back of the living room. "That's why most of what we have is from one European tradition or another."

Trevor nodded. "Exactly. And nearly all of the German traditions we have now started after the Anglo-Saxons left that area. In fact, most of the *anti-magic* traditions in the world today stem from the Anglo-Saxons. Very unpleasant people, back then. At least if you were a witch."

"Lovely lesson," Jessamine said. "But we need a plan."

"Are we even sure this is the right house?" Ed asked.

"Oh, absolutely," Reuben said, pointing at the window. "See the car?"

Ed looked. "Sure?"

"Tesla Model S 60," he explained. "Aluminum body, aluminum frame. No internal combustion engine—just a lot of copper wiring and lithium batteries. Most magic-friendly car you can easily lay your hands on in this country."

"I mean, they could just own a Tesla," Clara pointed out.

Reuben shrugged. "You don't see any others in this neighborhood. Median home price here is around six hundred thousand. That's a thirty thousand dollar car. Most of what you see here are big SUVs, European brands. It's not a guarantee, but it's a good sign."

"Can we see inside?" Jessamine asked Trevor.

He grimaced. "Tricky. It's stucco."

"Like concrete?" Clara asked.

"A little. That's not the problem, though. It's a wood-framed house. It's just they cover the wood with foam insulation—also not a problem—and then metal mesh or lathing. Sometimes both. Helps hold the stucco together. It's not enough to block magic, but it's enough to fuzz it. The roof probably has a radiant heat barrier as well, which is a little worse. And I can see from here that the windows have a metallic UV-blocking tint. Again, nothing that would *stop* us, but it makes things fuzzier. Let's see what we can get." He touched the glass with an index finger and said, *"X-ray mode."*

Another equation slid into the glass, and the target house suddenly became hazy and translucent. They could see several tall, dark shadows moving slowly back and forth.

"I count a dozen Paladins," Latoya said. "All in their trenchcoats."

That's the shadows, Clara realized. *Their coats block the magic, so they show up as shadows.*

"Two more in what I'm going to call the kitchen," Trevor said, pointing. "Not in trenchcoats. Interesting. Looks like they're working on computers." The seated figures were fuzzy, but clearer, and Clara could make out their heads and limbs more easily.

"They're all pretty tall," Sandy noted. "None of them likely to be Deuxm, unless she's one of the ones at a computer."

"She'll have gotten out of Dodge after we escaped," Jessamine said confidently. "We're not here for her. We're here for the lodestar."

"Can you detect that from here?" Clara asked.

Trevor shook his head. "No, not with this spell. And Jess' magic-detecting construct won't work at nearly this distance."

"So we assume it's in there and we can't see it. Which means we break in," Jessamine said.

"Teleport?" Reuben asked. "It'll be chancy with that many of them. The mesh in the walls will put us off-target on arrival. Could even smash through a wall."

"What if we—" Jessamine began.

"Mom, you can't be serious!" Clara said with alarm. "There's a *dozen* of them!"

"And they're going to be on alert," Sandy agreed. "They'll have those hand crossbows. Possibly even guns."

Jessamine frowned. "Okay. I'm open to suggestions."

"Glamour spell," Reuben said. "It's working well here."

"Not through the mesh," Latoya said. "I'm good, but that's a precision spell. And I can only do it eye-to-eye, which means only a few people at most. Three, max, until I get more practice."

"Sleep spell," Sandy offered. "Doesn't need to be precise."

"No, but those are pretty targeted," Trevor objected. "And you can only do one at once if you want it to be undetectable, which means the others would notice the ones dropping. Besides, look." He pointed to one of the shadows. "They've got their hats on, and they've got iron foil in them. You'd have less than a ten percent chance of having any effect at all between those, the distance, and the mesh in the walls."

"Poison gas?" Sandy suggested.

"Every gas spell I know needs an anchor," Jessamine said, frowning in frustration. "We'd need to get in to set it."

"What are those lines?" Clara asked pointing to the window. The house's walls seemed to have thin, gently glowing lines running through them at roughly waist height. Spurs led up to the ceiling, and an uneven web of the same lines snaked through the first- and second-story ceilings.

"Electrical," Trevor answered. "Metal, so it shows up, but obviously copper, so nothing we need to worry about."

Clara's memory tickled her. "Ed," she asked slowly, "did we learn something... there was a professor..."

"Professor Petrović," Ed said. "And yeah, you're right. I remember that class, now."

"For the rest of us?" Jessamine prompted.

"Petrović has this theory that magic can be projected along, and out of, thin strands of copper. Wires," Ed replied. "He has this idea of snaking wires everywhere and using them to project illusions, shields, sounds, all kinds of things. His theory is that you can feed the spell into any point of the wire and it'll spread along it. It's like how we can use copper for constructs, but instead of putting a spell *into* the metal, you kind of let it flow *through* the metal."

The team's eyebrows rose. "And does it work?" Reuben asked.

Ed shrugged. "He could get it to work about half the time over short distances. He made all of us try and we couldn't get anything. There has to be something different about the shape of the magic. Only one person figured it out."

All eyes turned to Clara and her memory obligingly bubbled up the information. "I know how," she said confidently. "I just didn't know *why*. But yeah."

"But we still have the problem with the mesh," Trevor pointed out.

"No we don't," Clara said, stepping closer to the window and pointing. "Look. Outdoor outlets. And they all connect back here."

"Circuit breaker box," Trevor said, nodding slowly. "That could work."

"So a glamour, then?" Latoya asked hopefully.

Clara shook her head. "I don't think I could do a glamour through that. Those are still too one-to-one. Or one-to-few, at least," she said, jerking her chin toward the kitchen where Aunt Evelyn was puttering.

"Poison gas," Jessamine said with some satisfaction.

"I'm not poisoning people, Mom," Clara said flatly. "But. . ."

"Sleeping gas?" Sandy asked.

Clara shook her head. "I don't. . . I feel like *creating* something that way would be hard. Maybe impossible. You'd need so much energy. . ." she trailed off, thinking. "Can any of you summon a sandwich?"

"Ma olen näljane, anna mulle süüa." Reuben said at once, holding out one hand. A sandwich, wrapped in white deli paper, appeared. "Corned beef on rye, anyone? No sauerkraut, can't stand the stuff."

"You made a reuben?" Jessamine asked, rolling her eyes.

"Your spell didn't include the name of the sandwich," Clara said sharply.

Reuben shrugged. "It's part of what I picture. The words are just to help shape the magic in my mind."

"It wasn't a complex spell. I saw it. Did it even use any energy?" she demanded.

He shrugged. "Not much."

"So look, this is exactly like the money," she said, turning to her mother. "You can't have just created that out of thin air. Not with that little energy. If you had truly created something, you'd have had to pull together all the atoms, all the molecules, that make a sand-wich. There's no *way* a spell that simple did all that so fast. This *came* from someplace. Conservation of matter and energy."

Jessamine looked uncertain.

"But it's magic," Sandy said, spreading her hands. "That's what it does."

Clara shook her head. "I don't think so. I think you're mostly just moving things around. That's still pretty magical, but it takes *energy* to create something from scratch. Way more than Reuben just used."

"What are you getting at, Clara?" Ed asked gently.

Clara turned back to the window. "The Professor's spells were all about manipulating what was already there, through the copper wires. Manipulating light, that kind of thing, right?"

"Sure."

"When you look at the magic—I mean, when I look at it, at least —you have to put a huge denominator on it to get it to flow through the wire and come out evenly. If you tried to do that with a spell that was already high-energy. . . I think it would melt the wire. Or blow up. Or not work."

"Okay. . ." Ed said. He could tell Clara was talking it out.

She nodded slightly. "What's taking up most of the space in that house, right now?"

"Air?" Ed hazarded.

"Air," she agreed. "Remember. . . I mean, I don't remember doing it, but the one spell I have in my head was for projecting sounds."

Ed nodded. "That one was impressive. It was like surround sound, once you got it working."

"So, all that spell did was manipulate air."

"I guess?"

"Well, sound is just air moving, right?"

"How does this help us right now?" Jessamine asked.

Clara gave her mother a tentative smile. "Well, what's air mostly made of?"

"Nitrogen and oxygen, as far as we're concerned," Reuben said. "A smattering of other gasses."

"A 'smattering?'" Clara teased. "Were *any* of you good in Ordinary science?"

"I have a *degree* in biology," Reuben huffed.

"What do you get with two nitrogens and an oxygen," Clara challenged him.

He blinked. "Nitrous oxide." Then he smiled. "Laughing gas."

"No, that's an anesthetic," Latoya countered.

"It's both," Reuben said. "Chefs also use it in chargers to make foams and stuff. All a matter of quantity."

"So how do you make it?" Clara asked. "Seriously. I don't know."

"I. . ." Reuben said, blinking quickly. "Aunt Evelyn!" he called. The woman can bustling forward, wiping her hands on an apron. "Do you have a smartphone, my love? Or a computer?"

She nodded, almost birdlike in her quick, small movements, and withdrew a smartphone from the apron's front pocket.

"Could you Google 'how to make nitrous oxide' for me?" He spelled it out as she typed. A moment later she offered the phone to him, but he declined. "Just hold it up so I can see?"

She complied, and Reuben leaned forward. "Start with ozone,

which means splitting a normal oxygen molecule in half. Unless we're talking the ozone layer itself, which we're not." He peered at the screen. "You'd normally heat ammonium nitrate. Or. . . well, a few other things work as well. But I think those mainly break down the oxygen." He frowned. "I did biology, not chemistry." He kept reading, motioning for "Aunt Evelyn" to scroll. "It occurs naturally. Nitrogen scavenges ozone."

Clara nodded slowly. "I think that'll do, then."

"Do what?" Jessamine demanded.

"I can turn the air in the house into nitrous oxide. Enough, at least, to make them all pass out. Everything we need is already there, and I should be able to just manipulate it into a new configuration. Not creating anything from scratch. Then we can just walk in."

Everyone was quiet for a moment, and Reuben shooed their "Aunt" back to the kitchen.

"That could work," Jessamine said thoughtfully. "If you think you can do it."

"It's math," Clara said with a grin. "What kind of concentration am I aiming for?" she asked Reuben.

"According to Wikipedia, two parts nitrous to one part oxygen," he replied. "Latoya, we're going to need your trick with breathing masks."

"Done."

"Okay," Clara said, quickly doing the math in her head. She stepped even closer to the window, staring at the house. Then she shook her head. "I can't see the magic through this. Is there another window?"

"The main bedroom should have a view," Latoya offered. She'd scouted the house after setting the glamour on its residents. She led Clara down the hall, everyone else trailing behind them.

The main bedroom window did offer a slightly obstructed view of the house down and across the street, but it was enough. Clara could see the front porch, and just make out the electrical outlet near the front door. The ambient magic was clearly visible to her as well, although. . . "I can't," she said, her heart falling. "It's too far. I need to be able to see the symbols."

"I could put an illusion on her," Latoya offered at once. "On a couple of us. We could—"

"If they're wearing their goggles, and I anticipate at least one of them is on watch, they'll spot that," Jessamine said.

"The odds are too good they have photos of Clara," Ed said protectively. "They'll recognize her regardless."

They all thought for a moment, staring at the house that was so close, yet just out of reach.

"We could—" Trevor began.

"Aunt Evelyn?" Clara called, turning from the window and pushing through everyone. "Do you have hair clippers?"

Clara and Latoya strolled slowly down the street, chatting quietly and laughing now and then. Clara's once long hair had been clippered back to less than an inch, something her mother had been furious about. Latoya, who'd already had a close-cropped haircut, was wearing one of Aunt Evelyn's wigs—a curly blonde number that fell to her shoulders.

"Good thing she had a wig we could use," Clara giggled as they walked.

"She had a *dozen,*" Latoya grinned. "This was the least awful."

They'd also borrowed some of Evelyn's clothes, which tended toward baggy. Hopefully this would all be enough to keep the Paladins from recognizing them.

They kept to "their" side of the street, walking slowly and gesturing broadly, pretending they were embroiled in some intense, hilarious conversation. As they passed the Paladin house, Clara quickly injected an eavesdropping spell into the electrical outlet by the porch. The ambient magic gathered into a precise set of equations, including the terms Clara had figured out that would spread the spell throughout the house's wiring. The exterior outlet would be the terminal point, and everything the spell picked up from inside would be transmitted to one of Uncle Jeff's collectible paperweights, which Clara had prepared before stepping out.

The spell in place, Clara and Latoya continued down the street, circled the block, and ducked back into their borrowed house.

"Anything yet?" Clara asked as they closed the door behind them.

"Absolutely," Reuben said, nodding emphatically. "For one, they're on high alert. They're scheduled to do another magic hunting run later today—meaning, using their 'holy relic' to try and find us. They've been going neighborhood by neighborhood, which kind of confirms they only have one lodestar. And it apparently needs time to recharge, because they've been tracking the time between runs very carefully."

"How long do we have?" Latoya asked.

"About six hours, which is plenty," Jessamine said.

"We *also* learned that they do, in fact, have numerous contacts within the local police, but they're all low-level. Patrol officers, basically," Trevor added. "Some people in dispatch to listen out for them."

"They're actually suspicious of government, which tracks to the narrative we've theorized they use," Jessamine said. "Like I said, until recently, the Paladins weren't big on recruiting. But Deuxm's gone all-out, and they mainly target poorer, disaffected people from smaller, poorer communities, predominantly in the Midwest, where there's already a population open to the anti-witch message. They look for people who are upset with their government, and ready to buy into anything that lets them fight back. So the story is that witches are the secret force behind the government, setting everything up to protect themselves and using the lower ends of society as energy sources."

"You're kidding," Ed said with disbelief.

Jessamine shrugged. "A lot of these people feel they've lost power in the world. They can either blame themselves and the systems they vote for, or they can blame someone else. And being a Paladin probably makes them feel powerful."

"Blaming someone else is always easier," Latoya said, shaking her head sadly.

"But we haven't heard anything that would prevent us from proceeding with Operation Giggle Gas," Sandy said.

"Is that what we're calling it?" Clara grinned.

"Had to call it something," Sandy replied with a smile. "So are you ready?"

Clara nodded, rubbing her hands together. "Yeah. I tested it outside a couple of times, and it worked. I mean, obviously I wasn't huffing the stuff, but it's nitrous, for sure."

"How can you be *sure?*" her mother asked.

"It's math, Mom," Clara shrugged. "That's just how it is."

Jessamine looked skeptical, but she finally nodded. "Okay. You and Latoya going to take another walk, then?"

"Noooo..." Clara said, blushing slightly.

"I thought that might be too obvious," Latoya said. "So we're going to kind of go opposite of 'low-key.'"

"Meaning?" Jessamine asked warily.

"Clara's going to run out, screaming at me. I'm going to run after her, screaming right back. We'll stop in front of the house next door —not exactly in front of the Paladins, but one over—and have a bit of a fight."

"You can cast a spell while doing all that?" Trevor asked, impressed.

"No," Clara said, causing his face to fall a little. "After a bit, we're going to make up. I'm going to start sobbing, she's going to hug me, and that's when I'll do it."

"Once the spell starts, how long?" Reuben asked, ignoring the look of disbelief on Jessamine's face.

"Ten minutes at most," Clara said confidently. "It'll run for an

hour past that with the energy I'm giving it, which will let it maintain the concentration. If we go in and close the door behind us, so
the air doesn't circulate, it should hold for a few hours, even."

"Plenty of time, then," Reuben nodded, doing some calculations
in his head. "So our—"

"You are *not* going to run out there and call attention to yourself!" Jessamine declared, eyes flashing.

"Mom, this is the best shot," Clara said calmly. "And Latoya will
be right there. If *anything* happens, we blow our cover and teleport
back to your workshop. Far away. You all can decide what to do
next."

"I'm the best at translocation magic after Alex," Latoya said
quietly.

Jessamine's lips compressed into a frown, but after a few
moments she nodded. "Fine. I don't see any other way. So. . . fine."

"When do we start?" Ed asked, his voice betraying his
nervousness.

"Right now," Clara said. "You guys should probably go make sure
our Aunt and Uncle don't freak out, because we're going to start
right here in the living room."

Clara slammed her way out of the house, screaming incoherent
curses and threats at her "sister." She ran down the short run of sidewalk and into the street, turning toward the Paladins.

Latoya followed in hot pursuit, demanding in fairly strong
language that Clara get back inside and talk about this. Clara
stopped at the designated spot, right at the foot of the neighbor's
driveway, and whirled. For nearly two full minutes, they
exchanged heated accusations, denials, counter-claims, and
threats. Then Latoya aid something in a low, urgent voice, jabbing
her index finger into Clara's sternum. Clara immediately burst into

tears, and Latoya gathered her in a tight hug. After a moment, Latoya turned and she and Clara walked back, hugging each other the entire way.

"Clock's ticking," Trevor said when they returned. "I started when you first hugged."

Everyone waited nervously, watching the living room window as the Paladin's magic-shadows continued moving throughout the house.

Four minutes later, they started dropping.

The ones still upright began panicking, clearly shaking their fallen comrades before they too succumbed to the gas.

Within six minutes, everything was still.

"Masks," Latoya said. She touched each of their faces in turn, her fingers spread to cover their noses and mouths. Each time, an incredibly complex set of equations churned and planted themselves on the recipient's face. Clara quickly memorized the sequence, and when Latoya applied hers, almost went cross-eyed trying to look down at the equations swirling around her own nose.

"I don't know if that's necessary," Jessamine said. "Ed and Clara aren't to—"

"It can't hurt," Latoya shrugged. "These will purify any air that you breathe. They'll last maybe ten minutes on their own. Everyone can trickle magic into them to keep them going."

"Use the crystals for that energy," Jessamine cautioned. "We don't know what we're walking to."

"I don't know if I can—" Clara started uncertainly.

"I'll get Clara's," Ed said. He'd kept two of the fully charged crystals. Jessamine, Sandy, and Reuben also had two, while Trevor, and Latoya had one apiece.

"Then let's go."

Latoya took a moment to refresh the glamour on their hosts, in case they needed to retreat here. "They'll come out of it in a few hours and think they spent the day napping," she added. Once that was taken care of, she joined the others out front. They trooped to the Paladins' house, where Clara and Ed were instructed to wait by the Tesla.

Jessamine walked directly to the front door, backed by her team. *"Boom,"* she ordered, miming a punch at the front door. With a burst of magic and a *crack,* the door swung inward and the five witches rushed inside. One of them slammed the door shut behind them.

A moment later, Sandy opened the door, stuck her head out, and waved. "She says you guys can come in. Everyone's asleep, but Clara, she wants you to make sure the spell will keep going."

Ed and Clara hurried inside, and Clara's eyes quickly took in the magic that was emanating from the walls, invisible to everyone but her. "It's fine," Clara said, shaping a bit more of the magic inside the home to keep the spell going longer. "The mesh in the walls isn't stopping ambient magic from getting in," she added.

"Okay, spread out. We need clues, and we need that lodestar," Jessamine ordered. "Latoya, you've got the mind-wipes."

"The what?" Clara asked softly as Jessamine and Sandy headed upstairs while Trevor and Reuben spread out on the ground floor.

"Mind-wipes," Latoya said. "Help me get his trenchcoat open," she added, kneeling next to one of the unconscious Paladins. "Ugh, these just *feel* gross, with iron plates in them."

Ed eventually knelt as well, as the three of them struggled to open the heavy trenchcoats. Latoya rummaged in the man's back pocket, withdrawing his wallet. "This is the key," she said, riffling through its contents. "Ah." She withdrew a small rectangle of plastic, about the size of a credit card, and held it up for them to see.

"Holy Order of Paladonic Hunters?" Clara said, wrinkling her nose. "That's not even a word."

"No, but they all get one. And see here? Member since 2010." Latoya sighed. "So I'm going to need to wipe a good bit."

"How does this work?" Ed asked. "We didn't get memory alteration in school."

"Advanced studies," Latoya said grimly. "And it's not exactly alteration. We don't know how to do that reliably. At least I don't.

I'm actually going to remove the last—" she looked at the card again "—decade and a half, almost, of his life."

Clara's jaw dropped. "Can he survive that, even?"

The older witch shrugged. "It's not always pretty. But it's the only way we know to take out the threat."

"That seems unethical," Ed said, clearly troubled.

"I don't love it," Latoya admitted.

"Show me," Clara ordered, standing. "But just take like five minutes."

"I can do an hour, reliably," Latoya countered.

"Fine."

Clara watched carefully as Latoya crafted her spell. Her hands moved in a complex pattern, and she whispered, *"Un gol, un gol, plin cu gri. Cu o oră înapoi, curățați drumul."*

"Romanian," Ed murmured as she worked.

Clara tuned out the movement and sound, and focused on the shape the magic was taking as it trickled from Latoya's body. The equation, once she accounted for the unusually odd distortions in the symbols themselves, looked. . . familiar.

"Stop," Clara ordered. Latoya looked up, blinking as her concentration was broken. "Do it again, but concentrate on making him forget something simple. Cars."

Latoya shook her head. "I don't know how to—"

"Just *think* about it," Clara said with frustration. "It doesn't have to work."

"Trust her," Ed said.

"Okay," Latoya said, breathing deeply. She began again, this time whispering a slight variation: *"Un gol, un gol, plin cu gri. Cu o oră în urmă, curățați drumul de mașini."*

"I've got it," Clara said. "Stop."

"What do you mean you've 'got' it?" Latoya asked.

"It's basically a quadratic equation," Clara said. She conjured a glowing image in the air.

$$ax^2 + bx + c = 0$$

"The first bit is the concept you want erased. The first time you did it, that was just zero. Well, basically. In my head, at least. The second is how far back to go. I could probably fine-tune it down to seconds, now that I see it." She paused.

"What's the third?" Ed asked.

"It's hard to explain. I'm. . . I have a theory, but I'm not sure. Latoya, can you try again? This time, make him forget something that hasn't happened yet."

Latoya frowned. "I don't—"

"Please."

She sighed. "Okay." With another deep breath, she began again. "*Un gol, un gol, plin cu gri. Înainte, plecat.*"

"That's it," Clara said, triumph in her voice. "You can stop."

"So what's it do?" Ed asked.

"It's a time dimension," Clara said. "I've seen that term before, but I don't remember where. The way she's doing it won't work, but it tried to alter that term. If I make it irrational. . . so look, this isn't really math, right? Just an analogy. I think. But if it's like I can picture it, we can make them forget *witches* and *magic,* not only from their past, but even in their future. Anything they encounter going forward just won't stick with them for more than a second or two."

Latoya's eyes widened. "Can you show me how?"

Clara turned to Ed. "I need. . . here." She reached down and took his hands, closed her eyes, and concentrated on the form she needed the magic to be in.

"Mrgmph," Ed gargled quietly.

Clara opened her eyes. "What's the matter?"

"You're manipulating *my* magic," he said heavily, color returning to his face. "Quite a lot, actually. But I think I got it."

"Can't you just do me?" Latoya said.

Ed shook his head vigorously, and then regretted it. "You

wouldn't like it. She'll still need to, but you if you can start closer to the right thing it won't upset you as much. Do. . ." he thought for a minute, his lips moving silently. "Try *Plecat, plecat, din când în când, vrăjitoare și magie a dispărut o întrebare. Uită, uită, acum și întotdeauna, vrăjitoare și magie, un subiect al niciodată.* That's the closest I can get."

Latoya nodded, mouthing the new words silently. "Okay. I think I have it."

"I'm still going to tweak your magic as we go," Clara warned. "Don't fight it. Whatever I'm doing, just lean into it and try and copy it."

"Okay," Latoya said nervously.

"Whenever you're ready."

Latoya began again, and Clara gently tweaked the spell as it began to work. After a couple of repetitions, Latoya had picked up Clara's intention and adapted, and her magic was flowing perfectly into the Paladin's forehead. It took more than a minute, but when Latoya stood, she looked confident. "I *felt* that work. Wait, what is it?"

Clara's eyes were wide open and she'd paled slightly. "I—"

"Clara?" Ed asked. "You okay?"

Clara just shook her head.

When Latoya had finally settled into the pattern Clara intended, the very air around them had lit up. The spell the older witch had cast had flowed across the walls, the floor, and the ceiling. Briefly, but Clara couldn't have missed it, bright as crisp as it was.

And just as Latoya had finished, something had whispered in Clara's ear.

"Veil."

It had sounded. . . satisfied.

"What's this?" Jessamine said, coming down the stairs and brushing dust off her hands.

"Clara modified the mind-wipe," Latoya said, still giving Clara a concerned look. Ed put his arm around Clara and was speaking softly to her.

"To do what?" Jessamine asked sharply.

Latoya explained.

Jessamine didn't look entirely convinced. "And you. . . are you confident this will work?"

"Absolutely. I'd have never managed the pattern on my own but. . . yes. Absolutely. I could *feel* it."

Jessamine stared at her teammate for a moment, and then nodded. "Okay. Do the others."

"Should we ask them about Deuxm?" Ed asked.

Jessamine shook her head firmly. "They won't know where she's gone. These guys operate in tight cells. They won't know about any others, and they certainly won't know her itinerary. Let's wipe these ones and move on."

"On it," Latoya said, moving on to the next snoring body.

Clara shook her head to clear it, putting the strange voice out of her mind for the moment. "Did you find it?" she asked her mother. "The lodestar?"

"No," Jessamine said grimly. "I'm hoping—"

"Not on this floor," Trevor said as he and Reuben emerged from the downstairs hallway.

"Then where in the—" Jessamine began. And then her eyes widened.

"The car," Clara said.

"The car," Jessamine agreed.

They both rushed outside. Jessamine strode to the back of the car, tapped the trunk, and ordered, *"Oscail."* The trunk opened obligingly, revealing a small wooden crate. It was about a foot high, and maybe eight inches on a side, with a hinged lid—not unlike the crate she kept the chain mail in, back in her workshop.

Jessamine flipped the lid open and sighed. "This is it."

The lodestone was a tarnished brass chalice, with perhaps a four-inch stem, a wide base, and a generously sized cup. The cup flared sharply outward near the top, only to flare back in again at its lip. Inside, resting on the bottom of the flare's widest spot, was a slim copper spike. The spike ran nearly from one wall of the cup to the other, and couldn't be removed without damaging it, due to the inward flare at the top of the cup.

"How's it work?" Ed asked.

"You fill it with liquid. Probably wine, given the era," Trevor said, coming up behind them. "And then it points toward concentrations of magic. Drive around in circles and you can triangulate."

"Mom, there's writing on the front," Clara said.

Jessamine closed the lid and tilted the little crate back. "It's burned into the wood," Jessamine said, puzzled.

"It looks like ancient runes," Ed said, leaning in to study the markings. "Look, that one's almost a—"

"Mom, what's wrong?" Clara said suddenly.

Jessamine had paled, her skin turning an unhealthy gray.

"That," she said in a strained voice, "is your father's writing."

"What?" Clara hissed.

"It's time you knew, Clara," Jessamine said, recovering her composure but keeping the crate tilted back. "Your father has the handwriting of a four year-old baboon with nerve damage."

"It isn't. . . runes?" Ed asked uncertainly.

Jessamine shook her head. "No, it's monumental laziness when it comes to writing things by hand." A sad smile crept across her expression.

"But what's it say?" Clara asked.

Jessamine choked back a sob even as we smile widened. "I'm guessing they ordered him to put a protecting spell on it."

"What's it *say,* Jess?" Clara demanded.

"It's Irish," she replied. "It says A Litriú Cosanta." VELLUM TRY TO DO IN SMALL CAPS

Ed let out an involuntary laugh.

"A Protective Spell," Clara translated.

"Jess!" Reuben called, strolling out of the house with Sandy on his heels. "We found these!"

Jessamine took the first item he handed her, a much-folded sheet of paper. She unfolded it, and sighed. "It's a map of Underhill."

"They have inside help," Sandy said, nodding.

"It's not accurate," Clara noted, peering at the hand-drawn map. "But it's close."

"Can you tell when it's accurate to?" her mother asked.

Clara waited, but her memory simply shrugged at her. "No. But someone back there might be able to. Headmaster Herrera, maybe."

Jessamine refolded the paper and tucked it into one pocket. "What else, Reuben?"

"This," he said, handing her a cardboard box that had been folded flat.

"A box?" Jessamine asked, confused.

Clara's brain automatically measured the box's dimensions. "Fold it back up, Mom," she said quietly.

Jessamine folded the box open, carefully closing the bottom flaps and holding them in place. Then her eyebrows rose. She turned, and settled the box gently over the wooden crate that held the lodestar.

It fit perfectly.

She removed the box and turned it around in her hands, examining the shipping label. "This was sent from a shipping service in Schaumburg, Illinois," she said in a near-whisper.

Clara's heart soared. "Dad."

CHAPTER 16

PREPARATIONS

"Okay, first things first," Jessamine said, plunking the lodestar on her worktable. "We need to wreck this thing."

The team, Ed, and Clara had clustered around the table. "I know a guy down at the dump back home," Sandy offered. "They have one of those machines that crushes entire cars."

Jessamine shrugged. "I'd worry a little about this magic being released that suddenly."

"It's got a *lot* of magic," Clara agreed. "I can take it apart, though."

"How does that work, exactly?" Reuben asked, leaning in with a curious expression.

"It depends," Clara said thoughtfully, shifting her vision to magic-mode and examining the artifact. "Hmm," she added after a moment.

"Good hmm or bad hmm?" Jessamine asked.

"Neutral," Clara murmured, pulling the lodestar closer. Then she straightened. "It's overcomplicated. The magic, I mean."

"Not surprising," Ed noted. "It's *old,* and back then they had some funny ideas about magic."

"You wonder how Paladins got their hands on it in the first place," Latoya said.

"You'd be surprised how many of these things wind up at estate auctions and yard sales," Reuben sighed, stepping back. "Back in the day, a decent number of clerics *were* witches. To them, prayers were spells. So these things wound up in church collections, at least until someone forgot what they were for. Then they'd kind of walk out the door and wind up on someone's mantle at home. Or they'd start in the hands of one monarch or another, trickle down to noble families, blah blah blah. The British Museum has at least a dozen items we know are magical."

"Overcomplicated is actually good," Clara decided, hauling the conversation back on track. "All I need to do is find a weak spot, change that equation slightly, and it should collapse the whole thing."

"Is that. . . dangerous?" Jessamine asked slowly.

Ed laughed. "You should have seen this doorknob, back before Clara's first term at—"

"It can be," Clara interrupted, giving Ed a mock-stern glare. "And I told her about that already. But yeah," she added after a pause. "It's a *lot* of magic. It has to go somewhere."

"And that is why we have the pit," Jessamine said confidently. "Reuben?"

"My pleasure," he said, picking up the chalice. He walked to the very end of the worktable, at the back of the basement, and bent over. Clara maneuvered past the others to see what he was doing.

A wood trap door, roughly two feet square, was set into the floor of the basement, hinging up to rest against the back cinderblock wall. As Reuben opened the trap door, Clara realized its underside was covered in multiple layers of silk. She leaned over. "What's in it?"

"It's three feet deep and lined with iron plate," Jessamine grinned. "Inch-thick. I had a human friend cut up one of those trench plates they use to cover up roadwork, weld it into a box, and drop it in. This used to be a French drain with a sump pump, but magic works better for keeping moisture out."

"Nice," Ed said approvingly. "That should absorb any backlash."

"And look up," Jessamine suggested. Clara craned her head back and saw that the ceiling directly over the pit had been reinforced with four inch-thick pieces of lumber. "In case shrapnel flies upward. Just don't lean directly over it when it goes."

"Got it," Clara said.

Reuben gently placed the chalice in the bottom of the pit and Clara got to work.

As she studied the intricate equations swirling within the brass artifact, she realized they reminded her a bit of a washing machine. The general mass of the magic was rotating evenly, clockwise, around the cup's outer surface. A thin branch fed into the copper spike's blunt end, threading through to its tip and back into the cup's wall. Here and there, "suds" of magic—overly complicated numerators with a dozen or so terms apiece—would bubble up, float along the overall magical current, and then sink back in.

When Clara and her adoptive parents had lived in Colorado for a few months, their rental home had been blessed with a washer and dryer in the basement. Well, they *thought* they'd been blessed—the washing machine turned out to be massively unbalanced, setting up a horrific racket and shifting roughly across the floor every time they'd tried to use it. Clara's Dad had eventually given up, and they'd gone back to using the coin laundromats they'd been used to elsewhere.

It seemed an apt analogy.

Clara scooped up some of the ambient magic in the basement and slowly attached it to the cup's existing energy. She gradually formed the magic into a complementary equation, one that she connected to a specific spot in the overall swirl. She left two variables open, and once the entire thing was firmly in place, moving along with the general flow, she started feeding in more power.

The cup itself began rocking gently back and forth, and then more violently as Clara fed even more power into it. The old metal reached a breaking point before long, shattering fiercely along unseen stress lines. Its sides crashed against the iron of the pit, and Clara watched as the freed magic was quickly absorbed by the iron and grounded into the earth. In her eyes, the metal plate glowed a hot yellow for several moments after the chalice's destruction, before finally "cooling."

"Well, that's that," Reuben said with satisfaction, reaching down to gather the jagged pieces of brass and copper. He dumped them into a burlap bag and handed it to Sandy. "Should be safe enough for your friend to grind up, now."

"Now we need to find Alex," Jessamine said, leading everyone back upstairs. They didn't fit any better into the small living room at the front of the row house, but the crisp, generous morning light was a lot nicer than the harsh glare of the basement's lamps. "Ideas?"

"Use the same spell we used to find you and Elsie," Ed said at once. "But we'd need to *go* there, and we'd need the triplets."

"We should ask Elsie, too," Clara said. "She'll be in the mood for some revenge, and it wouldn't hurt to have more magic that I'm comfortable with."

"I strongly doubt either set of parents are going to be good with that," Trevor cautioned. "It hasn't even been a week since we got them out."

"I can't do it without the triplets," Clara insisted. "There may be more of you, and you may be more experienced, but you can't amplify magic the way they can. And I'm used to working with Elsie and Finlay. Maybe he can come, too."

"This isn't—" Reuben started.

"I'll talk to their parents," Jessamine said. "Reuben, find us a base near that shipping company."

~

"I wish Finlay had come," Elsie whispered as the adults set the room up.

"I wish we could have gotten a bigger room," Latoya frowned. Their room was advertised as a one-bedroom suite, but it was really just an oversized regular hotel room, and it made a tight fit for the eleven of them. Trevor was spreading a map of the area on the room's small desk-slash-table.

"It's the biggest one they have, actually," Reuben sighed. "And it has the benefit of being across the street from our target."

"I honestly wasn't expecting two high-rise towers," Jessamine said, looking at the massive buildings through the room's large window.

"The shipping company is on the ground floor, along with a deli and a couple of other shops," Reuben said, joining her. "Assuming the Paladins are a little lazy, Alex can't be far. There are a dozen other shipping and mailbox places within a five-mile radius. If they were keeping him further away, it seems like they'd have used one of those."

"I think we're ready," Trevor said, poking one last bit of magic into the map's corners to hold them down.

"Let's do it," Clara said. "Guys," she added, turning to her friends, "I want as much magic as possible. Like when we raised the first Border. We don't know where they're keeping Dad or how much metal is around him, so we'll need to punch hard."

"Got it," Idalia said firmly. Her sisters nodded agreement.

Clara turned to the map. "Ready."

She saw the magic in the room swirl toward her friends, who were standing behind her. The triplets began to chant, with Ed and Elsie joining in.

"In mondhellem Schein und sternenklarer Umarmung,
    Verlorenes Kind, finde Trost, kehre in diesen Raum zurück.
    Flüstern webt durch tiefe Schatten,
    Von Magie geführt, sicher und gesund."

A blinding white braid of magic whirled around Clara. She took it up, fine-tuning its equations until it began to glow ultraviolet. "Concentrate, guys," she ordered the adults. They'd *known* Alex Holdaway, knew what his presence in the web of witch awareness should feel like. Clara grabbed her mother's hand and seized that awareness, showing it to the magic her friends were weaving. *Find this one,* she thought, shaping the energy, feeling it stretch itself into the distance.

Clara stumbled backwards as the magic narrowed itself to a point and stabbed at the map. Ed caught her, and Clara saw the massive energy dissipate as everyone released the spell. "I didn't—" Clara said, regaining her balance.

"You did," Ed said, pointing past her at the map.

Clara stepped forward and looked down.

A small pinpoint, still smoking, had been burned into the map.

Directly atop the northernmost high-rise building across the street.

"Well, that's convenient," Sandy said flippantly.

Jessamine frowned. "It isn't. That's what, a twenty-story building?"

"Twenty-one," Reuben corrected.

"So now we have to figure out which floor he's on," Jessamine growled. "Which office suite. Which—"

"Huh," Latoya said. She'd wandered back to the window and was staring at the building in question.

"What is it?" Reuben asked, joining her.

"Well. . . I mean, I don't know a lot about office buildings," she said slowly.

"I do," Trevor said, joining them and all but blocking anyone else's view. "What?"

"Well, don't the elevators go up the middle?"

"Usually," Trevor confirmed. "Hmm. We're too low down to see the roof. Um. Give me a minute." With a rush of magic, he was gone.

"Rude," Latoya grumbled.

Everyone dispersed a bit. Jessamine and Reuben sat on the end of the bed, while Sandy and Latoya sat on the small couch. Ed offered the single office chair to Elsie, who declined.

"Your parents were really okay with this?" Clara asked quietly as the adults began low conversations.

"Your mom is pretty convincing," Idalia said.

"My moms *worship* the Holdaways," Elsie said. "Although you know, it's funny..."

Clara's brow wrinkled. "Funny how?"

"Well, moms asked your mom if she'd promise I wouldn't be in danger."

"And?"

Elsie's lips twitched into a small frown. "She said she'd make sure I was as far from danger as her own daughter."

Clara's eyes widened slightly. "And that was... okay?"

Elsie shrugged. "Apparently."

"That wasn't much of a promise," Ed said, darting a glance back at Jessamine, who had stopped speaking to Reuben and was staring evenly at the classmates.

"I made a promise I could keep," Jessamine said cooly. "I try not to make promises unless I'm sure I can keep them."

"But Mom, that doesn't mean—" Clara began.

"Now we're ready," Trevor announced as he reappeared in another rush of translocation magic. He was accompanied by a short, middle-aged man carrying what looked like a heavy book wrapped in layers of silk. "This is Ernest, a friend of mine," he added with a grin. "Human, but obviously in on it. Use the table," he instructed.

Ernest slid into the office chair, unwrapping the silk to reveal a chunky black laptop computer. He opened it, then looked around the room. "Ah," he said, nodding with satisfaction as he spotted the wall-mounted large-screen television. "And the remote... ah, there." He got up, scurried to the nightstand to retrieve the television's remote, and then returned to the desk. A few moments later, the TV was mirroring what was on the laptop's screen.

The witches turned to the TV, keeping as far as they could from both it and the laptop.

"Now, this is us," Ernest said, clicking away on the computer's touchpad. The TV showed a satellite view of the area, and Ernest zoomed it in so that the north office tower filled the screen. "And this is the tower you're after."

Trevor peered at the image. "Yeah, see that little hut on the roof? Close to the middle? That's the top of the elevator shaft."

Latoya stood to get a better look. "Okay, but then what's *that?*" she asked, pointing.

Trevor stared for a moment. "Honestly, it looks like a second elevator shaft on this side of the building."

"Couldn't it be air conditioning or something?" Reuben asked, also standing to get a better look.

"No, those are the silver-gray boxes over here," Trevor said, pointing. He turned to the window. "Hmm. Ernest, can you do the rotation thing, and show the side of the building?"

"Street view," he murmured, fiddling with the laptop. A moment later the side of the building was displayed on the TV. He peered at the laptop screen. "You know, that *is* odd."

"What is?" Jessamine asked.

"Well, look," Trevor said excitedly. "The entire building is covered in blue glass, right? Look, you can see the top of the second elevator shaft. Right under it, those top two floors *aren't* faced in glass. They're just blank white panels."

"So you think the second elevator is just the top two floors?" Latoya asked.

"Ernest, give us the same view of the other building? They're twins, right?" Trevor asked.

"Mirror images," Ernest said, nodding as he manipulated the image. "Except for that. The south building doesn't have a second elevator."

"So that's an odd addition," Trevor mused as Ernest shifted the view back to the north tower. "How recent is your image?"

"Mmm. . . about nine months ago. Pretty recent, for this stuff."

"Can you go back?"

"To older images? Yep. I need a different app for that. Just a sec." They waited as Ernest opened a new application and located the towers again. Initially, it was the same view they'd seen before, but with a few taps, the images started changing slightly. Shadows shifted positions, the overall color tone of the image changed, and—

"There!" Trevor exclaimed. "Look!" The second elevator was gone, and the building's face was uniform blue glass. "How far back?"

"A bit over. . . well, pretty old. This image is almost eighteen years back."

"When Alex and I were captured," Jessamine whispered.

"Coincidence," Reuben said, although he didn't sound convinced.

"Trevor, do the thing with the window," Jessamine ordered.

"It won't help," Trevor said, shaking his head. "Those towers are made from a steel-girder frame. The floors are poured onto steel decks, and filled with steel rebar. The whole structure will be electrically grounded, which means magically grounded. That window treatment is metallic, too, just like the Paladin house. There's enough metal in there to absorb all the magic a hundred of us could throw at it."

Jessamine frowned. "Then we need to go in."

Trevor mimicked her frown. "Jess, you can't just wander into those buildings. You have to check in with security, and most of the time you need a key-card to even use the elevators. *Computerized* key cards. Not very witch-friendly. And—"

"I have an idea," Elsie announced, still staring at the TV.

"What?" Jessamine asked.

"There's a condition."

"A *condition?*" Jessamine asked suspiciously.

"I get to go with you."

CHAPTER 17

INTO THE FIRE

"I don't know," Reuben said uncertainly. "Eleven is a big team. And more than half of them teenagers? It's not—"

"I have a feeling," Jessamine said quietly.

Reuben fell silent at once.

"It's a big place," Ed said, clearly attempting to counter Reuben's concern. "And we need Clara to—"

"It's fine," the older man said, shaking his head softly. "There's a reason Jess leads the team. Her. . . feelings. We've learned to trust them."

"So how do we begin?" Trevor asked.

"There's no way we're not already on cameras," Sandy pointed out.

They'd left Ernest behind in case they needed an ally on the outside, and teleported to the roof of the northern tower. They were all standing facing the weathered, extra-wide doors of what looked like a freight elevator—the elevator that they suspected went down only one or two floors further.

"We open it," Clara shrugged, stepping forward. "It's metal, but so was the door on the Paladins' house back in Vegas. Girls, some magic, if you please, and don't be afraid to inject a little anger into it."

«Our pleasure,» the triplets said, stepping forward in unison as their eyes began to glow.

"A moment?" Trevor said, holding up a hand.

The triplets stopped, their mouths half-open and their initial chant unuttered.

"Ok?" Idalia said, shaking her head as the synergistic bond with her sisters fizzled.

Trevor stepped up to the elevator and began examining it closely. He traced a finger down the thin space where the doors met. He examined the heavy steel frame in which the doors sat. He hunkered down and ran a finger along the doors' threshold. Finally, he stood, stepped to the right of the doors, and jabbed a finger toward the doorframe.

With a *ding,* the doors slid noisily open.

Trevor looked back to the group, shrugging and holding an arm into the elevator. "Seems easier since they know we're here, if they're watching."

"A metal box," Jessamine growled.

"It's a metal box regardless," Reuben said heavily, stepping in. "Might as well, and we have the batteries. There's plenty of room for us all."

"Eggs in one basket?" Sandy said as she joined him.

"Pair off with the kids," Jessamine ordered as she led everyone else inside. "Ed, stay with Trevor. Clara, you're with me. Sandy, take Elsie. Latoya—I suppose you three are a set?" she asked the triplets. "Take the girls," she added as the triplets nodded. "Off we go."

"Only one other button," Trevor said, pushing it.

Jessamine squared her shoulders and stood directly in front of the doors as they slid shut in front of her. With one hand, she pushed Clara behind her.

The elevator descended smoothly, *dinging* again as it reached the floor below them and the doors slid open.

A short corridor, no more than two strides long, connected the elevator to an unusual round room. As the witches stepped in, they saw that the center of the room contained a circular, waist-high reception desk, behind which sat a prim-looking younger woman. Her brown hair was up in a tight bun, and a pair of fashionable horn-rimmed glassed perched upon her nose.

As they stepped into the round room, curved doors slid silently shut behind them, blocking off a return to the elevator. Now, the room's only other exit was a single door to their right.

"Hello," the woman said cooly. "You're not expected. This entrance is typically available by appointment only."

Clara caught her balance as the room seemed to. . . move. Around her, everyone else was also steadying themselves. The sensation went away just as quickly as it came.

"So you just sit here waiting for unannounced visitors?" Jessamine asked.

The woman shrugged. "We all have a—oh, dear." Behind the desk, out of the witches' sights, a teakettle had started whistling. The woman rummaged in a drawer, withdrew a towel, and used it to lift a red-enameled kettle up and into sight. She sat it on the desk's upper surface, laid the towel next to it, and took her seat.

A plume of steam was still jetting from the kettle's spout, hissing softly in the otherwise silent room.

"We're here for Alex Holdaway," Jessamine said, blinking at the odd interruption. "It'll be easier for everyone if you just take us to him."

"I don't know anyone by that name," the woman said. "But I can check the directory, if you like."

"Fine."

The woman's attention flipped down as she perused something only she could see. Then her eyes snapped back up to the witches. "Sorry, nobody by that name here."

"Then I think we'd like to look around," Jessamine said, her voice hard.

The woman shrugged. "I can call Security," she warned. She didn't sound especially worried.

"You've already done that," Jessamine said.

"Then I won't try to stop you," the woman shrugged. Her looked down again and began fussing with some papers, ignoring them completely.

"Let's go," Jessamine ordered.

They all walked toward the door to their right. It opened easily, and they all pushed through into a room that seemed completely dark. The door swung shut behind them.

"Aziz, light," Reuben muttered, but the room suddenly snapped into brightness as its overhead lights came on, revealing a half-dozen trenchcoat-covered Paladins.

Except these were. . . *more,* Clara saw at once. Their heads were fully enclosed in burnished metallic helmets with huge, green glass eyes. Flexible metal tubing snaked down their arms from a bulbous backpack, terminating in metal-and-leather gloves. Their trench-coats were newer than the ones she'd seen before, not only free of dust but made of some shinier material. *Ballistic nylon,* she realized after a split second.

"Stand down," one of them—Clara couldn't tell which one had spoken—ordered in a robotic voice. They all raised their right arms, fists clenched, pointing them at the witches. The adult witches began spreading out, those with charges assigned keeping the teen behind them.

"We're here for my husband," Jessamine said boldly.

Gas won't work, I bet they're on a closed loop, Clara thought furiously. The ambient magic in the room was all but nil thanks to all the steel around them: Clara couldn't spot anything more than a couple of anemic-looking, battered symbols drifting listlessly through the air.

"Stand down and you'll be taken unharmed," the robotic voice repeated. "Resist and we will incapacitate you. Or worse."

"We'll try worse," Jessamine said through clenched teeth.

Magic flared as Jessamine and her team tapped their crystal batteries. Much of the magic immediately fled toward the ceiling, walls, and floors, but Clara lassoed it with her mind and shoved it back toward the group, where it sank into the witches' bodies, writing uncomfortably. The adults crafted their spells in fractions of a second, and Clara almost absentmindedly corrected them, simplifying terms, reducing equations, tightening the math. The Paladins saw nothing of this, of course.

What they *did* see were five attacks cleverly designed to combat this particular foe.

With a shouted *"Φωτιά πετρελαίου!"* Sandy cast a black-green slickness at the feet of the Paladins, a viscous fluid that spread between their feet and then burst into flames. All six took a step back, putting them nearly at the room's far wall, but the fluid simply followed. And it kept coming as Sandy fed more magic into it, pooling thickly between the six armored humans.

"Ka Pahu Ka Moana!" Trevor shouted, and suddenly the thick, burning oil was splattering upward, adhering to the Paladins' coats.

In the same instant, Reuben yelled, *"Intensivieren!"* and the flames turned white-hot. Little plumes of black smoke began rising. The Paladins were now beating their coats to try and extinguish the flames, but it wasn't working—instead, they were simply spreading the burning oil to their hands and arms.

Jessamine had the last trick. *"Eisblöcke!"* she said sharply, and chunks of the ceiling—which seemed to be painted concrete, and not foam drop-ceiling tiles as Clara had expected—began cracking loose and falling directly onto the Paladins' helmeted heads. It certainly didn't kill any of them, but it definitely disoriented them, and half of them went down to one knee—giving the still-burning oil a chance to spread further up their protective uniforms.

The triplets must have been given a crystal, because the next barked spell was *«Bitte schmelzen!»* In Clara's vision, an impossibly concentrated plait of beryl-colored magic looped upwards, brushing the broken ceiling before it crashed down on the Paladins. At once, their metal backpacks and helmets began melting and sagging, glowing cherry-red with heat.

Some of the Paladins were screaming now, clawing at their helmets' latches and struggling to release their backpacks. But at least two kept their wits about them, once again aiming clenched fists at the witches and triggering some mechanism in their gloves. Orange-red goo shot out from their wrists, spattering Sandy and Trevor. Their magic sparked visibly, and Clara could see the ordered equations simply shattering.

Sprinklers hidden in the ceiling finally popped out and began soaking everyone with cold water. This didn't put out Sandy's magic oil-fire, but it did start dispersing the oil enough that the fire burned through its fuel more quickly, flicking out in just moments. Meanwhile, Ed must have tapped a crystal as well, because he thrust both palms forward and shouted, *"Ο Μωυσής έκανε λάθος!"* The water in the room rushed toward the witches, rose up before them in a wall, and then curled down to crash at the Paladins' feet. All six were knocked down now, struggling and slipping in the still-flaring oil.

"Give up?" Jessamine roared, her long hair plastering itself to her face and back. Not waiting for a reply, she raised one hand and yelled, *"Чай — водка!"*

Only Clara could actually see the magic: a block of equations, glowing a sullen brown and distended not into loops and curves but into angles and points, formed up over the Paladins. It encased the air, making it denser and heavier, before crashing down on them. All six Paladins were smashed flat to the floor, water and still-burning oil splashing in every direction.

None of them so much as twitched when Jessamine's magic dissipated.

"Trop c'est trop," Reuben muttered wearily, and the overhead sprinklers shut down.

"Status?" Jessamine asked, panting slightly. Everyone declared their crystals to be at three-quarter charge or better.

"What was that spray?" Reuben asked as Trevor and Sandy brushed the last of it off their soaking clothes.

"Some kind of gel with iron rust particles in it," Trevor said with a grimace. "Didn't hurt, but threw me for a loop. If they'd managed to get a lot of it on me, I dunno—might have been a bad day."

"Lavaggio a secco," Latoya ordered. Suddenly, everyone's clothes were dry.

"Conserve, please," Jessamine sighed.

"What? My crystal was full," Latoya shrugged. "You guys did all the work. I'm no good at physical combat, and this room was too small for illusions to do much good. Thank you for the assist," she added to the triplets.

"No," Idalia said with a smile.

"Problem," Johanna finished.

Latoya's eyebrows rose.

"It stops after a while," Ed assured her wearily. "Just try not to talk to them for a few minutes."

"You're just," Harriett said with a mock sneer.

"Jealous," Johanna said, mimicking the expression.

"Okay," Jessamine said. "Let's—" she turned back to the door they'd come through, only to find a blank, convex section of wall. "Where's the door?"

"Sealed us in," Trevor said. "And I don't see any others."

"It has to be this," Clara said, pointing to the right. Centered on the wall there was a nine-by-nine grid, each grid space about six inches square. "But I don't know how to open it."

Reuben walked over to inspect it, prodding each of the grids in turn. "None of them seem to be a trigger of any kind. Could it be magic?"

"Not much of a holy relic," Jessamine said doubtfully. "And with all the iron around here. . . still, Clara?"

Clara had already shifted her vision to examine the wall. "There *is* magic in it," she said slowly, running a finger along the grid lines.

"But I can't tell what it's supposed to do." She turned to the downed Paladins. "Are those guys gonna stay that way?"

"I got it. Kids, give me a hand," Latoya said. They began opening the Paladins' trenchcoats and casting the modified mind-wipe spell Clara had developed.

Veil, something whispered in Clara's mind, but she ignored it. There were more pressing matters before them. "So look," she said after a moment. "Each square has a very slightly different equation in it. They're all short, and I don't see how they connect to one another. But every time you touch it—" and here, she laid a hand in one grid square to test her theory "—the magic kind of spins away. When you remove your hand, it comes back."

"Maybe it needs a human hand?" Ed suggested.

Clara blinked. "I hadn't thought of that," she said, nodding slowly. "Possibly. Can we try one?"

"I got it," Jessamine said grimly.

"Mom, don't—" Clara said in alarm.

"I'm not cutting his hand off, baby. Reuben, give me a hand, here." They finished stripping the trenchcoat off a man Latoya had just mind-wiped, and dragged him over to where Clara was standing. "Any square in particular?"

"Just try one," Clara suggested.

"Hai dei fili che ti tengono fermo," Reuben recited, and the unconscious man—still in a dented and heat-damaged helmet—rose up from the ground like a puppet. Reuben moved his hands slowly, and the human's hands mirrored the witch's movements. With a bit of effort, Reuben was able to get one of the Paladin's hands planted in the lower-leftmost grid square.

Clara watched as the other squares brightened and their equations changed a bit. "This one," she guessed, pointing to a square that had brightened the most, and changed to more closely resemble the equation in the first square. Reuben complied, and Clara directed him to touch two more before the entire grid split in half, hinging inwards, along with the empty wall beneath it.

"Nice job," Jessamine said, patting her daughter on the back. "Latoya?"

"Just finishing. This took my crystal down about a quarter, by the way."

"Worth it. Let's go."

They stepped into a doorless hallway. It must have been intended as some kind of art gallery, because paintings were hung every few inches. Some were huge, like the one directly in front of them depicting a pastoral scene of shepherds guarding a flock, while others were smaller.

"No doors," Elsie observed.

"No," Ed corrected her, looking at the opening they'd come through, "disguised doors. This one was a painting of some kind of Renaissance wine party." He looked left and right down the hallway. "I'd guess the big ones are doors. Here," he gestured to their left, which was an enormous portrait of some monarch or other. "Definitely this one," he said of the shepherds, "and probably that one," he added, pointing to the right of the shepherds at a piece showing a medieval picnic. "Likely the one at the other end, too." That one showed the inside of an ancient church, with a haloed officiant dispensing bread to the crowd. "Which should we try first?"

"Shepherds," Jessamine said without hesitation. "It's closest. Clara?"

Clara stepped up and examined the painting. "There's nothing about it at all," she said with surprise. "Not a bit of. . . hmm. Wait a minute." She stepped closer to the painting, grasping its heavy gilded frame, and started tugging. "I thought it might swing away," she said after a moment. "There's something behind it, but I—"

Elsie stepped forward and pushed on the edge of the frame, sliding the painting sideways along the wall a few inches, revealing a square of aged stone set into the wall itself. In the center of the stone was a circular depression.

"Oh. Thanks," Clara said, focusing on the stone. "What made you think of that?"

"Literally every door in my moms' flat is a pocket door," Elsie sighed. "Every time I come back to school, I have to remind myself what *push* and *pull* mean."

"Can you figure this one out?" Jessamine asked Clara.

"This one's simpler. It's half an equation, like a lock. You need the other half, a key of some kind. You just put it in the depression."

"So if we *don't* have the key," Reuben prompted.

"Can you just disable it like you did in the dorm?" Ed asked.

Clara shook her head. "No, I don't think so. That was a doorknob. It was keeping the door closed, so getting rid of it let the door open. This is. . . it's hard to explain. The door *is* closed, and it needs magic to open it."

Trevor had been examining the square of stone. "This looks like something they pulled from somewhere else and brought here. The stonework is *really* old."

"The magic looks old, too," Clara agreed.

"How so?" Reuben asked.

"It's. . . finicky. It's all swirls and lace and. . . *pretention.* It's hard to follow."

"I'm sure those weren't the only Paladins in the building," Latoya pointed out.

"I have a feeling they're waiting to see what we do," Jessamine said, looking around. "I don't see any cameras, but that doesn't mean they aren't there."

"Can you crack it?" Elsie asked. "If not, we could always try just blowing through."

"And possibly injuring Alex, if he's on the other side," Jessamine said with a frown. "I'd rather—"

"No, I can get it," Clara interrupted. "I just need a second to find the pattern. Um. Does anyone have anything. . . soft? Like, clay? I think I can make the key, but it needs something physical."

"As big as that depression?" Harriett asked.

"Yeah."

"Just a sec." She reached into her pocket, withdrew something, and popped it in her mouth. "Give me yours," she told her sisters as she started chewing. The other two triplets complied, and within a few moments Harriett produced a white glob of well-chewed gum, offering it to Clara.

"Gross, Harriett," Clara said. But she took it anyway, staring at it in the palm of her hand for several long moments. "I need a little magic."

"Got it," Ed said. He put a hand on Clara's shoulder and began tapping his crystal.

Ambient magic spun around them, and Clara quickly grabbed it and forced it into the blob of gum. She began working the rubbery substance with her thumbs, pushing it this way and that as the magic sunk in. Then she reached up, slapped the gum into the depression in the rock, and *pushed.*

The painting swung away from the wall, and the wall. . . *folded.* Clara's eyes almost bent trying to follow the wall's motion, because it was moving in far more than the usual three dimensions. After a few seconds of *clicks* and *clacks,* the wall was gone, and the room beyond illuminated itself in soft, warm yellows.

"It's a library," Reuben breathed, taking a step in. "Oh, I would pay big money to just hide out in here for a while."

"We don't have time," Jessamine said, her voice tense and frustrated. "Let's try the next—"

"Company!" Latoya called.

The portrait of a monarch had swung away from them, revealing another Paladin, clad in the same helmet and other gear as the last batch had been.

"No," Elsie said calmly, followed by, *"Edrychwch y ddwy ffordd cyn croesi."* A visible wave of concussive force slammed into the man. The iron plates in his trenchcoat grounded some of the magic, but the rest was more than sufficient to send him flying back through the opening. The painting swung back into place, locking with a *click.*

"Tha dìomhaireachdan gu bràth," Reuben said, making an arcane

gesture at the painting. "Iron or no, that'll keep it shut for a good while. Where to next?"

"Picnic," Jessamine ordered.

Clara quickly examined the painting. "This needs three people," she said. "Must be something important. And they're each meant to have a key. But. . ." she trailed off as she interpreted the equations. "It's not as complicated. It's almost like music. Um." She paused for another moment. "It's just got to be done in sync, I think. Triplets?"

"Where's it go?" Harriett asked, stepping forward with her sisters.

"Here, here, and here," Clara said, indicating the spots on the painting. "It wants, like, a chord. I don't know music that well."

"Piano lessons since we were six," Idalia sighed. "Glad it was worth it." She took a breath. **«Ready?»**

The air *sang* as the triplets' three-in-one magic lanced out, chiming a C, E, and G. The frame of the painting began to resonate, tiny waves of magic spilling off it and grounding themselves in the steel studs of the walls. But the girls had hit it perfectly, and after a couple of seconds, the painting swung away from the wall.

"Armory," Trevor said at once as he and Sandy stepped into the room. Clara poked her head in and saw racks of black trenchcoats, rows of helmets on shelves, stacks of boots still in their cardboard boxes, and more.

Jessamine snarled. "We're wasting time."

"All in on the church, then," Latoya said, strolling to the end of the hallway.

Clara rushed to keep up. "There's no magic at all," she said, confused.

Latoya tugged at one side of the frame, and then the other. The painting swung away smoothly on the second try, revealing a second artwork. This one was a set of nested metallic discs, each one's center set slightly off from the one it sat within. The result reminded Clara vaguely of a diagram of the solar system.

"Oh, I love these," Trevor said, stepping up. "Purely mechanical.

Hmm." He leaned closer, and Clara realized that the edges of each circular plate were etched with tiny symbols. Trevor put one hand on the innermost disc and began rotating it, then worked outward to the next one, and the one after that. "It's basically a combination lock," he said as he worked. "These were huge in DaVinci's time. The engraving usually contains a key to the whole thing. I wonder where they got this? The only one I knew of this large was in the Vatican's. . . ah."

With a *chunk,* the wall swung away from them.

They stepped into a thoroughly modern office space. Gray, industrial carpet covered the floor, running from one lighter-gray wall to the next. Foam ceiling tiles ran between harsh fluorescent lighting fixtures. To their left was a small office, and Reuben stepped into it. "Nobody around, but it's been in use. Computer's still on." He began rifling through the papers on the desk.

Next to the office were two restrooms, followed by another office. Sandy took this one, also poking through the papers and folders that were stacked on the desk.

"Why aren't there any people?" Jessamine asked.

"I expect they've evacuated," Trevor said. "But look, there's another door at the end."

The rest of the group walked past the second office, and then stopped cold. A reinforced window, with wire mesh embedded in the glass, separated this hallway from the room beyond. In that room were three stern-looking men wearing black security uniforms. Their hands rested lightly on pistols at their waists. One of them stood on the other side of the door that connected their room to the hallway, as if daring them to try and go through.

The guard closest to them reached out to one side, never breaking eye contact with the group, and pushed a large red button.

A steel grate crashed down from above, all but covering the large reinforced window and the door. They could still make out the guards' eyes, tracking them.

"I guess we go back," Trevor said with mock cheerfulness. There were no other obvious doors or windows in the hall. "If anyone needs to go, now's the time."

"Not funny," Jessamine growled, turning back. "Reuben, Sandy, let's go."

"Nothing much of interest," Reuben said as he emerged from the office. "Meeting schedules, some shipping manifests, that kind of thing. I suppose if we had more time—"

"We don't," Jessamine snapped. "We need to—"

"Mom, wait," Clara said, stopping and looking around.

"What?"

"There's. . . we're missing something. The dimensions of the building don't add up. We've skipped a big section."

Jessamine focused on her daughter. "How so?"

Clara started drawing on the wall with one finger. Without ambient magic, she couldn't actually *draw,* but it helped her focus. Look, we came in from the exterior wall—the elevator. And then we turned right. But then we exited. . . *right* again. We should be outside."

"That round room was on a turntable," Ed said. "Had to be."

Clara nodded. "That makes sense." She considered it. "So it must have gone a hundred and eighty degrees around. So we actually exited *left,* fought the Paladins, and *then* went right." Her finger traced imaginary walls. "So if it was right again to get to this point. . . they herded us. I think we need to go back through that round room."

"The problem being," Reuben said heavily, pointing at the wall, "is that the door closed, and there's no lock on this side."

They all turned to look, and Jessamine groaned. "I'm just blasting through," she said angrily.

"No, wait," Clara said, hurrying to examine the wall. "There's a spell on this side." She cast about, looking for—"There! Look!"

In one corner of the wall, right near the floor, was another artifact set into the wall. This one was tiny, and as Clara crouched down to get a better look, she realized it was made of wood.

Reuben joined her. "No telling how old it is," he said slowly, rubbing a thumb over the worn surface, "but it looks well-used, at least. What's the spell?"

Clara's brows knotted in confusion. "I don't understand it. It's all. . . it's like it's *backwards*. And it's words. Well, maybe symbols. But not numbers."

"You mean like a mirror image?" Latoya asked.

Clara's brow wrinkled further. "No. . . it's *moving* backwards."

"Sketch some of it for me," Reuben instructed, releasing a bit of magic into the air.

Clara seized the power and a glowing replica of the wood's magic shimmered to life.

Reuben studied it closely. "It looks like Hebrew," he said hesitantly. "It's a right-to-left written language. That's why it seems like it's moving backward to you."

"I didn't know Jews *had* a magical tradition," Ed said.

"Oh, extensive, back in medieval times," Reuben said. "This looks like a simple locking spell. There's. . . oh, I can't quite recall it. An adjuration for opening locks. Hmm." He looked around. "We'll need some dust. Or dirt."

"Right back," Latoya said at once. She ducked back into the office she'd been searching, and came back with a palmful of rich brown dirt. "Potted plant. Will this do?"

"It should, if I can remember the adjuration correctly," Reuben said, taking a pinch of the dirt. "בשמות שנים עשר האנגלים, אני מצטער עליך לפתוח." he intoned, flicking the fingerful of dirt at the piece of wood.

Clara recognized the magic this time, the more familiar mathematical equations springing to life and following the dirt. Her mind tweaked and corrected it almost instantly, and when the first specks of soil hit the small square of wood, the wall *clicked* and folded inward.

"Nice," Reuben said. Latoya dropped the rest of the dirt onto the carpet, brushing her hands as they all moved back through the opening and into the painting-filled hallway.

Which also contained three more Paladins.

"Absolutely not," Elsie said, pushing her way to the front. The Paladins were already raising their fists, but before they could fire any rust-laden goop at the team, Elsie raised on palm and barked, *"Tân uffern tanllyd conflagration hylosgi coelcerth!"*

A *torrent* of flame blasted down the hallway, singeing paintings and making the witches recoil from its heat. Elsie's dark hair blew away from her head in the heat-infused wind, and everyone turned away from the overpowering brightness. When the flames died down, the Paladins were at the far end of the room in a smoking heap, piled beneath the smoldering remains of the monarch's portrait.

Belatedly, sprinkler heads popped out of the ceiling and began soaking everyone again.

"Trop c'est trop," Reuben muttered again, and the sprinklers sputtered once more and stopped. "I loathe being wet."

Jessamine pushed her way to the front, clapping Elsie on the back as she went. "Excellent work. You have a real. . . flare for combat magic."

Elsie grinned.

Clara's mother led them back into the room where they'd battled the six Paladins, all of whom were still unconscious. She turned to the convex section of wall. "We need," she said with authority, "to go through that."

"It's almost certainly lined with steel or iron," Trevor said, rapping the wall gently with his knuckles. "I'm not sure how we—"

"Couldn't we teleport to the roof and use the elevator again?" Ed asked.

Reuben shook his head. "Translocation magic would be dangerous from inside here. And I have no doubt the elevator is locked down."

«Stand back,» the triplets advised. **«Clara?»**

"Yeah, why not," Clara agreed. She stepped forward, raising her palms toward the curved wall. The triplets arranged themselves behind her, and everyone else stood well back. Clara *felt* the triplets draw from whatever crystal or crystals they were holding, and *felt* the thick ropes of magic come from them. In her mind, the room began glowing with a white, pearlescent heat.

She gathered that raw magic into her hands, forcing it to equations of breaking and shattering. Equations designed to break apart molecules, to crack *atoms* if necessary. Her math was tight, precise, and implacable.

She flung it at the wall.

«Oscail an bealach,» the triplets commanded at the same instant.

The wall didn't even fight back.

Where once there had been an outward-bowed section of wall now lay a thick, wide pile of white-and-gray powder.

"That," Harriett said happily as the glow faded from her eyes.

"Was neat," Idalia finished.

The eleven witches strode through, noting that the circular desk was now unoccupied.

The room's only door was to their left. "Which direction, Clara?" Jessamine asked.

"It has to be straight across. I don't think that door goes anywhere, now."

"Straight ahead it is," Jessamine said grimly. "Girls, do you have enough in your batteries?"

"For," Idalia said.

"One more," Harriett finished.

"Then let's do it," Clara said.

«Oscail an bealach,» the triplets repeated, once again sending Clara a torrent of synergistically amplified, three-in-one magic. The curved section of wall opposite them was reduced to dust, revealing another hallway.

"Bingo," Jessamine said as she marched past Clara, with everyone else falling in behind her.

"This feels more like a lab," Reuben remarked as they stepped past the ruined wall. "I'll check this one," he said, taking an office to their left. "I've got the two on the right," Trevor said.

The rest of the group continued around a dogleg turn. "Leave these," Jessamine ordered, jerking her chin at two empty offices on their left.

"That looks like a conference room at the end," Sandy said, starting to walk past Jessamine. "Oh."

They stopped in front of another security room. This one was smaller, and contained only a single, terrified-looking guard. He glanced to his right, where another giant red button lay just a step out of his reach. Behind the guard was another reinforced window, overlooking a room that reminded Clara of a hospital operating room.

A man lay on one of the two hospital beds.

"I wouldn't," Jessamine warned the guard. She held up a hand and started drawing magic from her battery, creating a glowing ball of energy.

Bawomb!

A wave of force so powerful, so concentrated that it actually made a sound, crashed onto Sandy and Jessamine from above. Both went to one knee, and Jessamine's magic was scattered instantly. A second later, a steel grate crashed down over the window and adjacent door

Clara looked up and saw an object of some kind embedded in the concrete of the ceiling. It was glowing hotly in her vision, vermillion equations boiling noisily across its surface. "Ed," she said, jerking her chin up.

"Nusileiskite čia," he ordered, gesturing at the object. Clara fine-tuned his magic in flight, and it neatly snipped the slab free from the ceiling. It crashed down just behind Jessamine and Sandy, sputtering angrily as its magic leached into the steel rebar in the floor.

"We're getting in that room," Jessamine said, her jaw clenched. Her eyes locked onto the guard through the slats of the steel curtain. "If you have backup, you'd better call them now. In fact, if you have family, you'd better call *them* now."

Clara looked past the grating, and couldn't see any ambient magic that she could work with. With this much metal around them, any magic that wasn't safe in a crystal or actively being used was being sucked into the building's structure. She quickly examined the fallen artifact, and saw that the casing that had held it in the ceiling was lined with a thick layer of silk. *Clever.* "Latoya," she said quietly. "Can you glamour that guard?"

"Not through all that," she said softly, crouching slightly until she could see the guard's eyes.

"But that's the only reason?"

"Uh-huh." The guard was beginning to sweat, his eyes flicking back and forth between the witches who were glaring at him.

"Then do it. I'll get it through the grate," Clara said.

Latoya hesitated, then nodded. "Here we go." She took a deep breath and began chanting softly.

"Faoi ghlas bog airgid na gealaí,
    A sióg wile, scéim mystic.
    Físíonn cogarnaí trí thrasna na hoíche,
    Grá agus dílseacht i trance.
    Teaghráin chroí ag imirt le fae allure,
    Ceangailte le draíocht, go deo."

Clara didn't bother translating; something in her memories recognized the ancient Fae spell. Instead, she focused on whirling the magic into a tight, pencil-thin beam. She pushed it through a slat in the steel grate, maneuvered it past the mesh embedded in the glass, and eased it toward the guard's forehead.

His eyes glazed over immediately. A moment later, he reached out distractedly and pressed a control.

The steel grating began rolling upward.

"I móinéir glasa áit a imríonn scáthanna,
    Draíocht sióg, idir oíche agus lá.
    Focail glimmered cosúil le drúchtíní titim,
    Croí ceangailteach i drall milis.
    Cogar géilliúil, corda draíocht,
    Rince na cinniúint, ag faeries grá."

Latoya continued her chant, and Clara focused on keeping the magic rolling. It was interrupted briefly as the grate moved upward, but Clara simply directed it through the next-lower slat, and then the next, and then the next, until the grate had retracted fully into the ceiling.

The guard pressed another button and the door began buzzing.

Sandy leapt up and grabbed the handle, pulling the door toward her.

"Wait here," Jessamine ordered.

"He'll be fine," Latoya said, letting the flow of magic trickle and fade. The guard's eyes remained glazed over, and he simply stood, swaying slightly back and forth, a faint smile playing over his lips.

A minute later, Sandy and Jessamine returned. Sandy was at the foot of a hospital bed, steering it through the doorways, and Jessamine was at the head, pushing. Hot tears were streaming down both their faces. "Let's go," Clara's mom ordered.

They rushed back down the hallway, retrieving Reuben and Trevor as they went. In the round room, Clara and Ed rushed to the sliding portions of the wall that blocked the elevator. These were easy to deal with—they simply wedged their fingers into the relatively wide gap and *pulled.* Then it was into the elevator, whose doors were still gaping open. Once they were in, Reuben jabbed at the "R" button until the doors finally closed and the elevator began moving.

"This can't be it," Sandy said nervously as the metal box ascended.

"I truly don't think they were expecting us," Jessamine said, her voice tense.

When the doors slid open, two more Paladins were waiting, standing just feet from the elevator opening.

But now all eleven witches had access to the rooftop's ambient magic.

Four of them lashed out at once.

"Cyfergyd," Elsie said.

"Gehirnerschütterung," Reuben snarled.

"Cerbokomocio," Ed snapped.

"Agyrázkód," Trevor ordered.

The two Paladins were blasted backwards in a wave of force that made Clara's ears ring. They fetched up hard against the walls of the building's main elevator core, sliding down into an insensate pile.

«Tóg abhaile sinn, bóithre ehterial,» the triplets commanded, and they were all surrounded by a wash of gentle, rainbow-colored magic that spirited them away.

CHAPTER 18
AFTERMATH

"He's coming out of it," Dr. Mumbai said.

They'd teleported from the rooftop in Illinois to Jessamine's row home in Philadelphia, and then almost directly to the nearest Border and into Underhill. From that Border, they'd risked the ire of the government and teleported to a small village named Twylage, where a witch doctor named Gian Mumbai had left his own dinner to see to Alex.

"Give him a little room," the doctor suggested gently as everyone clustered around Alex's bed. "They had him on a human drug named Propofol and it'll take him another half-hour or so to be fully rid of it."

Everyone except Jessamine and Clara backed off as Alex's eyelids fluttered open. He blinked a few times as his eyes focused, and then broke into a broad grin as he saw his wife. "Jess," he rasped.

"You're safe now," she assured him quietly, taking his hand in hers and squeezing tightly. "You're safe at last." Tears were trickling down her face. "And honey, I have someone who'd like to meet you." She nodded toward the other side of the bed.

Alex turned his head, and blinked a few more times. Then tears welled up in his eyes and spilled down his face. "Clara?" he asked, his voice tight. "My baby, baby girl!" he sobbed.

"Dad," Clara croaked as she leaned in and gave her father an awkward bed-hug. She lay her head on his chest, letting the crisp sheets soak up her own tears.

"How long, Jess?" Alex asked roughly, using his free hand to wipe his eyes.

"She's graduating in a few weeks," Jessamine said, laughing and crying at once. "The Thorns raised a pretty special girl."

Alex sniffed heavily as his wife bent down for her own hug, and for several long minutes, they just held each other tightly, a family at long last.

"I DON'T EVEN KNOW where they had me," Alex said. "But they kept me in that same facility for..."

"Seventeen years," Jess said, patting his hand. Once the drug had worn off, Dr. Mumbai had cleared Alex to walk, and everyone had relocated to a nearby inn for a meal and some rest. "What were they doing to you?"

"Research," Alex said heavily, slurping up a spoonful of soup. "They took decent care of me, I guess. I mean, they fed me, I got to exercise a little, but it was almost always the inside of that room, or somewhere else in the same building."

"What kind of research?" Reuben asked.

"Magic detectors. Magic suppressors. Shields against magic. You name it. They kept me drugged out a lot—there's a lot of hazy time in my memory. Sometimes they'd actually take me up to the roof, surrounded by iron and with an iron chain around one wrist, and make me cast spells at different artifacts they've come up with. They think they're—"

"Holy relics, we know," Jessamine said. "But Alex, they couldn't just *force* you to cast spells. They'd—"

"They were capable of being pretty. . . rough," he said, his eyes darting to Clara and her friends at one end of the table. "I resisted, early on, after they'd separated us. But then it got. . ."

"I understand," Jessamine said quickly, patting his free hand again.

"Risky to let you out on the roof, though," Latoya murmured.

"Not really," Alex sighed. "They got a pretty good feel for how much magic I could gather in a given amount of time, and they managed it pretty well. They never let me get enough to teleport down the hall, let alone off that roof."

"And it was all testing their relics?" Trevor asked with a frown.

"Mostly," Alex confirmed. "Seeing how much tolerance I had for iron nearby. How much tolerance I could build up, which wasn't much. But they have *hundreds* of artifacts. I'm pretty sure they stored most of them in that same building. Any chance you—"

Jessamine shook her head. "We were there for you."

"How did you know?"

She grinned. "A Protection Spell."

His eyes widened and he laughed. "The lodestar? Really?"

"Really. And they'd shipped it to Las Vegas, and we found the box with the label still on it. That got us to the building. Then Clara and her friends used a tracing spell to find you in the aether."

Alex's eyes managed to widen further. "Through all that metal?"

Jessamine grinned. "Clara's pretty special. And she has some pretty special friends."

"Apparently," he said with an answering grin. But it faded as he added, "Still, getting hold of their artifact storage would have been a massive win."

"I'm sure they're moving everything out even as we speak," Trevor said. "And that was our last real lead on permanent physical locations. It'll be back to waiting for them to make a move and then tracking them back to a bolt-hole."

"Oh, I wouldn't say that," Reuben said airily. *"Maintenant, où ai-je mis cette chose,"* he said, and a stack of manilla folders appeared on the table in front of him. He pushed his own soup bowl out of the way and began flipping through the folders. "Purloined these from that office I ransacked while you all were rescuing our damsel in distress. Something caught my eye... ah, here it is."

He flipped a folder open, turned it around so everyone could see, and pointed to the upper corner. "This address appears on a *lot* of papers. Shipping manifests, but also basic utility bills. This one's for the lease on that lab space they had you in, Alex."

Jessamine examined the page and then chuckled in spite of herself. "Of course it is."

"What?" Clara asked from the far side of the table.

"Apparently," Jessamine said with a wry grin, "the Paladins keep their billing office in Salem, Massachusetts."

"We're going to need some help," Reuben added.

❧

WEEK TWO WEDNESDAY AFTERNOON

"This is vexing," Jessamine said with a frown.

She and her team had spent all of Tuesday attempting to round up support for a move on the Paladins' Salem office, and they'd come up empty-handed.

"It's the government," Sandy sighed. "Nobody wants to support the counter-hunting effort anymore. The Witchers have everyone convinced we're just getting the Paladins riled up, and that if we leave them alone they'll settle down."

"They're not honeybees," Jessamine growled.

"I know, but they've pulled all the funding. No more houses in the Ordinary. I mean, you pay for your own place in Philly, but they're canceling the lease on my loft in New York City. My family's on the Witchers' side—they won't pay for it, either. I can operate from Underhill, but..."

Jessamine let out a heavy sigh. "But then it's Anchor to Anchor to get to the right Border, teleport from there, and no place to safely fall back and recoup if needed. No place to store supplies. I know, I know."

"Dan Saucedo and Elli Trevino were so frustrated, they handed in their resignations and disappeared. Neither of them enjoyed any kind of significant family financial support. Last anyone knew, they were going to Easter Island," Reuben said, reading off a list. "I got hold of Jim Perry. Says he was ready to step down anyway. I mean, the man *is* ninety years old, so I get it. Jeanette Jenkins was going to take over his team, but she was offered a position on one of the Council committees. Evan and Weijan are thinking of settling down near the capital."

"What about Kendall's team?" Jessamine asked.

Sandy shook her head. "Kendall and Claudette are expecting, and after. . . well, you, they'd planned to give it up. Reethi still hasn't recovered from that injury last year, and I think Ani is just tired of it all."

"Sora's out as well," Latoya said. "She barely even agreed to talk to me, and I got the definite impression someone had made some subtle threats against her family if she didn't give up the life."

"Witcher," Jessamine growled.

"Probably. But her whole team's out. Sasha, Kaoru, and Danbi, which actually surprised me. She *did* refuse to speak to me. And frankly, I think they're just freaked out. They were pretty close to Dimmick."

"Inside help along with a conspiracy to stop counter-hunters. And some good old-fashioned fear. Make the Ordinary unsafe for witches. Drive everyone *here*." Jessamine's eyes were flashing with anger.

"Unless you're in one of Witcher's private, protected resorts," Trevor added.

"So it's the six of us," Jessamine said flatly. "Against who-knows-what in Salem."

"I think you mean twelve," Clara said firmly. "No, hear me out," she said when her mother opened her mouth to protest. "We did fine in Schaumburg. You need the help. And personally, I want to see this through. What if this is, like, the Paladins' global HQ or something?"

"That's an office in the Vatican, we think," Reuben said, "but it could well be their North American headquarters. Or provide valuable leads. We've never run across any kind of central authority before."

"It could also be a holding company where the bills get sent," Sandy pointed out.

"Well, yes, but," Reuben said, holding up a hand. "I had Ernest run property records and do some digging. Here, he printed a map." Reuben rummaged in the stack of folders in front of him and withdrew a folded sheet of paper. It unfolded into a large satellite view of several blocks surrounding Salem Commons. One narrow street was circled in red ink. "This is the address on all those documents," Reuben said, tapping the map with a finger. "A lovely duplex that's been converted into office space. But it's owned by a holding company that also owns most of the rest of the properties on the street. So it's quite possible that this *is* some sort of central authority."

"What holding company?" Jessamine asked.

Reuben shuffled through papers again. "Protectoris, LLC."

Jessamine snorted. "Subtle. Okay, that doesn't sound like some kind of general real estate company."

"Ah, it's not," Reuben said, raising a finger. "They have small holdings all of the US. Usually single homes, scattered across the contiguous forty-eight."

"Any places we know?" Sandy asked.

He nodded. "A few are familiar, and I don't know why we didn't think of this before. But at least one of them was a Paladin bolt-hole from just before you were captured, Jess."

"It's eleven," Alex said quietly. Everyone turned to look at him. "I can't help here, Jess. It's too. . . soon. Maybe later, but. . ." he gave his wife an agonized, guilty look.

"Of course, no, I was being stupid," she said at once. "Of course you're not, I wouldn't even let you." Then she looked at the map. "But this street. . . Reuben, if they own everything, how do we even recon this without getting caught? It's a narrow street—and they'll recognize any of us on sight."

"Ah, I might have a thought there," Trevor said slowly. "I've a small group of human friends in Boston. It's maybe an hour south. I'm sure they'd be happy to drive up and take a look around. Are any of those houses on the market?"

"None Ernest could find," Reuben answered.

"So house-hunting isn't it. But they can just be tourists. There are plenty of museums and historic places in that area. I could even ask one of them to act lost and pop into the business office for directions or something."

Jessamine nodded slowly and pondered the map. "And we go in slowly. In pairs. Some up front, the rest through the backs."

"And what are you looking for?" Alex asked softly.

"Anything," Jessamine replied. "Records. Pointers to other cells. Hell, potentially Deuxm herself. Capturing her would be a real win for us. And in Salem, we're not dealing with steel-framed high-rise buildings. These are *old* homes. Wood framing. Brick and stone. All perfectly magic-friendly. We should be at a strong advantage."

"They'll have to wonder if we're coming," Latoya countered. "I mean, if we rifled their offices in Schaumburg, they know what's in them. They know we're not stupid."

"Knowing and being able to do anything about it are two different things," Jessamine insisted. "Trevor, can your friends go *now?*"

"I'll head back through a Border and find a landline," Trevor nodded, standing and hurrying out of the inn.

"Okay," Jessamine said, sliding the map into the center of the table. "Let's make a plan."

COUNTER-HUNT

"So were the witches here *really* witches?" Clara asked. It was a warm morning in Salem, and the team—the *expanded* team—had arrived in small, scattered groups.

"No," Jessamine snorted.

"Most weren't," Ed corrected her. "The big names—Elizabeth How, Bridget Bishop, Ann Foster—weren't. Typically, the women just had political enemies. Some were widows, and people wanted their land. Others just weren't well-liked by the people who'd accused them. But Enola Weakman was a real witch."

Clara wrinkled her brow. "I know that name."

"You should, you bought a biography of her in Linginham. That was our last trip there before you raised the final Border."

"Oh!" Clara exclaimed, remembering. "She was a mathemagician! She's the one who discovered Borders!"

"Really?" Jessamine said, scanning the thin crowd around them. "I didn't know that."

"She's the one who enabled Underhill to be what it is today," Ed confirmed. "And she's one of the few who made it through her trial alive."

"By using magic?" Clara asked. She didn't remember reading the biography she'd purchased.

"Ironically, yes," Ed chuckled. "The story is that she glamoured everyone and then moved to Underhill."

"Check in," Jessamine said distractedly.

Clara focused on the tingling magic that surrounded her right ear. It was a delicate, fragile spell, Latoya had said, but provided they didn't run across any substantial amounts of metal it would let them all communicate as they closed in on their target street.

"We're good," Trevor's voice echoed tinnily in her ear. He and Latoya had paired off. "We're holding one street over from the North end of the target."

"As are the triplets and I," Reuben said. "We're just turning onto the street to the West. There's a tourist shop here that's just opened —I think we can linger a bit."

"And Elsie and I," Sandy said. "We're finishing a cup of coffee, just at the head of the street to the East. We'll cut through someone's backyard."

"Clara and I are just turning onto the. . . oh, wow."

"What is it?" Reuben said with alarm.

"Nothing, nothing," Jessamine said quickly. "I just. . . I know we looked at the maps but the scale didn't hit me. This is a *small* street."

And indeed it was. The worn black asphalt lane was exactly big enough for one lane of on-street parking and one lane for traffic, although it was incredibly tight. The sidewalk was relatively wide, and made from charming red bricks. The houses sat just a few feet back, all with three or four steps leading up to covered porches of varying sizes. There were just eight houses in total, and the largest was the duplex they were heading for.

Trevor's friends in Boston had driven up as soon as he'd contacted them, and reported in less than two hours later. They'd managed to catch the business office just as it was closing, and confirmed that both sides of the duplex seemed to be used by the company. They'd described it as "pretty ordinary," with desks packed neatly into rooms that had once been intended for sitting, dining, and sleeping. They'd asked for, and received, directions to one witch-related museum or another, and briefly described the other houses on the block. Those, they'd said, seemed to be occupied by actual residents, although they didn't see anything unusual. Certainly no tall, trenchcoat-clad, goggle-wearing Paladins.

"Anything unusual, baby?" Jessamine asked quietly as they stood at the head of the small street.

Clara shook her head as she examined the lane, her vision in magic-mode. "No. The ambient energy looks absolutely normal. It's ebbing around the trees a bit, but it always does in the Ordinary."

"Everyone confirm your crystals are charged," Jessamine ordered. Voices checked in with confirmations; everyone but Clara was carrying a fully charged magic battery. With a crystal apiece, the triplets would be able to unleash true havoc at need, and Reuben would use his extensive knowledge of spells to help direct them. Clara would have felt more comfortable with that firepower at *her* side, but they'd agreed on the need to keep their groups unremarkably small.

"What about the duplex?" Ed asked nervously.

Clara scanned it again. "From what I can see from here, it's fine. The ambient isn't being drawn toward it, so it doesn't have tons of iron or steel. It looks. . . normal. *Everything* looks normal. It's eddying a lot near the cars, obviously, but that's it."

"Okay," he said softly, his voice tense. "When do we go, boss?"

Jessamine took a deep breath. "We go now. That's the signal, everyone," she added. "Positions."

Clara, Ed, and Jessamine began strolling casually down the street, on the sidewalk opposite the duplex. They knew the other teams would be moving into their positions as well: Trevor and Latoya would approach down the same street from the other direction, moving more slowly and stopping to chat in front of a neighboring home. Reuben and the triplets would be making their way into the backyard of a home on this side of the street, using magic as needed to keep themselves hidden from the homeowners. Finally, Sandy and Elsie would be making their way into the duplex's small backyard, forgoing magic and relying on the shrubs they'd seen on the satellite view of the area.

Clara's heart started pounding faster and faster as they neared the duplex. By the time they reached it, sweat was trickling down her back, her pulse was thudding in her ears, and she felt an almost irresistible urge to simply *run away.*

They crossed the street, passing between two cars that were parked alongside the opposite sidewalk, and climbed the few steps to the porch on the duplex's right-hand side. Without knocking, Jessamine tested the doorknob, found it unlocked, and pushed the door open. "Entering," she whispered.

The three of them stepped inside.

This space had clearly been meant as a living room: a small fireplace sat along the exterior wall, and a narrow staircase led to the upper floor. Two wooden office desks sat next to one another, both covered with neat stacks of paperwork and sporting laptop computers. One desk was unoccupied, but the one closest to them was being used by a middle-aged woman—a human, Clara's senses told her immediately—who looked up and smiled as they closed the door behind them.

"Hello," she said cheerfully. "Can I assume you're the ones we've been told to expect? I must say, I didn't expect two of you to be quite so young."

Jessamine frowned. "We're here to see Deuxm."

The woman nodded, her short hair bobbing energetically. "Of course, of course." She gestured down a narrow hallway that led between her desk and the stairs. "Just the next room down the hall. The old dining room, it's on your right. Powder room under the stairs on your left, if you need it."

"I. . ." Jessamine started. Then she shook her head and stalked down the hallway, Clara and Ed close behind.

Clara was scanning every inch the room, noting the still-normal ambient magic that flitted gently through the place. It avoided the cast iron radiators along the one wall, but otherwise seemed completely unremarkable.

The dining room had clearly been rearranged recently. Two desks were pushed up against one wood-paneled wall, and a small, round table had been placed in the middle of the room. Four chairs surrounded it, and in one of them sat Laura Deuxm. Next to her stood a Paladin, his trenchcoat securely closed, cap on his head, and heavy, complex brass goggles over his eyes.

Clara hadn't gotten a good look at Deuxm in the Las Vegas trap house, as the woman had been brightly backlit. Here, sitting in this charming old repurposed dining room, she looked. . . well, at least a *little* threatening. She looked tall—she looked like she'd loom over Clara if she stood, probably at least six feet tell. Her hair looked like it had once been jet-black, but now it was pure white. Her narrow face and prominent cheekbones gave her an angular, sharp look, and her dark eyes glinted with intelligence.

Clara realized she was sitting in a wheelchair.

"Well, well," she said easily. "Care to sit?" She waved at the three empty chairs.

"We'll stand," Jessamine growled.

"As you wish," Deuxm said with a shrug. "And to what do we owe the pleasure? Looking for clues on where to find our brothers and sisters?"

"For one." Clara could see the tension in her mother's neck and shoulders, and imagined she could almost smell her fear and anger.

"You won't find any. We've carefully sanitized the place since the debacle in our Schaumburg facility. Good on you for that one, though. Didn't see it coming."

"Don't leave shipping labels on your lodestar boxes," Jessamine said cooly.

"Lode—oh, the *quaesitor Magicae.* Yes. I do regret the loss of that. It was almost four hundred years old, did you know that?" She *tskd* softly. "No respect for history, I suppose."

"Not when it's used to hunt us."

"I suppose not." She turned her head to the Paladin. "That will be all, Brother Samuels. We'll be fine for a bit."

The Paladin nodded, turned, and pushed his way through a section of wall paneling that Clara hasn't even realized was a door. She got a quick glimpse of a very modern-looking kitchen before the door swung shut.

"You'll be *fine?*" Jessamine asked.

"Oh, absolutely," Deuxm said, nodding. She leaned forward, resting her elbows on the table. "Your friends outside are quite surrounded." At Clara's quick intake of breath, she added, "Don't worry, they'll be fine. We're simply holding them in place for the moment. The same as we are for you."

"You're not—" Jessamine started, but then the three witches felt a heavy *whump* in the air. In Clara's eyes, the room's ambient magic froze in place, and she could feel a. . . *pressure* of some kind, pressing gently against every inch of her skin. Jessamine stood a bit straighter. "A terminus ward?"

Deuxm's smile breaded as she nodded. "Courtesy of a very useful set of holy relics from the early nineteenth century, yes. My three other teams are each carrying one. Quite valuable in their own right, really, made of solid—"

"Magical artifacts, you mean," Jessamine snapped.

Deuxm shrugged. "To-may-to, to-mah-to."

"What do you want, then?"

Deuxm's smile widened even more. "To talk. Specifically to *you,* young lady. I'm told you're one of the. . . our term is *Keyholder.* You control the means in and out of whatever dimension you all come from."

Clara rolled her eyes as Jessamine replied. "We *come from* right here. I was born in Philadelphia."

Deuxm shrugged again, and her smile never wavered. "We can't exactly build a dogma around people from Philadelphia, can we? We know you at least have access to another plane. Another world.

Something of that nature. And *she*," Deuxm continued, nodding at Clara, "controls the portals. Passageways. Doors."

"Borders," Clara said without thinking.

Deuxm nodded. "Just so."

"And what could you possibly want with those?" Jessamine asked. "To invade? We know you've gotten maps."

"Inva—God above, no," Deuxm said, her eyes widening in what looked like genuine shock. *"Invade* you? Certainly not."

Jessamine blinked in confusion. "Then what—"

"Our hope is to *lock you all up in there,*" Deuxm said flatly. "And destroy whatever means you have of coming back, save one. I'm sure more of you will crop up on our side now and again, and we'd like a way to exile them."

All three witches were now confused. "But I don't—" Jessamine started.

"Yes, yes, the dogma is *suffer not a witch to live. Maleficos non patieris vivere,* if you prefer the Church version. And that will certainly remain our *public* stance on the subject. But the reality?" She shrugged. "My counterparts in Europe, Asia, and elsewhere agree that the task is simply too big. And modern principals are less. . . hmm, *forgiving* of putting children to death."

"You've killed plenty of us, over the years. Recently, even," Jessamine pointed out, and Clara at once thought of Dimmick and his team.

Deuxm nodded. "Of course we did. When attacked, we will defend ourselves. And we've been trying very hard to understand how to nullify your magic, to protect humans from it."

"You experimented on my husband," Jessamine said coldly.

"Yes, yes. And in doing so we learned a great deal about the relics in our possession. We've been able to confirm the scientific limits of your powers, and how things like iron disrupt them. Do you know we now have an exact recipe for low-carbon steel that's sturdier and more lightweight than raw iron plates, yet still interferes with your abilities? Oh, and we have *this.*"

Deuxm lowered one hand under the table, and another *whump* sensation slammed down from the ceiling. This time, Jessamine and Ed went with it, falling to their needs and gasping with shock.

"Mom!" Clara cried, leaning down to help steady her mother. She looked up at Deuxm. "What did you do?"

"Fascinating," the woman said. "You're unaffected."

"What did you do?" Clara shouted. She realized that all the magic in the room was *gone* and a cold feeling settled into the pit of her stomach.

"We're calling it a 'magic sink,'" Deuxm said. "First time testing it in the field. It's continuously feeding all the power in this area into a repository in our basement. I must say, I'm quite pleased with the effect."

"Repository?" Ed croaked, pushing himself back to his feet.

Deuxm shrugged. "Oberherr. Aldworth. Whatever he's called."

"You're. . . *empowering* Oberherr?" Clara said, helping her mother up.

"Oh, not exactly. The power feeds into *him,* yes, but he's chained to bare earth with pure iron. So it bleeds right back out again. Somewhat painfully, I might add."

"I'll kill you for this," Jessamine rasped.

"Oh, you would if you could," Deuxm agreed, nodding. "And I'll admit there's a good bit we still don't know about your unnatural powers. But wouldn't it simply be easier to work with us?"

"Where are you getting all the magical constructs?" Jessamine demanded, making a visible effort to stand straight and shaking off Clara's hand. "Where are you getting maps?"

"The *relics* have been handed down within our organization for centuries," Deuxm said. "Most were gifted to us. Directly from Heaven, so the lore goes."

Jessamine snorted.

"I know, I know, but we've had most of them simply forever, so who knows? Some few, we've managed to cobble together on our own. Little bits and pieces we've discovered here and there and managed to piece together into something useful. As for the maps, well... we've friends, here and there." She paused meaningfully. "We *do* know that humans can travel to your other realm, you know. Which gives us some leverage."

"For what?" Clara asked.

"As I said, we want you all out of here. Call it an offer of amnesty. Leave our world to *us*. Take your magic with you. If more of you can be born here, give us a way to exile them, to send them to you, and we will. Leave us in peace, and we'll leave you. Continue making a mockery of the natural order of things and we'll not only finish you, we'll come *after* you, over there."

"You can't," Clara insisted.

"Oh, I *can*, young woman, rest assured. It would be a bloody and devastating battle, I'm sure, but there are more of us than you know, and most are spoiling for a fight." She shrugged. "My way just seems easier, doesn't it?"

The witches exchanged a glance. Deuxm couldn't know about Underhill's lack of Creativity, couldn't know that locking all witched in Underhill would essentially be the start of their extinction. *No one can conceive a child in Underhill,* Clara remembered.

"It's our world, too," Jessamine insisted. "We're all—"

"We don't *care*," Deuxm snapped, her grandmotherly facade evaporating instantly, revealing the cold, calculating leader of witch hunters underneath. "We want you *gone*. What you do, what you *can* do, what you *are* is evil and reprehensible." Clara took an involuntary step backward at the sheer hatred in the woman's voice.

Ed stepped back also, and slipped a hand around Clara's.

"What would happen if we began firing iron cannonballs through one of your Borders?" Deuxm demanded, her lips twitching into a mad, hostile grin and her eyes flashing with animosity. "And I believe we *can*. What then?"

That means she's not sure. They've never tried it. Which made sense; the Borders would only open for a witch. *Although they've kidnapped so many,* Clara thought with a sudden, cold dread. *Maybe she's right.*

"Destroy them, these Borders. Leave us one. Or not," Deuxm added with a mild shrug. "If you'll feel safer, take them all down. I don't care. We'll deal with any baby witches as we find them."

Underhill would die, Clara thought with panic. *Would iron take down the Borders? Do they even know where the Borders are?* Her heart clenched tighter. *The maps. They* must *know.* "Mom," she said hesitantly.

Then she felt something.

Despite the utter lack of ambient magic in the room, despite the continuous, nagging pressure she could feel against her skin, something *warm* was flowing into her. Filling her, like liquid sunshine.

Her sense of witches returned, pushing its way insistently to the front of her mind. There was Ed, right next to her, and Mom on the other side. But there was Reuben, and the triplets. Trevor and Latoya. Sandy and Elsie. All close.

"I'm afraid I'll need an answer *right now,*" Deuxm was saying. Her voice sounded muffled in Clara's ears, as if whatever sensation was flooding her body was pressurizing her ears as well. "And we'll obviously need some kind of *surety* for your performance, if you take my meaning." She continued talking, but Clara was distracted by the gentle roar that now filled her ears and her mind. Whatever quirk of genetics or magic that had made Clara a mathemagician was now in full overdrive: Clara could *hear* the amber and turquoise power that was filling her, *smell* the sharp, bell-like tinkling of it, *taste* how it settled smoothly into her blood, coursing along as if it had never been anywhere else.

Traslonnú, someone said in her mind.

It sounded like Ed.

Clara opened her mouth to speak, saw Deuxm pause mid-sentence. Jessamine turned her head slightly to look at her daughter, her eyebrows crinkling together. She put one hand on Clara's forearm and—

"Mise agus mise, slán sábháilte. Tú féin agus tusa, imithe agus síos," Clara whispered. Ancient words in the mother tongue of Fae magic.

The world became a chaos of rainbow-colored wind.

Veil, another voice whispered.

In an instant, amidst the roar of magic surrounding her, Clara whispered a few more ancient words: *"Gabhaim abú ort gan féachaint."*

A satisfied sigh sounded in her mind as the magic reached up, forming elegant polygons made from equally elegant strings of equations. Numbers and symbols collided, reducing and simplifying until only a single term remained.

And then that term, that ineffable symbol that Clara had never seen but recognized immediately, exploded.

"THIS. . . is going to be difficult to explain," Jessamine said.

All of the witches had gathered on the pretty brick sidewalk in front of where the duplex had been. What remained was a neat rectangle of well-kept grass.

"Obviously we're not going to try," Reuben said. "In fact, I'd like to vote we all leave. In haste."

"What *happened?*" Sandy said, shaking her head.

Ed spoke up. "I was trying to feed Clara magic. From my crystal. I couldn't just release it into the air, they had something, some artifact, actively sucking magic down. So I just held her hand."

"I felt it," Clara said quietly. Her head was still ringing with whatever she'd wrought. "I heard you in my head. You said, 'Translocate.'"

Ed nodded. "I meant for you to take us out of there."

"I think I could have," Clara said slowly, taking his hand in hers. "I could feel you all."

"They had some kind of translocation magic ward on us," Reuben protested.

"On us, too," Clara said, nodding slowly. "I don't think it would have mattered. It was a *lot* of magic. And. . . something else."

"But that's not what you did," Elsie pointed out.

Clara shook her head as if in a daze. "No. The magic wanted. . . something else. You know the mind-wipe, Latoya? The new one we made?"

"*You* made, you mean," Latoya said. "Yes."

"Something whispered to me when I did that. 'Veil,' it said. It said it again."

Jessamine frowned. "Veil? As in. . . some kind of covering?"

Clara shrugged, leaning into Ed a bit. "Maybe. I had words, words in Gaelic." She thought for a moment, then shrugged again. "They're gone now. I don't remember them. But they got. . . mixed up. I think I started to try and teleport us all, but it. . . changed."

"The Paladins holding us vanished," Idalia said quietly.

"Ours too," Elsie said.

"Where did you send them?" Jessamine asked her daughter.

"I honestly don't know," Clara said quietly.

"Are they even *alive?*" Sandy asked.

Clara simply shrugged again, a single tear trickling down her cheek.

"Clara, is it. . . *every* Paladin?" Reuebn asked very quietly.

Clara shook her head. "I don't know," she whispered. "But I don't think they can find us anymore."

The other witches were quiet for a long moment, and then Jessamine nodded. She put an arm around her daughter's shoulders, hugging her even as Clara leaned even harder into Ed. "A Veil."

CHAPTER 20
GRADUATION

"Hey, kiddo, why the long face?" Theo Thorn asked Clara. "You did it! You graduated! This is a day to be happy!"

Clara smiled. "I am, Dad. And I'm so glad you guys got to come for it. It's just. . ."

"We've a lot of work ahead of us," Jessamine Holdaway sighed, patting her daughter on the back. "But it's for another day, baby. Theo's right. Today, take the victory lap."

Arlene Thorn's own smile looked a little forced. "So I take it the Paladin threat hasn't been eliminated?" she asked quietly.

Jessamine shook her head. "No, we've had reports of activity. At least, they've been spotted. Deuxm hasn't been sighted, yet. And with everyone already being so careful about being seen, we don't know if whatever Clara did—whatever 'Veil' was supposed to be—is actually doing anything." She shrugged. "But we'll figure it out."

Arlene's expression relaxed a bit, and she gave Clara a bear hug. "I'm so proud of you, honey," she said. She pulled back and Clara saw that her eyes were moist. "This is what we've wanted for you for so long."

"I hate that I missed you growing up," Alex Holdaway said, rolling his wheelchair closer to Clara to give her his own hug. "But I'm so proud of the woman you've become." His eyes were glistening as well, Clara saw.

"Our personal mathemagician," Elsie said with a grin. Her own moms were on the other side of the school's entry hall, where the graduation ceremony had taken place. They seemed to have cornered Headmaster Herrera in some kind of intense conversation that involved a lot of hand-waving.

The triplets' *entire* family had shown up, and the three girls had just broken free from the pack of them to exchange congratulations with Clara. "Our own personal synergy-maker," Idalia said, giving Clara a quick squeeze.

"So what's next, baby?" Arlene asked. "Advanced studies?"

Clara sighed and shook her head. "I'd thought so. I mean, I don't know what else I'd do. But the past few weeks. . ." she trailed off, looking at Jessamine.

Her bio-mom cocked an eyebrow. "Second thoughts?"

"It just seems like there's more important stuff to do. And I mean, I can really learn any spell I see someone do once or twice." She shrugged. "Seems like a waste to just hang out here, I guess."

Arlene's smile faded a bit. "Jess, I don't suppose you're going to lay down the sword?"

Jessamine shook her head firmly. "No. Now that Alex is back, we have access to the family funds. We're *well* funded. The team and I fully intend on reassessing the Paladin threat and making the Ordinary safe for any witch who wants to be there." She paused, and gave Clara deep look. "Baby, you know you'd be welcome with us. The team loves you and you bring a pretty unique talent."

Clara opened her mouth to reply, but Elsie beat her to it. "Only if I can come, too." Jessamine's eyebrows raised. "That's why Moms are hollering at Herrera. I told them and they think she put me up to it."

"We're joining, too," Harriett said suddenly, accompanied by vigorous nods from her sisters. "Our parents aren't delighted about it but. . . they *love* the Ordinary. They get it."

Finlay and Wolfgang walked up and looked back and forth between the triplets and Jessamine.

Jessamine's other eyebrow raised. "I don't recall it being an open invitation. Teams—"

"It's with you or on our own," Harriett shrugged. "Feels like it'd be better with you, but that's your only choice. Especially if Clara's in."

"I am," Clara said swiftly. She looked at Ed and began to apologize. "I know you—"

"Advanced studies aren't all they're cracked up to be," he interrupted with a smile. "And no way you're going to be a counter-Hunter without me."

Jessamine held up her hands in defeat. "Fine, fine, I get it. I suppose that's you as well, Finlay?"

He shook his head firmly, although Wolfgang frowned. "No. It's not. . . me. My family would never understand. Ma wants me to spend some time at home, and—"

"I think we should," Wolfgang said, but his tone was uncertain.

Finlay's expression was full of guilt.

"I have a suggestion," Alex offered. "I'm a long ways off from being an active counter-Hunter again. In fact. . . I may not." Jessamine looked pained, but said nothing.

They've discussed this, Clara thought.

"But that doesn't mean I can't, or won't, contribute," Alex continued. "From everything you've told me, it's clear you need a support team of some kind. You know, Reuben's not getting younger, and he's a great researcher. He and I chatted and. . . well, we think we'd like to be that support team. Help you do research, give you backup without being in the mix." He looked at Finlay. "I've spoken to your parents. If everything they've said about your grades are true, you'd be welcome to join us."

Finlay nodded slowly. "After some time at home, maybe?"

"Of course," Alex smiled. "We'll talk."

"We need a team name," Johanna announced eagerly.

"We do not need a team name," Jessamine said quickly. "The Council isn't even re-sanctioning counter-hunting. We certainly don't—"

"Rogue Scoobies," Idalia said at once. Her sisters nodded.

Clara laughed. "I like it."

"We don't need a team name," Jessamine insisted, although Clara could tell she knew she'd already lost.

"Well, before you all go off and buy team shirts or something," Alex chuckled, "can I suggest a wonderful dinner here in Underhill, before Theo and Arlene have to go home? Linginham is a short Anchor hop away and there are some wonderful restaurants."

"Will there be magical food?" Arlene said eagerly.

"Mom, you're going to love Lemon Impossibles," Clara promised.

EPILOGUE

"I haven't seen you for a while," Clara said.

The little blue elf shrugged, and glimmers of magic swirled away from him. The dream-forest was quiet tonight, softly illuminated by two moons. "More than you remember," it said. "You spent too much time," it added in a gently scolding tone.

"I know," Clara sighed. "But what's done is done. The final Border is up."

The elf nodded. "Magic is happy."

"Magic from the Ordinary."

The elf shrugged. "You did not see?"

Clara frowned. "See what?"

The air beside them swirled and hazed, resolving into an image. Clara recognized her parents—both sets—standing in Linginbaum's entry hall. She was there, along with her friends, but. . . "What's wrong with Mom and Dad?" she asked. "The Thorns, I mean?"

In the image, both Arlene and Theo were *glowing*. A fountain of light seems to pour from their heads, cascading around their shoulders and dissolving easily into the air around them.

"Magic," the elf said, entranced with the image.

"Mag—wait," Clara said, her mind suddenly reeling. "I've never seen them like that before. They're not witches!"

The elf shrugged again. "In the Ordinary, maybe not so obvious." It waved a hand and the image faded. "Here, much contrast. More obvious." It wrinkled its nose. "Not witches, no. Not children of Fae. Not magic," it added, holding up a finger. *"Of* magic." It nodded in satisfaction, as if it had just explained something very difficult.

"Of. . . wait. You mean. . . are you saying magic *comes from humans?"*

It nodded happily. "The True Fae," it said almost dreamily, "entice them here all times, humans. So bright!"

"So magic isn't from the Ordinary?"

Now it frowned. "Humans *in* Ordinary." Its tone implied that it thought Clara was being dense.

"Humans in—of course," Clara said, finally grasping it. "But they can come here, too. They can. . . wait, does that mean you don't *need* the connection to the Ordinary?"

"Need magic," the elf shrugged. "Witches here, humans there, magic there, Borders bring magic here."

"I—but witches can't be *only* here," Clara protested. "Underhill's Creativity is gone. We still have to go back to the Ordinary to. . . you know." She felt herself blush.

Now the elf's expression grew serious, and it spoke very quietly. "Creation," it said, nodding gravely. "A Great Power." It stared into Clara's eyes.

"A Great—wait, you mean like Ikwity? Creation is a *power?"*

"Missing long time," the elf said reverently. "Or sleeping."

"Sleeping," Clara breathed. A sense of excitement was building in her. "But maybe I could find it?"

The elf shrugged and made a flicking motion toward her. "Maybe."

Back in her bed, Clara's eyes flew open.

APPENDIX: LEMON IMPOSSIBLE RECIPE

Lemon Impossibles are basically a *very* sour lemon bar, and this variation has a cookie-style base.

Take a small and careful nibble to get a feel for just how sour they are! Then, munch on a miracle berry—a real thing in the Ordinary world!—and take a bigger bite.

Miracle berries are interesting fruits. Their molecular structure bonds with sour-tasting substances as well as the sweet-sensing taste buds on your tongue, making sour taste sweet for a brief period of time. When chewing a miracle berry, be sure to get it not only well-chewed, but also evenly spread across your tongue so that it can work its magic.

Miracle berries can be difficult to find in grocery stores, but Amazon and other online retailers offer them. Try https://amzn.-to/3NUMUCU for a brand I've used and enjoyed (that URL is case-sensitive).

INGREDIENTS

Base

- 4-1/2 ounces all-purpose flour
- 2 ounces powdered sugar
- 1/4 teaspoon diamond crystal kosher salt
- 8 ounces (1 tablespoon; 4g) freshly grated lemon zest
- 4 ounces (1 stick; 115g) cold unsalted butter, cut into 1/4-inch dice

Filling

- 3 large eggs, cold
- 1-1/2 cups egg yolks, from about 8 large eggs
- 9-1/2 ounces granulated sugar (reduce this to taste for an even more sour effect!)
- pinch of kosher salt
- 1/4 ounce (1 packed tablespoon; 8g) freshly grated lemon zest
- 10 fluid ounces lemon juice, from about 8 large lemons (or you can use genuine lemon juice from a container)

Garnishing

- lemon zest
- 1 teaspoon citric acid (if you're having trouble finding this locally, you can get it on Amazon at https://amzn.to/3vquqDX — note that the URL is case-sensitive, so type it carefully)

INSTRUCTIONS

- Pre-heat the oven to 350-degrees.
- Cookie base: Combine flour, powdered sugar, salt, butter, and lemon zest to a large mixing bowl. You can either use an electric hand mixer, food processor, or a pastry blender.
- Spray a 13 x 9-inch glass baking dish with non-stick spray.
- Using your fingers, press the cookie base flat onto the bottom of the baking dish.
- Bake the cookie base for about 20 minutes.
- While the cookie base is baking, make the lemon filling: Start by beating the eggs in the same bowl used for the cookie base (if you can't, it's okay to use a fresh bowl).
- Add the lemon juice, sugar, flour, and salt to the beaten eggs. Mix well.
- After the cookie base has baked for 20 minutes, remove it from the oven and slowly and carefully pour in the lemon filling.
- Return the lemon cookies to the oven and continue to bake for 20–25 minutes. They are done when the center of the filling has set firm, and the top of the bars are *just* starting to turn a golden brown color.
- Remove from the oven and cool the cookie bars on a wire rack.
- Garnish with sprinkles of lemon zest and citric acid powder—the powder is what makes these sour, so garnish to taste and for maximum effect! Use a knife to slice everything into evenly sized squares or rectangles, usually big enough for 3–4 bites apiece.

If you want to add the miracle berries (usually sold as halves) to the top of your Lemon Impossibles, as done in Linginham in Underhill, lay them gently atop the lemon bars after garnishing. But if you do this, remember that you can't eat the lemon and miracle berries in one bite! You have to pick a berry (or half) off, chew it and get your tongue nice and coated, and *then* bite the lemon bar.

APPENDIX: HOW TO MAKE AN AUTHENTIC PHILLY CHEESESTEAK

Residents of Philly all tend to have their favorite cheesesteak places —and the ones you see on Food Network shows usually aren't it! People get attached to their local neighborhood 'steak place, all of whom put subtle and different spins on their offerings. And a lot of what makes a "real" cheesesteak can only be found in Philly—the Amoroso's rolls, for example, which you can order directly from the bakery at https://amorosobaking.com.

And if you happen to visit Philly, Philip's, the shop that Clara, Ed, and Jessamine visit, is a real place at 2234 W Passyunk Ave.

But making your own excellent cheesesteak isn't hard!

The key ingredient is very thinly cut ribeye steak. If you have an actual butcher shop available, ask the butcher cut to cut a ribeye into thin slices using their meat slicer—you want lunchmeat-thin slices. You can do this at home without a meat slicer by partially freezing your ribeye and then slicing it as thin as you can get it using a sharp knife. Be careful!!

You'll also need to slice up any vegetables, such as if you'd like your 'steak 'wit.' Bell peppers and dill pickles aren't unusual in Philly, and depending on what neighborhood you're from you might even find mushrooms on your sandwich. Start by sautéing all of those together with a bit of butter or oil. If you prefer some of your mix-ins raw, like the pickles, just leave those out of the sauté and add them to the final sandwich.

If you have any larger slices of ribeye, cut them into smaller pieces. In a real 'steak place, the steak-cutting happens rapidly (and often loudly) using sturdy spatulas, right as they're sautéing the meat. That's difficult to pull off without a big, commercial flat-top grill, so you'll want to cut the meat ahead of time and then sauté it until it's well-done (it won't take long).

When everything's cooked to your satisfaction, warm your skillet to medium-high heat. Place some sliced & cooked meat in the skillet and top with the cheesesteak fixings of your choice, then top with a couple slices of cheese. Provolone is the standard, but plenty of folks prefer American (white or yellow), and yes, people absolutely use spray-cheese as well. Cheddar isn't recommended, as it doesn't melt quite as well.

Let all that sit for a couple of minutes to allow the cheese to melt. Once it's done, use a spatula to transfer it all to a sliced hoagie roll. Toasting the roll in advance isn't traditional, but feel free if that's how you like it!

Pro tip: cast iron skillets are excellent for doing this at home!

Now... you *can* go a step further. This involves wrapping your hoagie in a piece of aluminum foil, rolling it *very tightly* as you wrap it. If you're doing more than one 'steak, wrap them individually. Then toss them in a 250F oven for around 15 minutes. That'll toast the roll and really blend all the flavors nicely. When you take the sandwiches out, you can add any "raw" ingredients that you didn't include in the original sauté.

SAMPLE INGREDIENTS

Makes 6-8 sandwiches.

- 2 pounds Ribeye steak thinly sliced
- 2 medium onions sliced
- 1 green pepper sliced or diced (whatever your preference)
- sliced mushrooms to taste
- 6-8 hoagie rolls
- Provolone cheese
- 2-3 tablespoons butter
- salt & pepper -or- steak seasoning to taste
- aluminum foil

INSTRUCTIONS

This is a shorter version of the above, where you sauté everything in one skillet: veggies first, followed by adding the steak.

- Preheat your oven to 250 degrees.
- In a skillet over medium/high heat, sauté the onions, bell peppers, & mushrooms in the butter. Set aside. Wipe out the pan, and return to high heat Add the ribeye steak & season with either salt & pepper to taste. Cook for a couple of minutes. Set aside
- On each side of the skillet (on low/medium heat), layer the cooked ribeye, onions, bell pepper, & onions Cover with 3-4 pieces of provolone cheese. Allow to sit about 2 minute for the cheese to melt. Transfer to a hoagie roll. Roll very tightly in a square of tinfoil. Bake for 15 minutes.

APPENDIX: THE LANGUAGES OF MAGIC

For witches that aren't lucky enough to be a once-in-a-generation mathemagician, words and motions, along with mental images, help shape raw magic into spells. The words are especially important because they lend specificity and meaning to the witch's efforts. Notably, the *actual words used* aren't critical—what matters are the images and feelings those words conjure in the witch's mind. Words also make it easier for one witch to teach a spell to another, although as our heroes learn in school, there's still some trial-and-error to get the right "mental state" in place for a spell to work.

Nearly every ancient human culture—and a few not-so-ancient ones—have magic traditions that they shape and preserve using words. Many of these spells, such as teleportation, are very similar across cultures, using different sounds to create the same mental readiness. As our world modernized, many cultures traded spell-words, and sometimes settled on a particular one as being the best one for the job. That might mean an Irish witch learning a few words in Lithuanian, for example, and that's become very common for modern witches.

Here are some example spell phrases—can you guess what

language they're in? Answers follow!

- Lotnaidí thosaigh!
- Olyan fényes, mint a nappal
- Parolu al mi mallaŭte
- Στιβαρό σαν πέτρα
- Exsurge, dormies
- Iš čia į ten žaibiškai
- Захищений світлом
- Powołany do życia
- Gaoth on chuan, seideadh làidir is luath

Some languages have become well-known for being perfectly suited for specific tasks. French magic, for example, is almost always the choice for hospitality magic, while German magic is often preferred for precision and strength. Irish Gaelic, the language of the Fae, is used for some of the most fantastical spells, including many that involve glamour and illusion.

ANSWERS

- Lotnaidí thosaigh! (Irish)
- Olyan fényes, mint a nappal (Hungarian)
- Parolu al mi mallaŭte (Esperanto)
- Στιβαρό σαν πέτρα (Greek)
- Exsurge, dormies (Latin)
- Iš čia į ten žaibiškai (Lithuanian)
- Захищений світлом (Ukranian)
- Powołany do życia (Polish)
- Gaoth on chuan, seideadh làidir is luath (Scots Gaelic)

Pro tip: you can use Google Translate to get approximate translations for these phrases, as well as the spell phrases in the story. Machine translation isn't perfect, but it'll give you a rough idea of the words forming the spells.

APPENDIX: THE SALEM WITCH TRIALS

The Salem Witch Trials, which ran from February 1692 to May 1693, were one of the most egregious abuses of justice and power in Colonial American times. More than two hundred people were accused of practicing witchcraft, thirty found guilty in sham "trials," and nineteen executed by hanging. Women were disproportionately targeted —fourteen were murdered, compared to five men. At least a half-dozen more victims died in jails, usually under cruel and inhumane conditions.

Enola Weakmen, mentioned in this story, is fictional, but the other witches mentioned in the Salem scene were real people.

You can read more about the Salem Witch Trials at https://en.wikipedia.org/wiki/Salem_witch_trials.

NOTES

267

1. A PALADIN PROBLEM

1. Read the story in "Classmates," available for free at DonJones.com.

Award-Winning Fiction

Daniel Scratch: a story of witchkind

- Kirkus Starred Review
- Winner, American Fiction Awards—Best Fantasy (2023)

Clara Thorn, the witch that was found

- Winner, American Fiction Awards—Best Young Adult (2023)
- Runner-Up, American Fiction Awards—Best Fantasy (2023)

Find these books and more at DonJones.com

About the Author

Don Jones spent two decades writing tech books before he finally penned his first sci-fi novella, *A History of the Galactic War*. His well-reviewed and award-winning novels span fantasy and science fiction, with a focus on world building and relatable characters.

Connect, get free novels and short stories, and learn about upcoming releases by visiting Don's author website at DonJones.com.

ALSO BY DON JONES

stories of witchkind®

<u>Age of the Adherents</u>:

Daniel Scratch • Master of the Tower • The Fifth Axis

<u>The Order</u>:

The Order of Some • The Conspiracy of One • The Truth of All

~

Clara Thorn

Clara Thorn, the witch that was found

Clara Thorn, the witch that fought

Clara Thorn, the witch that won

~

Endless Sky®

Truthsayer • New Worlds

~

The Never: A Tale of Peter and the Fae

~

Find more at DonJones.com

www.ingramcontent.com/pod-product-compliance
Lightning Source LLC
Chambersburg PA
CBHW071223210726
48293CB00002B/552